ALEYARA'S DESCENT

CHRISTOPHER L. BENNETT

PUBLISHED BY
eSpec Books LLC
Danielle McPhail, Publisher
PO Box 242,
Pennsville, New Jersey 08070
www.especbooks.com

ISBN: 978-1-956463-67-5
ISBN (ebook): 978-1-956463-66-8

See Bibliography at the end for previous publication notes.

All persons, places, and events in this book are fictitious, and any resemblance

Cover and Design: Mike McPhail, McP Digital Graphics.
Interior Design: Danielle McPhail, McP Digital Graphics
Cover Background:
Copyeditor: Greg Schauer, John L. French

To Xuân Stanek,
for being my muse in the early years.
May Motai watch over you.

Contents

The Moving Finger Writes

The Moving Finger writes; and, having writ,
Moves on: nor all your Piety nor Wit
Shall lure it back to cancel half a Line,
Nor all your Tears wash out a Word of it.
— The Rubáiyát of Omar Khayyam
(trans. by Edward Fitzgerald)

Miar woke from cryosleep with difficulty, struggling to full awareness. It was usually this way; her metabolism was more attuned to frequent light naps than this profound dormancy. But the long sleeps were needed, for Miar was a messenger to the future.

As she engaged in her usual awakening ritual—an intense, cleansing stretch, a long drink of nutrient fluid (hesitant at first, then deeper drafts as her stomach acclimated), a licking-down of the fur that had become matted while she slept—she noted the automatic systems performing with their usual efficiency. Acoustic, olfactory, and visual readouts brought her up to speed on the ship whose arrival through the F'teondrou timehole had triggered her revival, confirming that it had been scanned for weapons and found safe. The station had already opened its landing bay as an invitation. Once the small warp skiff was inside, an interface with its computer and a brain scan of its single occupant would facilitate translations. And then the alien's questions could be asked.

But something was different this time. As Miar scanned the readouts, making a quick meal of a meat bar, her large, tapering ears perked up in surprise as she noted the message stored in the computer, awaiting her perusal. It registered as a standard Marrhwai transmission protocol—standard in her native time, making it a definite relic in the present (whenever that might currently be). Thankful that the computer was taking its time with the translation matrix, Miar cued up the message.

Afterward, she sat in stunned silence for long moments, gazing abstractedly out at the stars wheeling madly inside the timehole. When she finally remembered the waiting alien, she signaled the computer to let the being enter. She gathered herself as best she could, needing to be at her most balanced to provide the necessary guidance. Still, her tail fur was entirely too ruffled when the bipedal visitor arrived.

His name was Jared Yung. He called his species human. For years, he said, he had charted the many tunnels through spacetime, traveling back through one, forward through another, jumping from era to era on a dithyrambic course through a hundred millennia of galactic history. The timeholes were Jared's life, their potential his obsession. For the latter part of those years, he had searched relentlessly for their creators, desperate for the answers he hoped they could give him. He did it the logical way — going ever backward. Find a hole that would send him far back; travel through space to another, older hole whose destination was even farther back. Thus, at last, he had found the creators, in the person of Miar of House Prrisht'cheo, science-priestess of the Marrhwai.

"I don't understand," the gray-haired human told the white-furred Marrhwai. "For decades I've traveled through the past — not just to study history, but to rewrite it. Improve it.

"I'm not a fool," he hastened to add. "I was a geologist to start with, not a physicist, but I've had many years to become an expert on temporal theory. I know a moment in time can't be erased or undone. That's common sense. For something to change, time has to pass — one state is succeeded by another, a before and an after. And a moment in time can't come before itself.

"But it can come *alongside* itself. Two versions of the same moment, simultaneous by definition. Coexisting in parallel timelines. I've tried to create such parallels, to right wrongs, to use my foreknowledge to avert catastrophe in at least one version of history. But I have met with failure at every turn.

"I tried to prevent the birth of Lorenz Vale, a dictator who slaughtered millions in the name of spiritual purity. I tried — I am not unattractive by my species' standards — I tried to seduce the woman who would be Vale's mother into coming away with me so she would never meet his father-to-be. But I failed to reckon with the fact that she already had a suitor — a highly jealous and abusive one. I barely escaped with my life. And millions of lives more stayed lost." He rubbed his jaw, still feeling the blow years later and millennia earlier.

"I tried to stop the assassination of the Kilisith ambassador and prevent a war that devastated five worlds. But the 'assassin' I stunned turned out to be an innocent bystander whom the real assassin was able to frame because I left him unconscious near the scene.

"I tried to divert the asteroid that destroyed the civilization on Madgren II. But I arrived too late, and my ship's engines were too weak to change the asteroid's course in the time remaining. A people on the verge of greatness were thrust back into barbarism despite my best attempts."

Miar listened silently, inwardly grieving tragedies that for her had not yet occurred, but that she knew she could never prevent.

"I even attempted to head off the birth of the Barjian Tyranny," Jared continued. "I visited Barji Prime in its pre-spaceflight days, worked in secret to try to change the factors that led to the warlords' rise. But I was discovered, and if anything, the knowledge that an alien was influencing their culture helped foster the xenophobia that later drove their blitzkrieg through the stars." The human looked at her with an emotion that, even over the gulf between species, Miar could recognize as pain of immeasurable depth. "I try very hard to convince myself that I didn't *cause* the Barjian Tyranny—for otherwise I could never live with myself."

He sighed sharply. "I have tried for years to change history for the better. When I failed to make any major changes, I tried to make smaller adjustments, on a more personal scale. I thought that if, perhaps, there were some inertia to history, something that prevented grand revisions in its flow, maybe some minor alterations would go unnoticed. But no matter how small a change I attempted, one way or another I still failed. In all this time, I have had not one success.

"Why must I lose every time, Miar? Is there something I've overlooked, something I've failed to do? Please tell me, what am I doing wrong?"

The tall, elegant Marrhwai studied him with sympathy. "Your only mistake, Jared Yung of the human species, was in trying to change the past at all. The past is done—and it cannot be undone. Once a word has been spoken, no power in all the universes can unspeak it." She had recited the same words many times over—yet this time, after the message, they bore a more personal weight. She hoped her distraction was not evident to the human, grateful that her species' modes of expression were as yet unknown to him. Though she imagined that would change before long.

"I'm not trying to 'unspeak' it!" the human cried. "Just to create an alternative alongside it. There *are* parallel histories. Centuries of physics say so."

"There are—but they only branch off from quantum-scale events, where a single particle can exist in multiple states at once. There is no way to create or access them through macroscopic actions. Indeed, since their differences are on a subatomic scale, they would probably proceed almost indistinguishably on the scale of beings like ourselves. Even if you could enter one, you would perceive no difference.

"But you could not. By interacting with the past, you correlate its quantum state with your own. That very correlation of states is what creates our experience of a singular timeline to begin with. Merely by entering the past, you ensure that the only future you can create is your own."

"No! I can't accept that." He rose and paced the room as Miar herself often did when her ancestral hunting instincts grew restless. "You're not telling me anything my people's physicists didn't know a thousand years before I was born. There *must* be something more! Some deeper insight. You built the timeholes—you *must* know something!"

"Nothing that changes the elementary laws your scholars determined long ago."

Wishing she could give him comfort, Miar gazed at Jared, studying his demeanor, the tension in his facial muscles. She had been here before with other travelers. Often, what they truly needed was simply an understanding listener.

"You have a great need to undo the past, Jared," she observed gently. "It is very... personal. What lies in your own past that so compels you to attempt rewriting the galaxy's?"

Jared held her unblinking gaze. In his body language, in his scent, she could perceive him overcoming his resistance, responding to her gentle tone, deciding to trust her. "I've never had the heart to tell anyone before," he said. "But this is the end of the line, one way or another. I suppose it's... time."

"What we have here is *not* two black holes orbiting each other," Jared Yung announced to the crew members assembled in the *Lynx*'s conference room. The youthful, black-haired science officer gestured to the display, which showed a pair of "puckers" roiling the starscape behind them as they followed a highly eccentric, elliptical orbit around one another more than fifty times a second, with the center of mass inside the larger one's event horizon. "What we have is a black hole being orbited by the mouth of a wormhole."

The crew reacted with amazement. "A wormhole," Captain Claudia Yung breathed. "We've found a wormhole. Instant transport across untold parsecs."

Jared grinned at his big sister's change of heart. When the intense gravity waves from the orbiting singularities had required the *Lynx* to drop out of stardrive, the captain had met the accidental discovery with impatience. The resource assessment survey of the Origem Loop was already behind schedule, and the last thing she had needed was another delay that might jeopardize their contract with the Cosmographic Survey.

Her attitude had changed when Jared had discovered stars shining within the smaller hole—a glimpse of the space at the far end of the wormhole. A discovery of such magnitude would more than make up for a lack of punctuality.

But Claudia didn't know the half of it yet. "It's much, much more than that, Captain. This isn't just a shortcut through space." Jared paused, as much for effect as for breath. "We are orbiting a time machine."

The crew reacted with shock and disbelief. "That's impossible," scoffed Tchael, the Shirriesh medical officer.

"Not at all," Jared countered. "The principles have been known since the twentieth century. It's all relativity."

"That old saw?" Tchael shot back. "Obsolete for centuries."

"But it's still a good enough approximation to explain why the wormhole's builders—and it had to be built, there's no way they can be stable naturally—why its builders put it in such a tight, eccentric orbit around the black hole. And by the way, we still haven't figured out why the orbits aren't decaying, with all the gravity waves—but I'm digressing again." Claudia gave him a wry look, though he could tell she shared his enthusiasm.

"The wormhole moves so fast in its orbit, and is subject to such strong gravity from the black hole, that it's severely time-dilated by both factors. Time in the mouth moves about half as quickly as time out here. *But*—the two mouths are connected through the wormhole, not through normal space, so the other mouth doesn't 'see' the movement of this one relative to normal space. As far as it's concerned, this mouth is stationary, so time for them goes at the same rate. And that mouth's motionless relative to the fabric of space around it. So a clock outside the far end of the wormhole would read the same time as a clock *inside* this mouth—which is running well behind our time, by about half the wormhole's age. So by going through the wormhole, we'd end up in the past."

The crewmembers took a moment to absorb the convoluted concept. "In theory, perhaps," said Grace Mbaye, the chief engineer. "But how do you get in? It's only a few thousand kilometers from the hole at most, and racing around it over fifty times a second."

"You'd have to enter at its farthest point from the black hole—that must be why the orbit is so eccentric—and you'd need a very fast ship and very good navware. But it can be done. I sent a probe through two hours ago, and its readings of star positions, periods of known pulsars, even the cosmic background temperature all confirm that it's on the edge of Barjian space about twenty-eight hundred years ago—meaning the hole's been around for nearly six thousand years."

Claudia did some figuring. "Twenty-eight hundred years. That's about when the Barjian Tyranny was ended by the Kushi, wasn't it?"

Jared grinned. "Almost exactly. Imagine the possibilities for historical research! Imagine actually *talking* to the Kushi Liberators!"

"Whoa, hold on, little brother. This is a resource survey, re-member?"

"And a time machine is one hell of a resource. So we should really survey it. Come on, you want to pass up the chance to get it named after us?"

The captain gave him a skeptical look. "The Yung Hole?"

"Unh. Okay, bad idea."

"Worse idea—imagine the disaster if we changed things somehow. Maybe prevented the Liberation."

He scoffed. "Don't worry, sis. I've been reading up on the physics, and unmaking the past like that is pure fiction. Traveling through time is like... watching a prerecorded ball game. Watching it again won't let you change the outcome, because the game was only played once. It just looks to you like it was played again."

"So if you go back and see a past event..."

He nodded. "You're seeing its *first* and only occurrence for the sec-ond time. You can't change it, because you were there already anyway, part of what happened all along.

"Well," he added, "depending on what theory you listen to, there's a chance you could split off a parallel timeline where you *could* change things. But nobody in this timeline would ever know it. So our history would be safe no matter what happened back there."

Now Claudia was getting excited. "So we could go through?"

"I think we should try sending a warp skiff rather than the whole *Lynx*. Easier to navigate around the black hole, especially on the return trip. And needless to say, we mustn't use our stardrive anywhere near the holes. The vortex it creates would—"

"Needless to say," she echoed. "We can all imagine. But aside from that, you think we could do it?"

"As long as the skiff's quadruply-redundant navware doesn't fail utterly, we can do it."

"Then we're doing it."

Over Claudia's resistance, Jared convinced her that he should be the one to go through. He regretted it for a moment as the skiff dove headlong into the cosmic Scylla and Charybdis before him... and then all was calm. Jared could tell within moments that he had moved through space; the stars around him were marginally more densely packed, as though he had moved several thousand light years closer to the galactic center. He absorbed it for a moment, then turned the skiff around. Behind was a single, motionless pucker in the starfield—but in the center he could see stars wheeling by madly. "I made it!" Jared cried.

"Oh, come on, Jared," came the captain's reply, beamed through the timehole. *"You're the one who assured us it could be done. Don't tell me you didn't really think so!"*

"Oh. Well, I didn't mean—"

"Forget it. You're there! Back in time! Twenty-eight hundred years before you were even born! How's that for pulling a fast one on the universe?"

"Point taken, Captain," Jared smiled. "All sensors operational."

Jared began thrusting away from the timehole, hoping to get better readings away from its gravitic distortion. "By the way, Claudia," he told his captain, "it occurs to me that since I'm now alive nearly three millennia before you, you can no longer claim the privilege of being the older sibling."

"Ahh," came the wry response from the future. *"So that's why you were so hell-bent on going."*

Before he could think of a suitable comeback, something registered on his scans. "I think I'm picking up drive emissions. Consistent with multiple ships. I'm moving to get a better look."

"Be discreet, Jared. If you interfere and create a new timeline, we might never get you back."

"At last, you'd get your wish of being an only child."

"But I'd have to explain it to the CS. Not to mention Mom."

Before long, the screen was focused on a new set of stars—some of which were moving, drawing closer. Soon their signatures began to resolve—and Jared gasped. "Barjian. No question."

"My God," whispered the captain. As the ships came closer, Jared could see that some of them bore the distinctive hull damage of Kushi particle rays. *"They must be fleeing the Final Rout. If they—"*

Jared's eyes widened as the alarms went off, the readouts showing a targeting laser painting his skiff. He swerved as one of the ships fired a pulse of light. The deadly plasma bolt shot past—but its radiation wake hit the skiff's systems hard, sending the readouts into chaos.

"Jared?" came Claudia's tense voice over the radio.

"I'm okay! I've taken damage, but—"

"Jared!" the captain's voice interrupted, more urgently. *"Are you there?"*

"Yes! Captain, can you—"

"We've lost your telemetry, my God, are you there?!"

"Claudia!" But it was no use. He was no longer transmitting.

But he was still receiving. After a moment of silence, Claudia's voice sounded tightly: *"If they're that close to the timehole, they must have detected it. Could they figure it out?"*

"The Barjians were brutal, but brilliant," came Grace Mbaye's sober reply. *"They'll work it out faster than we did."*

A sigh from Claudia. *"We can't let that happen."*

"No, Captain."

Jared could imagine her looking about the bridge, gauging their responses. *"I suppose we all concur. I wish I could be glad about that. Because there's only one thing we can do."* Her voice shuddered. *"I never thought I'd break a contract."*

"No!" Jared cried; but of course nobody could hear him—not even the Barjians, who must have let him live this long only because the timehole had distracted them.

After a long pause, Claudia spoke once more. *"S'kaa, initiate forward thrust, using this vector."* A pause as she transmitted the figures. *"Then activate stardrive at... these coordinates."*

The pilot's voice, frightened: *"Captain?"*

Softly: *"It's the only way, Elbir."*

After a moment: *"Program laid in. Awaiting orders."*

Jared squeezed his eyes shut, not wanting to hear this, yet unable to bring himself to cut it off. Claudia's voice came through the intercom once more. *"All personnel, this is Captain Yung."* It was a shipwide page. *"As you know, we have discovered a gateway into the past. It could have made all our names... it could've been a grand adventure for our kids someday.*

"But there is a Barjian fleet closing in on that gateway. I'm sure you all know what that means. We've seen the scars of their violence in so many of the systems we've surveyed. We've thanked them for blowing away planetary crusts so we could get to their minerals more easily. Easy to joke from a distance. But try to imagine what just one Barjian phalanx could do in our time, in a galactic arm that's been at peace for centuries. Hopefully, with that in mind... you'll be able to forgive me for what I'm about to do.

"You have been... the finest crew anyone could ask for. You have been my friends, my loyal partners in our endless search for knowledge. And I cherish you all." The tears burned Jared's eyes. *"Elbir,"* he heard her say, *"initiate course."*

"Course initiated, sir."

Jared knew what was happening without studying the readouts. He could almost see the *Lynx* launching itself between the singularity and the wormhole mouth, engaging its stardrive.

A black hole and a wormhole are very similar things. A wormhole is essentially a two-ended tunnel through spacetime; a black hole has only one open end. The Lynx's gravity drive created a link between the two holes—and they became one. The starship, the black hole, and the wormhole mouth all vanished from the universe, the lost mass compensated for by a huge release of energy in the form of gravitational shock waves that would be felt for parsecs around.

And 2800 years earlier at the other end, the Barjian fleet found itself rushing headlong into what had just become a black hole.

"If I hadn't found that timehole, if I hadn't insisted on going through, then my sister and the forty other people aboard the *Lynx*

wouldn't have died," Jared said with difficulty, his throat dry. "So ever since I've... I've tried to use the timeholes to save lives, to make things better. Maybe even... work my way back to that place and time and prevent the *Lynx* from finding the timehole. Destroying it before... before Claudia does."

Miar understood that he spoke of destroying it as his sister had, by sacrificing himself. "Jared, your motives are noble, but your methods are futile. As a scientist you must know what you try to do is impossible. Your obsession with changing events behind you merely prevents you from moving forward."

He scoffed. "Forward! I'm eighty thousand years in my own past." He resumed his pacing. "It's not even really about saving Claudia and the *Lynx* anymore. Not *just* that. I just... I can't accept that everything is predestined. That free will is just an illusion."

Miar looped her gossamer tail—her species' form of laughter. "On the contrary, my friend. The *absence* of free will is an illusion created by time travel. As you told your sister—as you will one day tell her—when you loop back to overlap your own past, its events appear to follow an unalterable destiny, when in fact they are simply occurring for the first and only time.

"Free will does exist, Jared Yung. You do make your own decisions. But each decision... can only be made once."

Jared sat silently for a long moment. "I can't accept that," he finally said.

"You must. Your own experiences are proof."

"No, there must be a way," he countered intently. "I mean—if the past can't be changed—why would your people have built the time-holes in the first place?"

"So that generations to come could learn from their past." Miar stepped over to the human, placing a soft-furred hand on his shoulder, fingers curled into a fist to protect him from her claws. "That is what the past is for, my friend—not to be changed, but to be learned from. If you erased the past, you would erase its lessons."

Again the pain showed clearly in his small brown eyes. "Some lessons should never have to be learned," he breathed.

Miar coughed softly, betraying her impatience. This one would be a challenge to convince. But she needed him for what lay ahead, so she would have to keep trying.

"You are not to blame for the past, my friend," she told him. "Do not torture yourself for things you cannot help. Better to focus on what you can do than on what you cannot. Especially now—for you may have a vital role to play in the events that lie ahead."

Jared tilted his head, the skin above his eyes rumpling. "I don't understand," he said.

So Miar showed him the message.

"Greetings, Miar of House Prrisht'cheo," began the Marrhwai on the screen: white of fur, blue of eye, her forehead crowned with a dark gray marking in the form of an inverted Y. Jared looked between the strikingly feline alien beside him and the one on the screen. Even to one unfamiliar with the Marrhwai, they were clearly the same individual.

"I am indeed your older self," the recorded being confirmed, *"but I speak to you from the past."* The future Miar spoke with haste and urgency. *"You are needed, Miar. You must use the incoming spacecraft to travel to the uptime end of the Niquelahr timehole. You and the human Jared Yung have a vital part to play in the defeat of Kirish Grayshadow. You must leave promptly. Space and time coordinates follow."* The message ended, replaced by text Jared could not read.

As he stared at Miar, absorbing what he had seen, she copied the message to a data crystal and transferred it to the carrypouch on the belt that was her only garment. "Come swiftly, Jared Yung. I will answer any questions as best I can on the journey, but—" Her tail looped. "I have it on reliable authority that we must depart at once."

"Who is Kirish Grayshadow?" Jared asked as Miar led him briskly to his ship. Even though she had been in cryosleep for decades, he had to struggle to keep up with her determined, long-legged stride.

"Kirish, who called himself Lord Grayshadow, was a tyrant far in the Marrhwai past. He placed himself on a pedestal above the rest of us and demanded our tribute and devotion. Those who would not submit were slashed beneath his claws."

"But...." Jared felt new hope as they entered his small craft. "This means your future self is telling you to do the very thing I've tried to do for so long! And it sounds to me like she succeeded, like she knew what was going to happen because she'd lived it! We *can* change history after all!"

Miar lowered her head. "No, Jared. Kirish Grayshadow's reign ended when he used the Niquelahr timehole to travel to the future, intending to bring back advanced weapons to use against his enemies. He never returned from his mission—and apparently you and I are part of the reason. We are not about to change history, Jared—merely to play our part in it. Just as you played your part in the history of Earth, Madgren, Barji, and all the other worlds you have visited."

Under Miar's instructions, Jared set a course for the timehole that would take them on the first leg of their journey into the past—not F'teondrou itself, of course, since that could only take them forward, toward Jared's time.

If Miar was right, there was no point in ever returning there.

Jared slept deeply after showing Miar the basics of his craft's operation. When he awoke much later, he found Miar studying the message from her future self once more. It contained frustratingly little information, yet at least Miar could take comfort in the fact that she would surely survive whatever happened. But would Jared?

"We passed through the Wromm'shalla timehole while you slept," Miar reported, "and are now en route to the S'vitralneo hole. Once through it, we shall be in the right time, and need then only travel through space to Niquelahr."

Jared acknowledged the update brusquely. "I've been thinking," he said. "Your arguments make sense, from a physical point of view, a logical point of view. They hold together. They almost seem inevitable. But there's a question they don't answer."

"What is the question?"

"Every time I've attempted a change, it's turned out I lacked exact information about what I was trying to change, and so blindly became a part of the very events I was attempting to alter. But it can't always be that way. In all the times that anyone has traveled into the past, there must have been instances where a traveler knew exactly what had happened in a given time and place and was in a position to change it.

"When I was nine, I was trapped for two days in a maintenance tunnel of a space habitat. I know exactly where I was, exactly when it happened, and I know I saw no other person in all that time. Theoretically, I could go back to that precise time and place, and be somewhere I know I wasn't."

"Since you were not there, something would happen to prevent you."

"But that's exactly my point. *What* would prevent me? And what would prevent people in other situations from making other changes? What possible physical mechanism could there be that would specifically prevent the *exact* actions that would alter history, in *every* possible instance where it was attempted?

"The universe doesn't work that way, Miar. Its laws operate on particles and energy fields, not on choices and specific actions. You yourself said we have free will. If I'm in a past where I know exactly what happened, what force could act in every possible instance to confound my free will so as to prevent me from changing it? Fate? Magic? Angels? Certainly not physics, since physics doesn't work that way."

Miar watched the stars for a moment before answering. "Physics works differently in different conditions. On an open plain, you are free to run in any direction—but only in two dimensions. Run off a cliff, though, and your freedom to choose your direction is abruptly far more constrained—even though exactly the same physical laws apply.

"There are degrees of freedom, Jared. None of them are absolute."

"So you're saying time travelers are more constrained in their choices than those who haven't... jumped off the cliff."

"Yes."

"But the same question applies. What specific physical process would operate to restrict our choices or their outcomes to make sure we didn't change anything?"

Miar pondered, absently pawing at her squirrel-like tail. "You raise good questions, Jared," she admitted. "As for how the impersonal workings of the universe could target specific choices... all I can say is that we are part of the universe. Our bodies, our brains, and our thoughts are made of the same energies that form all the universe. Our actions and our lives are expressions of those energies in interaction. We are all part of a greater whole."

"So free will is an illusion after all?"

"That is not what I said. Our will is part of the larger whole—no less than any other factor, yet no more. If that does not feel like freedom to you, it is only because you have not yet accepted that you are part of the universe—and it is part of you."

Finally they arrived at Niquelahr, where the timehole mouth whirled madly around its partner singularity, churning the starscape beyond — so much like Jared's first fateful sighting, so long ago in the far future. Nearby, but far enough to be safe from the gravitic turbulence, was the Marrhwai station: a vast glittering wheel, turning with slow majesty in contrast to the frenzied gyration of the timehole, with lush yellow-green jungles apparent through the sky windows of its inner rim. Yet the gleaming hull was scarred, the windows pitted and blackened, the jungles ablaze within. In spite of all the tragedies he'd witnessed, Jared was shocked. Miar simply rumbled softly in her throat, a purr of infinite sadness.

They made their way to an intact docking port, careful to avoid detection by the large ships moored on the other side of the wheel, and made their way cautiously inside. Soon they came upon the bodies. Dozens of Marrhwai corpses lay scattered about the streets, savaged by tooth and claw, microwave and particle beam. Most of them had white or black fur, or a mix of both. Many of the white-furred ones bore gray or black splotches upon their foreheads.

Jared gazed between Miar and a young female corpse, barely out of cubhood. Miar answered the unspoken question in his eyes. "This was the home of House Prrisht'cheo," she confirmed. "These are my children, and their children, and theirs. Of all of them, I was away when it happened."

"My God. Miar...." He trailed off.

Miar folded her hands and lowered her head. "Why do you think I chose to sleep my way through the ages, alone in that station? I had nothing to hold me to this time."

"You knew this would happen."

"I didn't know Grayshadow was the cause. Only that Niquelahr station had been destroyed by unknown raiders. All the bodies burned before the atmosphere was lost."

Jared shook his head. "If only we could have been here sooner...."

Miar whirled on him, her eyes those of a predator poised to strike. "'Could have been' is a phrase wise time-travelers learn to expunge from their language," she hissed. "It is nothing more than self-torture." She tried to gather herself. "We must accept the tragedies of our past, learn to move beyond them, or else we simply eat ourselves from the inside. *Let it go,* Jared Yung! End your mad obsession with putting the flame back in the candle! All you do is burn yourself."

Suddenly there was a high-pitched growl, and they whirled. Seemingly from nowhere appeared a Marrhwai tigress, a fearsome beauty striped in brown and black, with a rakish splash of copper atop her head. Her eyes, captured ring nebulae of gold and jade, blazed at them—then softened as she focussed on Miar. "You are Prrisht'cheo?" she asked tentatively.

Miar stepped forward proudly, tensed for battle. "I am Miar, science-priestess, matriarch of House Prrisht'cheo," she declared.

The tigress relaxed. "Thank the Sky that at least one of you survives," she sighed. "I am Tashar, also of House Prrisht'cheo."

Jared looked between the two dissimilar Marrhwai. "You're related?" he asked Miar.

"Kin by house if not by blood," Miar answered curtly. "Tashar? I know the name. A litter-sister of Kirish Grayshadow."

Tashar hissed. "To my shame."

Miar spoke to Jared, without turning from Tashar. "She often spoke against his cruel acts—even fought him at times. Only blood loyalty kept her alive. But when Kirish mounted his expedition to the future, Tashar accompanied him."

"I joined him so I could stop him," the tigress explained. "But it has done little good. He found his future weapons, and used them to slaughter the Prrisht'cheo—his own house!" She spoke with the indignant disbelief of a child. Despite her ferocity, she had a youthful quality. "Many of his soldiers joined my revolt, but we were out-gunned." As if in illustration, an explosion resounded nearby, shaking them. "We have to seek cover," Tashar said quickly. "Then you can tell me how you survived, and who your alien friend is."

Tashar absorbed their story with wide-eyed fascination. "Then... you knew what you would find when you arrived?" she asked Miar with deep sympathy.

"When my future self told me where and when I must go, I recognized it. But I had to come."

"To live the death of your house a second time...." Tashar nuzzled her gently. Despite all the battles she'd fought, there was a depth of kindness in her. "Time travel reeks," she concluded. "No wonder you want to change things, Jared. I, too, yearn to undo all this horror. It's not fair that we can go back but not make anything be different!"

"Sometimes it is necessary to be part of what always was," Miar said. "Judging from my message to myself, Jared and I will help in the defeat of Grayshadow."

"You're just about the only ones left who could, other than me," Tashar said. "This place is falling apart, its defenders cut down. I'd have abandoned it already if I didn't still need to stop my brother."

Jared placed a hand on Tashar's soft-furred arm. "We'll do anything we can to help."

Tashar purred and nuzzled him. "Thank you. But what can we do?"

He peered through the crack in their hiding place at the shielded, two-person hovertanks that roamed the streets hunting down the last resistance, the soldiers inside occasionally blowing apart buildings, sculptures, and gardens for no reason. "How would they react if they saw me—an alien? Would they shoot first, or would they be curious?"

"Curiosity is a strong trait in the Marrhwai," Miar said.

Jared smirked. "Somehow that doesn't surprise me."

"They would want to see what you were," Tashar added. "Knowing Kirish, he would want you alive to question. To *play* with," she sneered.

"Would they drop the shields to take me into a vehicle?"

"They would have to."

He took a deep breath. "Then I guess you've got yourselves a diversion."

Choosing his moment carefully, Jared waited until all but one of the tanks were out of sight, then ran out into the view of the remaining one's occupants. "Hey, over here!" he cried, waving. The turret swiveled to cover him, and he ducked behind a broken tree—but no energy bolt spewed forth. After a moment, the tank began to approach him. He ran in the predetermined direction, hoping Grayshadow's soldiers would consider one tank enough to stop a single unarmed alien.

Soon he let them corner him. The hovertank settled to the ground, its shield disengaged, and one of the Marrhwai soldiers—the first live male he'd seen of their species—came out to investigate. "And what are you, then?"

"I am the cat who walks by himself," Jared replied, "and all times are alike to me." His translator was set to receive-only; if they knew their tongue were programmed into it, they'd know he'd had contact with Marrhwai.

The soldier coughed irritatedly, and raised his gun. "You understand this, don't you?"

Jared cowered melodramatically. "Lions and tigers and bears, oh my!"

The Marrhwai moved in and pulled him forward. "Come on, let's get you inside. Lord Grayshadow will have questions for you."

"I've been to London to visit the Queen."

The soldier grunted and shoved Jared into the entranceway—only to find it occupied by Tashar, who leapt on him as Miar finished incapacitating the other one. Jared grinned. "Tyger Tyger, burning bright."

Tashar was nothing if not a fast operator. Before they knew what hit them, several of the other tanks had been disabled by fire from what they had thought was one of their own. Miar and Jared took command of two reasonably intact ones, and together the three of them effectively neutralized Kirish's armored force. Miar took no joy in it; there had already been more than enough death.

Soon they walked amid the ruins, searching for survivors, hoping to find some who were not of Grayshadow's troops. But Niquelahr was silent save for the fires. Kirish's plan to conquer worlds had been halted, but this tragedy had not been averted. "You and I are truly the last of the Prrisht'cheo," Miar finally told Tashar, her tail drooping, as they stood in the entrance hall of a ruined museum.

"Maybe not," the lithe tigress countered. "There is still my brother to be found. May he be alive so that I can kill him!" Miar could not approve of the sentiment—but neither could she condemn it under the circumstances.

"The first part of your wish is answered," came a new voice. With that lightning speed of hers, Tashar was facing it before the second word ended. Miar and Jared spun more slowly, and found themselves face to face with Kirish Grayshadow.

For that was who it had to be. He was massive, powerful, his sleek coat a gray so profound it was Shadow incarnate—but where the light hit it, it shone like polished silver. His golden eyes, like flames piercing the fog, burned with baleful savagery. He wore a breastplate emblazoned with the emblem of Lord Grayshadow: a mighty blue tree, the sacred *n'wele*, with a silhouette of Kirish upon its highest bough, poised to pounce.

Kirish continued, a cold purr in his voice as he levelled his rifle at Tashar. "As for the second part... you are welcome to try."

Tashar hissed, limbs tensing for a leap. Kirish narrowed his eyes, perfecting his aim.

"*Stop!*" Miar strode between them, throwing her haughtiest, sternest gaze upon Kirish. "How dare you threaten your own litter-sister with such cowardly weapons?! Do you not have the honor to take her on with your own claws?"

Even the mighty Lord Grayshadow was cowed by her regal presence, this radiant force of white light. But he recovered himself and said, "I had enough of that when we were cubs. I outgrew it long ago."

"Only because I was too fast for you!" Tashar taunted.

"Outgrew?!" Miar scoffed. "A spoiled cub like you? You mewl for attention and worship, demand to have everything your own way, and lash out when you don't get it." From the corner of her eye, she saw Jared quietly circling to Kirish's right, moving for a fallen rifle. She kept her gaze firmly on Kirish, however, and prayed the young, impetuous Tashar could do the same. She stepped up her imperious lecture, striving to hold his attention. "And through your childish ignorance of the balances of life, you destroy whole houses with your petty tantrums. You are no emperor. You are a monster!"

"Simply a matter of perspective," Kirish purred. He aimed his rifle between Miar's brilliant blue eyes.

"No!" Jared cried, grabbing the rifle and firing in haste. It took Kirish in the right leg, and the tyrant fell, his wild shot hitting the ceiling. In a flash, Tashar leapt over Miar's head and was upon her brother.

Miar ran to Jared and pulled him away from the falling debris as the ceiling crumbled. She half-carried him outside, and as the building started to collapse, he cried, "Tashar!" In his eyes, she saw a fresh horror piling atop all the others he'd known.

But as the building toppled to dust, a brown-black streak burst from the cloud. Tashar rolled to her feet in front of them, coughing daintily. "Let's get out of here," she advised, licking blood from her claws.

With the fall of Kirish, his surviving troops lost their will to fight on. They retreated to their ships and fled the station and the timehole. Marrhwai history never recorded their fate.

But before Miar and her allies could leave Niquelahr, she knew there was one thing she had to do. The message from her future self had used Marrhwai protocols, not human. That meant she had sent it—was about to send it—from Niquelahr's facilities.

They found a barely functional communications center. As Tashar removed the body of the comm operator, Jared noted Miar's manner. He was coming to recognize Marrhwai expressions now—especially pain. "Miar?" he asked.

"My grandson," she breathed, twitching an ear in the direction of the body.

"I'm sorry."

Miar nodded, and moved to the console, gathering herself to send the message that had brought her here. Jared looked up, a thought striking him. "Miar—this is our chance."

"Our chance to do what?"

"To find out once and for all. We have exact knowledge of what's about to happen. We know what's on the message you sent. But you *can* change it. All you have to do is say the words differently!"

Miar gazed at him sadly. "I do not remember the exact words. Whatever I end up saying will be what I have already heard."

"Then—then I'll stand behind you. We know I wasn't visible on the original message. If I'm in it this time around, that will be a change. A small one, but still a change of history. And it would be so simple. And maybe it can help us figure out how to make bigger changes. Miar, we might still be able to find a way to undo this tragedy— and others!"

"Jared, you know this event has never happened before. There is nothing to undo—merely a thing to do."

"But *what could stop us?* Miar... all I have to do to change history is to stand behind your shoulder. What could possibly prevent that?!"

Then came the snarling cry: *"Creature!"* He whirled to see a broken Kirish Grayshadow lying in the doorway, gun aimed at Jared's heart, deadly madness in his eyes. And Jared knew his question was about to be answered.

But then there was a blur of white, a weight knocking him aside. The gun screamed... and Miar lay still.

Tashar appeared in the inner doorway, saw what had happened, and leapt screeching at Kirish to exact her vengeance. But his own had exhausted his last breath, and there was nothing for Tashar to do but wail.

After a time, Jared and Tashar stood silently together over Miar's body. "This means... history *was* changed," Tashar realized. "Miar never sent the message."

Furrowing his brow, Jared knelt by the body and retrieved a data crystal from Miar's pouch. "What is it?" Tashar asked.

"A copy of the message," he said. Had Miar forgotten she carried it? Or had she simply accepted the futility of trying to change what would only happen once?

Their eyes met for a moment. Tashar nodded, took the crystal, and moved toward the console.

Then she paused. "Wait — we don't have to send it. You can still prove that history can be changed."

"If we don't send it, Miar won't come. You'll die, along with millions of others in the past." He nodded. "Send it."

"We don't have to send *this* message," Tashar realized. "I could send a message saying the same thing, or you could. It would be a change." She checked the systems, then sagged. "No. The cameras and microphones are down. Only the crystal playback works."

"I guess... that was inevitable," Jared decided.

Yet even as he said it, he realized Miar was right; this was not the result of fate. This was where the choices of countless different beings had led, one free choice after another. Yet the sum total of those free choices had whittled down the probabilities bit by bit, until Jared and Tashar were left with only one remaining choice. Perhaps that was the true paradox. The only constraint on one being's freedom was the sum total of everyone else's freedom.

As Jared reflected on Kirish, on the Barjians, on all the tyrannies he'd seen, he realized that was the way it should be. No one should believe their own choices existed independently of the free choice of others.

"Quickly — send the message before this whole system collapses." He watched as Tashar set the station's powerful comm-laser to where Miar's station would be hundreds of years from now, hundreds of light-years away, and beamed the message into space. The loop was finally complete.

✸

They left in Jared's ship, letting Niquelahr burn, a pyre for Miar and House Prrisht'cheo. They traveled forward, to Miar's station at the F'teondrou timehole. "There's nothing for me in Niquelahr's time, or in my own," Tashar had explained. "And someone needs to carry on Miar's work, to take the lessons and legacy of the Marrhwai into the future."

Jared kept her company as she got settled, as she learned the station's systems, as she reviewed its records to learn the questions she would be asked and the answers she would need to give. "And where will you go now?" she finally asked the human.

Jared stared out at the timehole, a crystal ball floating in the dark, a thousand future stars spinning in its depths. "Forward," he answered at length. "Somewhere in space and time is a place I once called home. I don't know if I can remember the way back—but I'll find it if it takes another lifetime."

Tashar nuzzled him softly. "May the Sky light your way home, my friend."

He stroked her head fur. "And may you be a bright beacon for lost travelers like me… out here in the forest of the night."

Jared returned to his ship and prepared it for departure, not without reluctance. Tashar caught a quick meal in the station's galley while ship and station collaborated on the calculations for the risky trip forward. But as she groomed herself after her meal, a thought suddenly struck her, and she raced to activate the comm before the human left.

"Jared, I just realized," Tashar began. "The message! The message we sent to this station was a recording of the one this station received! Miar never said the words on that recording. So *how can they exist?*"

On the screen, Jared sat in silence for a long moment. Finally, he smiled and said, *"Don't worry about it. It's all in the past."*

And then Jared Yung steered his ship into the timehole and was gone. Tashar watched him vanish into the future and stood for a while, gazing into the timehole at the whirling stars of a place and time that were not hers. It struck her that this place and time were not hers either—but then she changed her mind. From now on, this was home.

At last, with her ears folded into a smile, Tashar laid back into the cryochamber to begin the long wait for the next traveler through time. For she was the past, and she had things to teach the future.

Abductive Reasoning

The odds of a wafer-ship being struck by a microsingularity in deep space were, like both of the entities involved, too minuscule to notice on a cosmic scale. So naturally it happened to Cjek'darrit while she was in a hurry—and right in the middle of her shortcut through an uncivilized part of the galaxy. The spillage from her damaged vacuum-energy sails would send her badly off course and critically deplete her reserves if she couldn't bring it under control—but of course, the sails were the one component her onboard nanites couldn't self-repair.

What hurt most was the irony. Her creche-mates only reconverged at the home star once every few hundred galactic microrotations, and Cjek'darrit had skipped the last reunion because of a silly argument with her wing-sister—an impetuous choice she'd regretted ever since. And so, in her determination not to miss the next reunion, she'd made the equally impetuous choice to divert through undeveloped space, far from anyone who could receive her distress signal in time.

Her only recourse was to head for the nearby star's third planet, which showed signs of a technological civilization—though it looked like a primitive one that hadn't learned how to generate power without befouling its ecosystem. Logically, if it were advanced enough to have the materials she needed to repair her sails, it would probably be part of the Galactic Coalition already. So Cjek might have to resign herself to waiting however long it took for the Coalition to receive her distress signal and send help—or for this civilization to develop starflight on its own, whichever came first. Either way, it would mean another missed chance to make amends with her sister—and who knew if she would be granted another?

At least she managed to bring the wafer-ship through its atmospheric deceleration in one piece. As she wafted toward the ground,

Cjek's scans revealed a sparsely populated area—some sort of agricultural zone, hideously wasteful of land and resources—with only a few crude wooden structures nearby. She hoped its population was sparse enough that she could remain unobserved as she reconstituted herself, giving her a chance to size up the local culture before deciding whether and how to make open contact.

But her bad luck hadn't ended yet. The strain of descent triggered a surge of energy from the breached vacuum sails, causing them to emit brilliant beams of varicolored light and a loud, descending hum. She damped it as quickly as she could, then vectored in for a landing in the middle of a field of tall, slender crops—an excellent source of organic compounds from which to build her new body. The wafer-ship housing her consciousness biochip was ideal for spaceflight, but too tiny and fragile to operate planetside without the protection of an organic shell.

Still, the body would be vulnerable while it was incomplete, so she kicked her replication nanites into high gear, prioritizing speed over stealth. The synthesis process unavoidably released additional lights, sounds, smells, and clouds of vapor, and she could only hope the vegetation around her would provide sufficient concealment.

Once the neural interface between her biochip and the body's sensory cortex was online, Cjek'darrit opened her newly made eyes and found herself in a neat, circular burned patch in the middle of the vegetation field. Engaging the motor cortex, she rose and tested the limbs of her new conveyance—a flesh form comfortably like the one she had been born in so many embodiments ago, yet optimized for the biochemistry and environment of this high-gravity, ultraviolet-bombarded world. The nanites had fashioned a functional skintight garment from fused plant fibers to provide additional protection for the body.

As soon as Cjek neared the edge of the field, her echolocation registered the hesitant approach of a bipedal animal swathed in a similar fabric covering with bits of metal attached—no doubt one of the operators of this agricultural compound. Once again, she cursed herself for her impatience. Yet after a moment, accepting that she'd been observed by an indigenous sophont, Cjek decided there was no reason to delay contacting the creature and learning what she could from it. A portion of her wafer-mind had already scanned the broadcasts and data systems of this planet and had not flagged any clear indications of usable technology, but most of her available processing power had been devoted to constructing a translation matrix. She might be able to use that matrix to gain additional knowledge from a native. Thus, after loading the dominant local tongue into her language center, she stepped out to greet the unidentified farming organism.

The bizarrely vertical-bodied bipedal creature—a "human," according to the translator—carried an illumination source in one of its hands. As soon as the light beam fell upon Cjek'darrit, the human's single pair of eyes widened for a moment, then shut firmly as the creature went very tense, its hands clenching tightly by its sides. Realizing she'd frightened the poor thing, Cjek loped gingerly toward it on all sixes. *Hello,* she thought in Teoi'kath, hearing it emerge from her mouthparts as "Hello."

The human's eyes briefly snapped open, then clenched shut once more. "I-I'm ready," it whispered. Based on broadcast visual images, her nonverbal interpreter protocol suggested its manner was frightened but somehow eager as well. Cjek suspected the protocol's accuracy left something to be desired.

"I'm glad to hear it. Ready for what?"

The human finally relaxed its eyelids and got its first good look at Cjek'darrit. Its reaction translated as the expected shock—and then a more unexpected reaction. Disappointment? As though Cjek were not what it had expected to see.

"*You* know," the human finally answered. "Don't toy with me. I know all about what you aliens do. The abductions. The tests. The implants, the impregnations, all of it! And I'm ready," it went on defiantly—but still with that undercurrent of desire. "Do your worst!"

Cjek's first reaction was excitement. No sooner had she landed than she'd found a lead on a possible means of rescue. It seemed too good to be true.

But then the details of the human's description began to sink in. "Wait a minute," Cjek said, the matrix providing the proper idiom. "Are you telling me that space travelers are performing invasive medical experiments on intelligent creatures without their consent?"

"Of course you are! Everyone knows it! Even the government knows it, but of course they're keeping it a secret from the rest of us. The politicians and the aliens, you're all in on it."

Cjek wondered how everyone could know something that the government kept secret. She also wondered how it—no, *he*, the interpreter advised her—could seem so ardent about something he was so vehemently condemning. Perhaps her translation software needed an overhaul. "Look here, friend. That sort of thing would violate half the laws and ethical codes in the Galactic Coalition. So be careful with those accusations.

"I, for one, have never been to this planet. It's not even on my charts." She raised the front half of her body to vertical, pushed herself up further on the tips of her middle limbs' long fingers, puffed up the featherspine crest on her head and back, and splayed her short, fanlike tail to its full width. "I am Cjek'darrit of the Fourth Rank, Subline Red, Left Wing. I am an Iteoi from the stellar system Ruch'danni. I had an accident in space. My sensors detected evidence of industrialization on this world, so I came here to search for repair equipment. And you are?"

The human stared for a moment, then came to some form of attention. "Roy Vincent Duncan!" he exclaimed. "Citizen of the United States of America of the planet Earth!" A tiny, winged arthropod landed on the side of his face, somewhat spoiling the effect.

"Okay, okay, these ears work fine. Roy, is it?"

"Roy Vincent Duncan!" he shouted, frightening the arthropod away. "Citizen of—"

"Roy it is, then. I'm Cjek. Now listen, why don't you take me to your—" She paused, for Roy perked up at that for some reason. "—Your house," she finished, "and tell me more about these aliens abducting your people. If someone is doing something so immoral to your kind, the galactic authorities ought to be notified!"

That last was added merely to get the human's cooperation. Cjek'darrit tried to be a decent enough citizen, but she was no crusader. Whatever species had undertaken to experiment on Earth's indigenes might not be willing to help her leave the planet if they feared she would report them. And any such report would take at least a micro-rotation—about two hundred of this planet's years—to generate action, given how far removed this sector was from the normal lines of galactic communication. By that time, the experimenters would probably have concluded their study anyway. So what would be the point?

Once they reached Roy Vincent Duncan's farmhouse, the human had overcome his shock and evinced deep excitement to be conversing with a real live alien. But he soon remembered his mission to inform Cjek'darrit about the heinous alien experimenters. More winged arthropods flew through the door in both directions as the Iteoi followed the human inside. They were probably drawn to the aroma of decaying food that pervaded the interior. Cjek tiptoed gingerly through the clutter on her rear four limbs, wishing she could balance on just the rearmost pair as easily as Roy could.

"Here," Roy said, beckoning Cjek toward a back room. "I have the photos in here."

"A whole room? Don't you have a data network connection?"

"And let the En-Ess-Ay eavesdrop on my every move? Oh-h, no. They won't get me that way."

Something about the room they now entered reminded Cjek of religious shrines she'd visited on other worlds. The walls were festooned with images, some depicting circular objects or vague patterns of light. Most, however, depicted pale bipedal forms, and it was these that Roy pointed out to Cjek'darrit. "You see?" Roy asked.

Cjek ruffled her crest in confusion. "See what? There are only humans depicted here. Naked humans."

"*Humans?*" Roy exclaimed. "They're aliens!"

"Where?"

"These!" He pointed to them directly. "Anyone can see they aren't a thing like us!"

"What are you talking about? They're upright bipeds with two arms and an oval head pointed at the bottom. A very distinctive head shape you have; I've never seen anything like it. And they balance on hind limbs the same as you — do you have any idea how rare that is? Two eyes, a horizontal mouth… ten fingers," she finished, holding up all but two of her own dozen. She gave him a quick sonar burst to look beneath his clothing, then consulted the communications records she had downloaded on descent. "Granted, they lack external sexual characteristics, but that could just mean… oh, no. No, Roy, I need to find aliens. I don't have time to indulge your fetish for images of unclothed immature females."

"What? No, it was just the one time. And I was holding them for a friend. And the government planted them anyway! No, I swear, countless people have seen these aliens. Look, look." He gestured at the wall dominated by the images of bright lights and circular shapes. "These are their ships."

Grasping for hope, Cjek reasoned that experimenters visiting this world might choose to incarnate themselves in bodies mimicking those of the indigenous civilization. The emulation was imperfect, but the approximation might be intended to put the natives at ease, or might simply be a practical adaptation to the conditions of this planet (though how teetering on two limbs could be practical in this high gravity was beyond her). So she might as well give the human the benefit of the doubt—for now.

Roy pulled back when Cjek's prehensile tongues shot out from her stubby probosces to ruffle through the photos of the alleged spacecraft. Soon, she swiveled her left eyes to focus on the human. "You've got to be kidding."

Surprise seemed to be Roy's dominant emotion. "Well—I know they're a little blurry...."

"They're *all* blurry! Doesn't anyone on this planet know how to use a camera?"

"They, they go by so fast—"

"You're putting me on, right? I mean, look at these. There's no design similarity at all, other than the circular shapes." Cjek reared up onto her hind legs to study some of the higher images, using both tongues and forehands to shuffle through them. "No consistency. There's no way these could all be produced by the same race."

Roy's mouth gaped. "You mean there are multiple species visiting us?"

"Come on, there'd have to be dozens. I can't imagine an ordinary planet like this attracting *that* much attention—especially with this inconveniently high gravity," she added with a grunt as she lowered herself to a more comfortable quadrupedal stance.

"Besides—nobody uses cumbersome craft like these for interstellar journeys. The power requirements would be outrageous. And why bother, when you can store your consciousness biochip and a nanofabrication suite on a wafer-ship half the size of your hand?"

The human looked at his hand. "Then how do they get the abductees inside?"

"How big do you think these things are, anyway?" Cjek engaged her optical analysis software to evaluate the printouts again. The results were not encouraging. "This one has a diameter about a fifth your height, and it's about eight human-lengths from the camera. This one's on a wire—right there. Wait... this one looks like one of those metal things on the wheels of your vehicle! Wire... wire... this one's a cloud!" What kind of sick joke was this creature trying to play on her in her time of need?

"But—" Roy sputtered. "But look!" He led Cjek into another room and activated a video device, inserting a silvery disc into an adjacent machine. "Watch this. It was taken from an airplane at night."

"What? I see a point of light moving around on a black background."

"But look at the *way* it moves! No Earthly vehicle could change direction that fast, be that maneuverable! It's clearly cancelling inertia!"

Cjek made a noise analogous to clearing her throat. "How did you say this was recorded?"

"Some passengers on an airplane saw it. They had a camera, and—"

She stared. "A *portable* camera?"

"Yeah. Handheld."

Cjek's assessment of this creature's intelligence was plummeting with its every utterance. Being ignorant of interstellar spacecraft parameters was one thing, but not even grasping the difference between an erratically moving object and an erratically shaking camera? "You're just wasting my time now, Roy. That's probably the second planet in your system! I saw it while I was coming in—it's quite bright."

"But—but millions of people have seen UFOs! The brilliant lights in the sky, the colors, the—"

"Wait, wait a minute. Brilliant lights in the sky?"

"Uh-huh."

In spite of herself, Cjek was becoming amused by this whole pathetic situation. "Oh, Roy, Roy, give us aliens some credit! If you were a space traveler studying a planet-bound species—and you didn't want them to know you were there—would you go flying around their night sky *in brilliantly lit vehicles*?!"

"You did!"

"That was an accident! And I wasn't even trying that hard to hide."

"Well, they... they don't care if we see them!"

"But you said they were conspiring with the government to keep all this secret."

"That's 'cause—that's 'cause the government has some of them prisoner! Area 51, Roswell, you know!"

Cjek focused all four eyes on Roy, puckering her probosces as she processed all this. "So... they have a whole fleet of advanced, powerful spacecraft right here on your planet, and little enough regard for your species to treat you like laboratory vermin—and yet they're not willing to attack your government facilities to free their kin. Instead, they've agreed to keep their presence secret to protect their kin—yet they casually advertise their presence in your night skies. Meanwhile, your own government is aware that a foreign power has invaded its soil to conduct immoral medical experiments on its populace, and has sided with the invaders against its own taxpaying citizens." By the First Rank, this was almost worth the risk of missing her reunion again. Was his whole species this lacking in critical reasoning skills? If so, it was no wonder the Coalition hadn't bothered to contact them.

"They, they've taken over the government! They put things in people's necks, see—"

"But you just said the government was controlling *them!*"

Roy was unable to find an answer. Cjek took pity on him. "Look... if you're doing a clandestine survey, you set up a gravity-lens telescope in a nearby system. If you're a little more daring or want more resolution, you put receivers in the outer cometary cloud and monitor the radio signals. If they don't broadcast outward, or if there's some other reason for an on-site survey, you hide out underground."

"Yeah! Yeah! There's a *big* UFO base at the North Pole!"

"Then," Cjek went on as if Roy hadn't spoken, "if you need to do aerial reconnaissance, you send out robot probes designed as small flying creatures—insects, you would call them. Or perhaps you even..."

She trailed off. Had the answer been right in front of her this whole time? She looked up at the tiny, buzzing creatures that circled the room's dim light source. Scanning through the recognized interstellar contact frequencies and protocols, she soon got a ping in return. Most of the insects in this domicile were genuine, but Cjek'darrit felt great relief as two of them settled atop her head and sent a tightbeam transmission to her biochip within.

<Your appeal is acknowledged, Cjek'darrit of the Fourth Rank. We apologize for not initiating contact, but we are programmed as passive observers.>

<Understood. Are you authorized to help me repair my vacuum sails?>

<Certainly. We are obliged to assist any Coalition citizen in need, as well as to minimize disruption to the experiment.>

<So you *have* been experimenting on these beings? Abducting and probing them?>

<Our experiment is strictly observational, evaluating the development of a technological civilization in isolation from interstellar contact. Our femtosensors have pervaded the dust of this world for thousands of its years. We

have no need to abduct the humans; we are inside every one of them at every moment, passively observing every last detail of their lives.>

<And these humanlike forms that Roy insists are aliens?>

<Mere folklore. Humans' superstitious beliefs in extraterrestrial visitation tend to conform to dominant entertainment-media images of alien life. This particular image was originally published as a speculative projection of future human evolution, filtered through this regional society's prejudices in favor of intellect over animal traits, as well as its prejudice in favor of pale skin. It was then co-opted by cultists such as this one, whose beliefs were then popularized by the entertainment media, creating a feedback loop that entrenched the image in their culture.>

"Yes, yes, I don't need a sociology lecture, just get me off this planet!"

She realized a moment later that she had spoken aloud. Roy was staring at her warily. "Who were you talking to just then? Is it *Them?* Are they listening right now? Are they coming to probe me?"

Cjek trilled with laughter. "Oh-h, Roy, Roy. You have no idea. They've been inside you since the day you were born."

It was the wrong thing to say. "No. No!" Roy cried, erupting in panic and running from the room. When Cjek got her laughter under control and loped out after the poor creature to try to calm him down, she found him confronting her with a pair of metal tubes connected to a handgrip. "Stay back! You've been one of them this whole time, haven't you? Trying to find out what I know! Trying to make me doubt! Well, you won't take me!"

She stepped toward him, one hand spread forward placatingly. "Oh, seriously, Roy, why would I need to discredit you if I were just going to—"

The tubes erupted in a chemical explosion that expelled a number of dense metal pellets at dangerous velocity. Her thoughts accelerated to track their approach, but this body was too massive and the local gravity too high to allow her to dodge in time. All she could do was isolate her biochip from the body's pain receptors before impact. Judging from the feedback she did receive as the pellets penetrated her body, that had been a wise choice. The pellets tore through several major organs and tendons, and the hydraulic shock waves that propagated through the body's flesh and fluids overloaded its muscular and circulatory systems, causing it to collapse into immobility. It would take some time for her nanites to rebuild the flesh, and they were still depleted from the exertion of synthesizing it in the first place. She doubted Roy would give her the luxury of self-repair in his current state.

Luckily, the observers were still with her. *<Leave the body,>* they suggested. *<It has served its purpose. Come with these drones in your wafer-ship and we will see you on your way home.>*

Cjek'darrit thanked them and began making preparations to jettison her space-going form from its ruined shell, the most short-lived body she'd ever inhabited. But she couldn't resist making the effort to animate its vocal tract one last time to address Roy. "I'm fine, by the way," she told him, making him convulse in shock. "No hard feelings. This isolated state has clearly made your species delusional, so I don't blame you. But don't worry, I'm going now. Keep the body. Show it to your friends—well, to the people who share your beliefs. Tell them what I've told you. If you're going to obsess over aliens, you might as well get your facts straight."

Before Roy could overcome his panicked paralysis, Cjek allowed the body to expire and ordered her nanites to hollow out an exit pathway for her wafer-ship. The insect drones took the opportunity to ask, *<You disapprove of our isolation experiment?>*

<It doesn't seem to be doing this species a lot of good.>

<Our methods are within the letter of Coalition law. We merely observe; any harm they suffer is through their own choices and actions.>

<That's a convenient rationalization.>

<It is true that the lack of the stabilizing influence of the Coalition has allowed certain negative drives to manifest in amplified form. But it has allowed positive drives to amplify as well. The same imagination that leads this human into delusion inspires others to conceive extraordinary new approaches to physics, sociology, and art. The problems they create for themselves imbue them with a passion to find solutions. Their unique perspective could benefit the Coalition greatly once they reach it on their own.>

<Maybe. But is it worth the cost?> As her wafer-ship rose from her corpse, she took one last look around Roy Vincent Duncan's abode. <It's a terrible thing to be alone too long.>

With that thought in mind, she flew off with the drones, ready to resume her journey back home to her family. This time, perhaps, she would stay for a while.

Roy stared at the corpse of the alien for a long time before deciding what to do. Should he photograph it, freeze it, take samples? Should he contact his allies in the UFO community and reveal these new truths to them?

But what truths? No saucer, no abduction, no probing? Wafer-ships and passive observation? This bizarre, uncategorizable clutter of body parts instead of a proper Gray? No black helicopters showing up to silence him?

He sighed. "No one would ever believe me."

So Roy Vincent Duncan took Cjek'darrit's corpse out to the crop circle it had come from and burned it. Then he spread the ashes around the cornfield in a more intricate pattern of circles and lines. A week later, he razed the faster-growing corn that had resulted, neatened up the edges, photographed the whole thing, and drove down to the local library so he could log on and tell the world what had *really* happened when the saucers had come to take him.

What Slender Threads

Dain Bakor stifled a roar of frustration as she ducked under the cover of a fallen piece of metal roofing, dodging a drone for the third time within the past few minutes. Silently, she cursed Gareth Malhotra for his persistence. Bad enough that his lies and betrayals had left her no recourse but to end her time on Earth; now he wouldn't even leave her alone to go through with it.

She cursed herself, too, for she only had herself to blame for letting things reach this point.

Once the whir of the drone subsided, Dain eased out of hiding and made a break for a nearby alley. Halfway down its length, she froze and pressed against a wall as one of Gareth's teammates crossed into view at the far end. The ginger-haired agent was lissome and androgynous with light amber skin—close enough to Earth-human to fool the natives, but with the precise, fluid body language of a cyborg from Diju. As she'd suspected, Gareth also had masters from a more advanced braneworld.

Dain held very still, hoping the deep shadows would shield her from the Dijuno's large cybernetic eyes. Soon, the agent moved on, but Dain held her position until she could be sure that any further drones under the cyborg's mental control had also gone past. She fought her instinct to dash straight for the transbrane capsule, forcing herself to turn away from it when she exited the alley. She had already let Gareth's team track her most of the way there before she'd caught on that she was being followed. She realized now—far too late—that he must have let his true intentions slip deliberately, to spook her into running for home. Like a fool, she'd reacted exactly as he wanted.

Luckily, the Irddru's agents had located the crossover site in a large, decaying industrial district on the outskirts of the Baltimore-

Washington metropolitan area—a cluster of heavily constructed, metal-laden factories and machinery sufficient to shield the energies of the capsule's passage from detection. Its torn-up streets were a maze, so her convoluted path thus far would have told them little. With care and luck, she could put them on a false trail, then lose them and report home at last.

"This is unnecessary, Dana."

Dain jumped at the sound of Gareth's voice. After a moment, she realized that her own guilty conscience wouldn't echo off the walls; he was speaking through the drones, trying to flush her out. She slowed, softening her footsteps and keeping an eye on the rooftops and overcast skies above.

"I'm sorry I had to deceive you," Gareth's voice went on, *"but we don't need to be adversaries. What I told you before wasn't a lie. We* do *share a connection. The Irddru enslave your world. They're planning to do the same to ours, and they're using you to do it."*

His gentle, coaxing voice only made her clench her fists tighter, digging her nails into her palms. She felt so stupid that she had let him charm her into lowering her guard. The less attention that was paid to lowly government worker "Dana Baker," the better it had been for her cover at the research agency. But Gareth, one of its key physicists, had reached out despite her aloofness, appearing to accept her as few other Terrans would accept a woman of her exceptional height and muscularity, in this society that prized half-starved females with childlike features. Despite all her caution and training, he had worn down her defenses until she'd welcomed him into her life, even beginning to desire him as a lover. The only mercy was that he had insisted on "going slow," no doubt repulsed by the prospect of sex outside his species.

"We can help each other, Dana," his voice echoed. *"We're all orbiting each other, affected by each other's gravity. Our lives resonate with each other, even when we believe we stand alone. And so we're all responsible for one another."*

Dain nearly laughed, for their very surroundings proved how little responsibility Earth's humans took for their own kind. This coastal area was mostly abandoned now, as the population moved inland to escape the flooding and increasingly violent storms the Terrans had unleashed through their own negligence. The fools would surely be better off once they were conquered.

"Whenever you mentioned your mother and sister, Dana, I could see the fear you tried to hide. What have the Irddru threatened to do to your family if you fail them?"

Dain stumbled, then froze, waiting to see if the drones had detected the noise. She cursed herself again for letting Gareth get to her. She knew full well that if she let herself get captured — worse, if she allowed the transbrane capsule to fall into Terran hands and set back the infiltration of their world — then her family's death would be the least she deserved for her incompetence.

"Why should the Irddru hurt me?" Mayu had asked her older sister more than once, when Dain had dragged her back from playing in forbidden zones or tried to get it through her head why she shouldn't dance in public. "If the big bird-lizards are so powerful and wise, why would they be afraid of a child having fun?"

"Children are a danger to themselves," their mother told them when she finally realized Mayu was smart enough to understand. "Not just you, but all Zumela. Primates like us… we're too young a species to master ourselves. The Irddru have three million more years of practice at being civilized on their world. Their rule might seem unforgiving, but it's only because we need to learn discipline."

Mayu scoffed. "How do I put anyone in danger by dancing?"

"You remind people of the old rituals, the ways that almost destroyed us. It's not your fault, love, but you need to trust in the Irddru's strictures. They know best."

Back in their tiny shared bedroom, Dain explained it differently. "You have to be smart, Mayu. Play the game, think like them. Get ahead within the system, and then you can find ways to do what you want."

"Easy to say when you're the big sister. You never let me do what I want."

"You think I get to do what I want? I can't, because I'm always running myself ragged to save you from your own stupidity! Next time I should just let the Irddru throw you in a work camp!" She stormed out, unable to face the pain in her sister's eyes.

Once Dain was confident she hadn't been located, she resumed her course away from the crossover site. Gareth's voice did not follow her; perhaps she'd managed to get ahead of the drones. Taking a chance, she broke into a run.

Two blocks on, she rounded a corner, then skidded to a stop. An overturned van and a pile of debris blocked her way. Turning back, she saw a large male figure dropping from the roof above, landing in a crouch to cut off her exit. As he straightened, she saw that he was armed with a hefty plasma rifle and a holstered Earth pistol. He struck a relaxed pose and gave her a lazy grin.

"Hi there. Dana, right? Or… no, Serejen Ru says if you're Zumela, it's probably Dain. Or maybe Deya? Tell me if I'm getting close. Oh, I'm Roak, by the way. I'm from Dabaas."

She knew the Dabaarai's reputation as mercenaries, though she'd never met one until now. Roak had a large, robust build, stockier than a Zumela's, with a heavier brow and jawline and coarser hair. He probably didn't go out in public much on this planet, though he spoke the language well. No doubt he was an enforcer, brought in when there was violence to be done in the shadows. The Irddru used her own people in that capacity often enough.

Dain braced herself. "You won't take me without a fight."

Roak took that in, his relaxed attitude unchanged. "Sure, we could do that. Or you could just take us to your transbrane capsule like Gareth wants. I get paid either way, but the second way's easier for both of us."

"You get paid," she countered angrily, "but it costs me everything."

"Oh. Okay, I get that. You've got something to fight for." He strolled forward. "Let's make that happen."

Somehow, his casual, unperturbed manner was more intimidating than overt hostility. No doubt he had reason for his confidence. Dain probably had a moderate edge in strength, but she was trained for infiltration, not combat.

The tension built in her body, then broke. She turned, ran, and used the fight-or-flight adrenaline to vault atop the fallen van. She dropped to the pavement on the other side just as bullets speared the air above her head. As she made a mad dash toward the next corner, she heard Roak trying to clamber over the van. By the time another shot rang out, she was already out of Roak's sight, too far ahead for him to catch up. But as she fled, she heard a faint call, loud but polite:

"Okay, then! Good luck!"

She almost laughed. She supposed he was happy as long as he got paid. She could respect that. Her incentive wasn't so different—the allure of living on a more advanced world, enjoying its abundant food and health care, its spacious private dwellings, its entertainment media, its endless variety of coffee beverages.

"What's the point?" Mayu asked when Dain explained the benefits of their masters' offer. "Once the Irddru conquer that world, all those amazing things will be lost. You'll even be helping to end them! How does that make sense?"

Dain sighed. Mayu was in her early teens now, but still as stubborn as ever, continuing the same long argument even here in the dingy barracks of the work camp she'd inevitably gotten herself sent to. Nothing seemed to penetrate her skull.

"It just means I need to make the most of them while I can," Dain told her. "It'll be better than what we have now, at least for a while. And if I do what the Irddru want, it'll make things better for you and Mama too."

"Oh, very noble. You're the one always complaining that you have to take care of me, wishing you could just think of yourself. Well, now you get your chance—while it lasts. You get to live in luxury and not care who it hurts."

"You ungrateful—It's your own fault for getting caught! For years Mama warned you to let the past die. You never listened, and now I have to do this so they'll let you out of here!"

"No." Mayu shook her head angrily. "Don't make me your excuse. Not for helping them do that to a whole world. Do it for yourself. Play the game, get ahead, just like you always say. Because you're playing to lose in the end, and I don't want that to be because of me."

Her sister had still been too young to understand, too lost in her simplistic ideals. But Dain had taken her at her word anyway. After all, those who fought for higher, more abstract causes just got themselves (or their families) killed. Life was short anyway—better to live for the moment than suffer for causes beyond yourself. Mayu still childishly believed it was possible to do both.

Hearing another drone, Dain veered again, frustrated at the Dijuno agent (no doubt the Serejen Ru that Roak had named) for making it so hard to double back to the capsule. She needed to get under cover.

Ducking into a shaded airway between factories, she found the nearest locked door and pulled on its handle. The rusted lock was designed for mere Terran strength, so she broke it with little difficulty.

She found herself in the gloomy, dusty interior of an abandoned factory, a great echoing space smelling of stale air, rust, and organic decay. Arrays of dirty windows along the side walls of the long, narrow space admitted fitful, gloaming light, with many panes boarded and some broken. Hulking machines crouched in the gloom like vast, dozing beasts of metal, casting wakes of deep shadow into the passageways between them. It would be an excellent place to elude a pursuer — or for a pursuer to lie in wait.

Dain lifted her gaze and spotted catwalks overhead, with stairways leading up from ground level. She took slow, wary steps toward the nearest one, hoping to claim the high ground before anyone else did.

A loud rustle and the sound of running feet made her spin, ready for an attack. She saw only a gaunt, stumbling figure in tattered clothing, retreating deeper into the gloom. No doubt it was one of the many people left homeless by this world's inefficient economy and uncaring leaders. Dain had glimpsed others squatting in this abandoned district when she had first come through months before.

Still, this one had seen her. It might be safer to chase the person down and kill them before they could tell Gareth's team…

No. A body crushed by superhumanly strong hands would be a louder testimony to her presence than a frightened wastrel wishing only to be left alone. She was safer letting the vagrant go.

Reaching the stairway, she ascended as quickly as she could without making noise on the metal steps. It proved futile; as soon as she reached the catwalk, Gareth stepped out from behind one of its brick support columns.

"Hello, Dana." He was armed with an electroshock pistol, too far for her to reach him before he could fire. But he was close enough to speak normally, and for Dain to see his familiar, handsome features.

"You might as well call me Dain."

"Then I'm pleased to meet you properly at last, Dain."

"You won't be pleased for long. You won't get what you want from me."

"This doesn't have to be a fight, Dain. As I see it, your masters are the real threat here, not you."

"The Irddru *saved* my world! We were in chaos. War, poverty, pollution, almost as bad as the mess you've created here. We were weak, divided—we reached for more than we could handle, and we broke ourselves. Only the Irddru were strong enough to put us together again." The words poured from her, almost beyond her control. It disturbed her how strongly she felt the need to justify herself to this man. "They tamed us, gave us order and peace for the first time in our history. They'll do the same for you. You should welcome them!"

"You call that peace? How many Zumela have they executed or worked to death in labor camps over the years?" She winced at his words. "How many of your people have been forced to fight and die in their conquest of other braneworlds?"

"The prerogative of the strong. If we want better treatment, we have to prove ourselves worthy—otherwise we're no use to society anyway."

He took a step closer. "Do you really have so little regard for your own people?"

Dain moved her eyes inconspicuously, sizing up the construction and state of the rusty catwalk, the distance to the ground and to the nearest large machines. "We would have destroyed ourselves without the stability they brought. We owe them our lives!"

"And that gives them the right to take those lives at a whim?"

"Only if we fail to repay our debt!"

She caught the faint whir of a drone from behind and to the side, realizing that Gareth was keeping her talking to let Serejen Ru close in, perhaps with a sedative dart. She continued to harangue Gareth so that her step forward seemed like an emotional gesture, matching his. "If I fail, my family dies, yes. But that will be your fault for getting in my way, Gareth! For tricking me, using me." One more step. "You're no better than they are."

She kicked out and shattered the rusted bracket that secured the catwalk to its nearest support pillar. The catwalk heaved, sending Gareth off balance. Dain leapt off with all her might, landing atop one of the abandoned factory machines, whose function she couldn't begin to guess. She rolled to her feet facing the way she'd come, spotting the drone closing in. Her foot struck something—a piece of sprinkler pipe that must have fallen from overhead. She grabbed it and hurled it, knocking the mentally-controlled drone from the air. She hoped it caused the Dijuno pain.

"Dain!" Gareth called. He had retreated to a more stable part of the catwalk. She prepared to jump down out of his view, but she spotted Roak rounding the corner at the end of the aisle between machines. She jogged the other way to get some speed and distance, then jumped across the gap, tumbled along the top of the next machine, and came down clumsily to the floor on its far side. She had to hope she could lose Roak in this gloomy maze.

"I'm sorry I had to trick you, Dain," Gareth called, his voice echoing through the factory. "I took it no further than I had to. That's why I... why I had to regretfully decline your advances. I couldn't use you that way."

Dain froze. That was unexpected.

"But I'm trying to stop aliens from invading my world," Gareth went on. "You're trying to help them invade it. It's not symmetrical."

The source of his voice was in motion, the echoes making it hard to pin it down. She took a chance that the same would go for her. "You work for aliens too!" She ducked under a bank of heavy pipes, out into the next aisle. It was clear for now.

"I work *with* them to keep braneworlds free."

Dain scoffed. She kept him talking while she surveyed the aisle, trying to spot an exit route from the factory. "You think Earth is free? You're interdicted, Gareth! The Dijuno and the others who police brane travel — they forbid travelers from coming openly to offer you aid and commerce, forbid your people from even knowing about other branes." She decided to head for the long side wall opposite the catwalk. Perhaps she could slip through one of the broken windows. "You're complicit in their lies, hiding the multiverse from your people."

"That is not exactly true," said a new voice. Dain pulled up short as Serejen Ru emerged before her. The Dijuno's ginger head had a thoughtful but untroubled tilt. One raised hand drifted idly before Ru's chest, fingers dancing as the large-eyed cyborg spoke in a professorial lilt. "Our policy is to shield inhabited worlds against conquest from other branes. Earth's humans, given their history, currently fall into the category of potential conquerors."

Dain chuckled, amused that this slender creature believed it feasible to stand in a Zumela's way. She lunged and swung at Ru, but her fist passed through empty air. The Dijuno had anticipated her move and dodged with effortless agility. Dain pressed her attack, but Ru evaded every swing and kick with a grace reminding her of Mayu's dancing. "Yet we have contacted individuals who are ready to know, such as Gareth," Ru went on in a casual tone. "Those with sufficient knowledge of brane cosmology to extrapolate the truth, and sufficient ethical maturity and empathy to be trusted with it. Those with the potential to guide Earth's civilization to a point where it can join the community of civilized worlds."

"Lies and flattery!" Dain panted. She halted her attack, recognizing its futility. Ru wasn't even winded. "Earth's history is even more fraught with war and cruelty than Zumé's was. They're too weak in body or mind to thrive without a firm controlling grip."

Ru's head tilted further. "Have you and I not just demonstrated that brute force is not the superior approach?"

Dain stared. Ru was almost as frustrating to argue with as Mayu.

Before Dain could answer, Gareth emerged from behind a bank of pipes and moved to stand beside Serejen Ru. "The difference is that Ru's group recruited me," he said. "They didn't compel or threaten me. If you fail in your work, Dain, the Irddru will kill your family. If I fail in my work... the Irddru will probably kill my family. Do you see the connection we share?"

Dain broke for the other end of the aisle, but Roak came into view, blocking her only way out. She skidded to a halt, weighing her options. "There's no connection!" Dain cried to stall for time. "All our species, we look similar, but we're not related. We're different down to the DNA!" She stepped closer to Roak, trying to appeal to him. "Don't you see? You have no reason to serve these Terrans. We're all just rivals for each other's land and resources. As soon as any world harnesses open strings and achieves its first transbrane crossing, as soon as they learn there's an endless number of habitable planets just a brane jump away, the race for conquest is on. They'll come for your world soon enough."

Roak furrowed his heavy brow. "Sorry, I'm a bit confused. Which is it?"

"What do you mean?"

"First you said the Irddru conquered worlds to help them. Now you say there's no reason for anyone to help other worlds. If the Irddru told you that too... well, then they're lying about *something*." He shrugged. "All I know is, these guys are paying me. That helps me, and it helps my kid sister back home." He smiled. "She's saving up for medical school."

Dain was taken aback. He had a sister too? And his eyes when he spoke of her were filled with pride, not fear.

"In his own uncomplicated way, Roak has illustrated how the Irddru's propaganda works," Serejen Ru interjected. "They teach conflicting ideas simultaneously, encouraging paradox and confusion. The more their subjects doubt that anything is true, the less they will be motivated by any committed belief, and thus the easier they are to deceive and control. It is a common pattern of oppressive regimes across the multiverse."

"You're trying to make me doubt too," Dain countered, her head darting around to take in the three of them.

"Doubt can be healthy," Gareth said, "as long as it comes from within and makes you think for yourself. I believe there's doubt in you. They wouldn't have to threaten your family otherwise." He took a step closer. "We can help them. If you cooperate with us, take us to your transbrane capsule, we can work with you to free them."

"More lies," she said, though with little conviction. "You can't guarantee you can keep them safe."

Gareth held her gaze. "No, I can't. All I can guarantee is that we'd try to find a way."

Dain hesitated. The Irddru would have offered her that guarantee, and she would have known it was a lie yet had no choice but to accept it. Gareth had trusted her with the uncomfortable truth.

But that was not enough. "Why would you even try? We have no shared heritage or history. There's nothing connecting us."

Her opponent smiled. "You've already admitted that there is, even if you didn't realize it. An endless number of habitable worlds just a brane jump away. Why do you think there's always a planet there instead of empty space? Worlds of the same size and mass in the same orbit, in universe after universe. Always staying in sync with each other despite orbital perturbations. Orbiting suns of the same mass and temperature, their evolution affected by identical supernovae and flares, identical asteroid impacts and tectonic shifts.

"There *is* a connection, Dain. It's gravity. I wasn't just speaking metaphorically before. Do you know why gravity is the weakest fundamental interaction?"

"No." She would have to make a move soon. Which path gave her the better chance of escape?

"Because its strings aren't bound to the D-brane of our universe, of any universe. They're closed loops, free to propagate through higher dimensions. While other particles are stuck to the fabric of just one universe, gravitons leak out across all of them. The extra gravity we used to attribute to 'dark matter' is really the echo of masses in neighboring branes, leaking through like your neighbors' conversations through your apartment walls. And so a large mass in one brane universe attracts a large mass in the next, and so on. Which means that every universe has an Earth-sized planet right here, subtly pulling on every other one so they stay aligned. As a result, they have almost the same land masses and generally similar evolution, with the same environmental changes selecting for very similar adaptations, and the most probable mutations usually winning out over time."

"Not always. The Irddru's world —"

"Is in a distant enough D-brane for the resonances to be weak," Serejen Ru interposed. "At such removes, the probabilities often resolve differently. Flightless avians retain foreclaws and evolve sapience before hominins, as the Irddru did. Or pachyderms —"

Gareth held up a hand to forestall Ru. "But it's all variations on the same themes," he added. "All because of gravity binding the braneworlds together. The weakest force of all… yet it draws tiny particles together to form vast and powerful wholes. The weak working together as one can shape a universe — even transcend it." He took a step closer. "This is what fascists like the Irddru don't want us to recognize: that by joining together, the weakest masses can overcome the strongest few." He reached out his empty hand.

He made her want to believe him. He had always made her want to be with him. Seduction? Entrapment? Or had he always been sincerely trying to win her as an ally?

No! She shook off her doubt. She knew of only one sure way to keep her mother and Mayu from dying because of her.

She lunged at Roak. He was the strongest of her foes, but she understood that strength better than Ru's calculated dance or Gareth's mind games.

His momentary surprise let her swerve out of his line of fire and close on him. She struck his heavy jaw with a left cross and knocked the rifle from his grip.

Roak recovered quickly, chuckling as he rubbed his jaw. "Okay, then. This should be fun."

His carefree manner while she fought for her life incensed her, particularly since the ferocity of his blows belied it. She parried as best she could, looking for an opening to beat him to the weapon. But though her strength and reach were greater, he was a professional, and the blows he got through left her dazed. Her urgency let her push through the pain, and she finally knocked him down with a spinning kick, then used the opening to run to the plasma rifle.

Gareth and Ru were running to Roak's side, helping him back up. Hefting the rifle, she swung its barrel toward them, but they ducked behind a machine. Roak's arm poked out, holding a handgun. His head appeared, and she fired to force him back.

Dain looked up at the catwalk crossing overhead, this one even more corroded than the first. She fired a plasma burst at the point where it joined to its brick support pillar. She jumped free as the catwalk and much of the pillar crumbled and fell, creating a barrier between her and her pursuers. She started for the exit.

A high-pitched scream from behind her made her hesitate. She turned to see a gaunt homeless female cowering under the catwalk steps. She got only a brief glimpse—long enough to tell it was an adolescent barely older than Mayu—before the steps and more of the brick pillar collapsed on top of the girl.

"No!" Gareth cried, intensifying the twinge of guilt that ran through Dain. But it was this world or hers. She had to think of her own and only her own. She ran for the door while she had the chance.

Before she reached it, she realized she wasn't being chased. She stopped and turned to see Gareth and the others gathered around the pile of rubble, trying to pull it off the homeless girl. Roak strained at the heavy chunks of brick and metal, but they barely budged.

"So much for your pretty philosophy about gravity!" Dain screamed at Gareth. "It kills, just like any other force!"

"Forget philosophy!" Gareth cried. "Come help us!"

She stared. "What?"

"We can't do it without you! Please, Dain!"

It had to be another trap. They couldn't care more about some random, forgotten person than about the transbrane capsule. Gareth's society had abandoned this woman, so why wouldn't he? It could only be a trap, so she forced herself to run.

At the exit, she froze, turned back, and saw that they were still struggling to free the girl. They didn't even seem to care that Dain was getting away.

It had to be a trap.

It had to.

But if she felt trapped, how did that girl she'd buried feel? How did her sister feel?

"It's not like I *want* to keep bailing you out of trouble! It's your own fault for never listening!"

"Then don't! If I'm such an inconvenience, just forget about me! Leave me in this camp to rot! Go look out for yourself, like you always say!"

"I would if you just let me!"

"What's stopping you, Dain? Huh? What's it matter to you anyway?

"Why should you care?"

Before Dain knew it, she was by the others' side, the rifle abandoned. She worked with Roak and Gareth to heave away the biggest chunks of debris, until Serejen Ru was able to send in a pair of drones that gently lifted the girl between them and maneuvered her free. Once she was laid out on the ground, Roak went to work; apparently, he was a trained combat medic as well as a mercenary.

Dain could have run. Instead, as she stood next to Gareth, panting and drained by more than just exertion, she asked, "Why did you do that? You're waging a fight with countless worlds at stake. Why did you jeopardize that for the sake of one insignificant person?"

Gareth gazed back. "Why did you?"

Dain didn't answer until minutes later, when the ambulance that Ru had remotely summoned arrived to take the girl to the hospital. "I'm ready to lead you to the capsule now."

Once Dain guided Gareth and the others to the secret location deep in the steam tunnels beneath the factory district, she was stunned to find the heavy, spherical transbrane capsule already secured by several of Serejen Ru's drones and a small multispecies team. "I apologize for deceiving you yet again," Gareth said. "You thought you were leading us away from here, but by tracking your movements and extrapolating the area you tried to avoid—even reading your microexpressions and ideomotor responses when we mentioned the capsule to you—Serejen Ru's drones were able to triangulate its location. It's an old magicians' trick to feign mind-reading. You can't resist involuntarily glancing and tensing your muscles toward something you're thinking about, even when you try to hide it."

Dain stared at him, betrayed. He had lied to her after all. But his reasons for doing so confused her. "Then why keep up the pretense?"

"We had to confirm that your willingness to cooperate was genuine."

"Why does that matter if you already captured the capsule?"

Gareth placed a gentle hand on her arm and smiled. "Because this was never just about the capsule, Dain. It was about freeing you."

She resisted believing him. "You mean recruiting me. So I could fight for your side instead of theirs."

"A choice you made on your own. Now that you know what we fight for."

"What you lie for. What you manipulate for. No matter how noble you seem, I can't trust you, Gareth."

"You shouldn't. I'm too charming by half. I'll lie, I'll seduce, I'll do whatever it takes to defend my world — and others like it, others we may need one day as allies. I would've done worse than lie to you if you'd made it necessary. Because I believe in our purpose.

"So don't trust me — trust the cause that drives me. And let it drive you too."

"All I want is that you keep your promise. Try to save my family."

"We will try. But that will require your help. And once you take that step, for better or worse, there will be no going back."

"There are uncounted braneworlds where I could hide from the Irddru. You can't compel me to remain on your team."

He smiled. "No. But I have a feeling something else will."

She thought of the girl… the strange, alien Earther girl in whose face she'd seen her own sister. A girl she'd risked her sister's safety to protect… because she knew it was what Mayu would have wanted her to do. Because she'd realized, at least for a moment, that there was no difference between them. And if that was so, then the same was true of all the others Gareth and his team were fighting to protect, on this and every other braneworld. Even universes apart, they were connected.

If that gulf could be bridged, then maybe the one between Dain and Gareth could be as well — though only if he could prove he was willing to meet her halfway.

She stepped forward and laid a hand on the transbrane capsule. "My family first," she insisted. "Show me what you're capable of. After that… we'll talk."

Conventional Powers

Emerald Blair took deep, calming breaths as she listened through the wall, using her amplified hearing to size up the horde on the other side. She'd withstood her share of challenges in her short career as a crimefighter, but she'd never faced a group this large before. They were numerous, alert, and eager for her to the point of frenzy. Surely they would eat her alive if she let them.

"Just the way I like it," Emry whispered. She drew back her right fist and shoulder, braced her green-booted feet, and thrust forward with all her weight, grateful for the elbow-length gloves she'd recently added to her light-armor outfit. Moving faster than the unenhanced human eye could see, her fist smashed through the sturdy composite like it was balsa wood. She carried her momentum forward into an even mightier kick that shattered the lower part of the wall, then launched herself through the opening, knowing her noisy entrance had drawn the attention of everyone in the chamber. Spotlights swung to bear on her as she landed with a tumble and came up on her feet, hands planted on her hips as she faced the stunned multitude before her and delivered her battle cry:

"Looking for trouble? You just found her!"

The crowd cheered wildly, rising to give her a standing ovation. *"Let's hear it for Emerald Blair, the Green Blaze!"* cried Kelly Hayashi-Chandler, the press agent for the Troubleshooter Corps.

As the audience began chanting Emry's championym, Kelly came out from behind her clear protective shield to give the young Troubleshooter a hug and a kiss on the cheek. "You're a natural, kid," the slim, short-haired woman whispered in her ear before ceding the stage.

I sure hope so, Emry thought. Still, the crowd's adulation buoyed her confidence. Her innate exhibitionism did the rest. Emry took a running leap that propelled her nearly four meters into the air, catching herself on the lighting scaffold. She knew it could hold her weight; the convention hall was built strong to accommodate showy superhumans. Holding on with her left hand and foot, she leaned out and blew kisses at the crowd. "Hel-loooo, Ceres ModCon 2108!" she belted, hearing a squeal of feedback before the audio pickups lowered their gain in response to the sheer volume of her brassy soprano. "Yeah! I love you too! Whoo-*hooooo!*"

She glanced over at the banner above the stage, a portrait of the Green Blaze in a dynamic action pose, falling through the air inside a Stanford torus filled with towering skyscrapers, firing a stylized shock laser at unseen pursuers while shrapnel from an explosion tore at her skin and light armor (which wasn't nearly so tight or flimsy in real life). She *wished* her hair were as long and lustrously fluid as shown, and she doubted she could manage to look so spontaneously sexy while fighting for her life. Still, she loved the power the artist had conveyed. She looked as though she had just hurled herself off a skyscraper with no thought to what came next, completely in the moment and not letting little things like plans or gravity distract her. *It's like he sees into my soul.*

Emry spotted a number of Green Blaze cosplayers jockeying for her attention. They came in multiple ethnicities and genders, but all had hair or wigs in various shades of red, only a few coming close to her own leaves-in-autumn hue. Some had based their costumes on her real light armor, a sleeveless, flame-patterned green jerkin with matching knee boots, tight black trousers, and a brown utility belt worn at a rakish angle. Others wore the scantier tank-top version from last year's rush-job biopic *Blazing Banshee*, while some sported still more revealing variations of their own. One well-endowed woman cosplayed as her porn-comics parody Ephemeral Bare, the Scream Daze, wearing a utility belt, green boots and g-clip, and nothing else. She certainly succeeded in catching Emry's attention as she bounced up and down. *Those can't possibly be real,* Emry thought, but she still enjoyed the view. *Vack, what does 'real' even mean around here anyway?*

After leaping back down to the stage, she called out to the cosplayers. "You like the gloves? A little something for next year!" The cheers surged to a new crescendo, and she laughed. "Yeah! My people! Keep it comin'!"

Emerald went on to entertain the crowd with a few more displays of power, including the old superhero standby of bending a steel bar in her bare—well, gloved—hands. (ModCon safety rules prohibited bullets, locomotives, and mighty rivers within the convention center.) She invited the civilians in the audience to take her on in a tug-of-war, holding her own against sixteen people at once before she let them pull her over the line.

Once the crowd settled down, Emry called up her speech notes on her retinal HUD and began her address. "I can't tell you all how much it means to me to be here on this stage. To me, ModCon is one of the most important events for the transhuman community here in the Belt. And the Corps agrees, which is why the TSC and ModCon have been sponsoring each other for almost a quarter-century now. It's more than a trade show for new medifica—sorry, modification tech and medical advances."

Vack! She couldn't afford to fumble like that. This was an uneasy time in the Belt, with tensions high after the failure of last year's attempt to build a stronger coalition of transhuman states (which had turned out to be a sinister plot to mind-control their leaders). The Troubleshooter Corps had not been immune from the turmoil, and the people needed reassurance that it still had their backs. Many—including Emry—had questioned the Green Blaze's suitability as the TSC's representative under the circumstances. She was a novice, known more for her juvenile-delinquent backstory and her sexual escapades than for any great heroic feats so far. She had exposed the mind-control plot but had failed to capture its masterminds, a mixed victory at best. But her classic superheroine looks and her flashy personality made her popular with the public, and she was one of the three or four most physically powerful Troubleshooters the Corps had ever had, so the TSC's new director Lydia "Lodestar" Muchangi had chosen her to symbolize the Corps's renewed strength and vitality as it looked to the future. Now it was up to Emry to live up to Lodestar's faith that she could deliver the substance as well as the style.

Willing herself to relax, Emry continued. "It's more than a place for the Belt's mod peacekeepers to exchange information and techniques. Even more than a place for the Troubleshooter Corps and other major security providers to scout new talent—though, believe me, I'm lookin' forward to tomorrow's power trials as much as the rest of you! Yeah, all you local heroes out there," she ad-libbed, "I'm gonna have fun kickin' all your fine asses — and I hope a few of you are good enough to kick mine!"

The audience roared again, reassuring her. Many local peacekeepers, both conventional law officers and costumed freelancers, attended ModCon every year — though never so many at once that their home habitats were left unprotected. The power trials were the main event, a series of friendly competitions letting the attending superheroes show off their strength, speed, fighting skill, problem-solving acumen, and other assets — both to entertain the audience and to catch the eyes of law-enforcement recruiters. A trophy in the ModCon power trials was a mark of prestige coveted by amateur and regional superheroes, a way to make their names and advance their careers.

"Whoo! Yeah! But you know… okay, settle down now… It's also about more than just entertainment. Believe me, I'm as big a geek as anyone here. I'm gonna go home with all the swag I can carry, and you know I can carry plenty!" She flexed her muscular arms as the crowd cheered. "But all the comics, the movies, the games, the toys… They mean something special to us mods. Superheroes give us a foundational mythology, ahh, a source of identity that real history and heritage don't provide." She stumbled over the words, which were a bit too formal for her comfort. Luckily, the rest came from her heart, even if it was pre-scripted. "And they've always meant a lot to me. ModCon was where some of my earliest superhero fantasies were incubated, when my mom and dad first brought me here when I was seven. I only wish they could be here now to see me standing before you all as a real, working crimefighter." She blinked away tears. "It's humbling. It makes me more determined than ever to live up to the faith that you and the Corps have placed in me as the Green Blaze. I've learned… the hard way… that the realities of this work are often more bitter and painful than the fantasies, and that doing real good often comes with a heart-breaking cost. But being here at ModCon, sharing in this with all of you… it fills me with the hope and wonder and spirit of adventure that make this crazy job worthwhile. Thank you all!"

The crowd gave her a strong ovation; it seemed her sincere enthusiasm had helped to win them over, as Lodestar had gambled that it would. After the applause, Kelly opened the floor to questions. By custom, the local heroes went before the fans, for the advice they received could make a difference in their work. Emry was just thirteen months past her apprenticeship, but many of the talented amateurs needed all the help they could get.

The first question came from Kyojin, a towering celebrity heroine from Vestalia. "Is it true," the square-jawed, short-haired giantess asked in awe, "that you're the strongest woman in history?"

Emry chuckled. "In my weight class, probably. The strongest there is?" Her eyes roved over the giantess's powerful frame with frank interest. "Well, you'll get to test that tomorrow at the trials, honey."

The next questioner was even more delicious to look at, a blond man with a powerfully muscled build. He wore an abbreviated harness-and-briefs outfit displaying a considerable majority of his tanned skin, which gleamed with a silky sheen. "Green Blaze, hi," he said. "I'm the Decider, and I defend the Eichsfeldia colonies, near Vesta."

"Ooh, I'm deciding something right now," she purred. The audience laughed. "What can I help you with, Conan?"

"I have a question about costuming. My partners in law enforcement back home think I should wear more protection on the job. But I've got bulletproof skin, superstrong bones and muscles, augmented speed and reflexes... I don't think they appreciate how much of what we do is about display. Now, obviously you like to show your skin too," the Decider went on, gesturing toward her plunging neckline. "You've got amazing upper body development—in more ways than one—so why *would* you want to cover up?"

She grinned. "Aww, thanks."

"But I notice most other Troubleshooters' costumes don't really show off their bodies, even when they've got a lot worth showing. Is it just that you're more durable than the rest?" the Decider finished.

"No, there are plenty of Troubleshooters as tough as me—though none tougher," she added with a wink. "But dressing well is about the right outfit for the right occasion, y'see. Sure, you want to show off what you've got. But that's for public appearances, community outreach, merchandise. When your life's on the line—more important, when other people's lives are on the line and they need you in one piece—then extra protection's a good idea. Remember, nothing's bulletproof, just bullet-resistant."

She demonstrated how her light armor could transform for action, sealing the jerkin to the collar and unfolding to protect her midriff, then go back to a more revealing mode for the cameras. "So my advice, Dessy, is to get yourself a more flexible look. There are some good light armor engineers around the con—go shop around, make some contacts. I love the bod, really, but that's all the more reason to keep that gorgeous anatomy intact."

A pixyish Eunomian heroine called Spindizzy asked a follow-up about the propriety of showing skin while visiting habs with tighter modesty standards, such as Al-Battani or Besht. Emry described her long-sleeved tunic and some of the colorful headscarves and wraps that she had for such occasions. "Costume variants and accessories are part of the fun of being a superhero. The toy companies sure love it!"

The next question came from Doctor DeMeter, a prominent hometown heroine here in New Queens, the most populous member of the interconnected bundle of habitats called the Ceres Sheaf. A graceful, West African-featured woman with long, intricately braided hair, Ekundayo DeMarais wore a cornstalk-green jumpsuit with a wreath-patterned sensor headband and an equipment belt with a cornucopia buckle. Emry was instantly captivated by her beauty and poise—which made her question come as a blow. "With all due respect, Green Blaze, a lot of us didn't come here for fashion tips or displays of strength. We're trying to make a real difference in the Belt, at a time when tensions have grown higher than ever, with extremist groups in both mod and baseline communities stirring up hostility against each other. Even the Troubleshooter Corps has been compromised, and though you've made a visible show of cleaning house these past few months, the public's faith in your neutrality and efficacy has been eroded. We need to know that we can still rely on the Troubleshooters for inspiration and moral leadership.

"So tell us, is this all we have to expect from the Green Blaze? Are you here to rebuild our faith in the Corps, or merely to be a colorful distraction from its problems?"

The question cut right to Emry's worst fears. As much as being here was a dream come true, as much as she'd studiously pumped up her enthusiasm for it, on some level she had to wonder if she'd been sent here because she hadn't yet proven herself fit for more serious responsibilities. How could she win her colleagues over with mere words when she had so few deeds to speak for her?

"I admit I've still got a lot to learn, and a lot to prove," she admitted to DeMeter and the crowd. "That's part of why I'm here. ModCon is a way for us crimefighters to learn from each other, to make each other better," she said without consulting her notes, "and I'm really looking forward to learning from all of you.

"And you know, ModCon duty's nothing to be ashamed of. There's a lot of new modtech here to tempt thieves and spies, a lot of local heroes whose enemies have tried to target them here in the past." As she spoke, a group of individuals dressed in black attire rose as a unit from their seats in the rear and began to come forward. *Oh, now what?* Keeping an eye on them, Emry went on, putting more weight into her next words. "Our being here, um, it's as much about our mutual security as about having a good time. It's important work, looking out for each other as well as for the public. That's why I'm so proud that Lodestar trusted me to represent the Corps this year."

The black-clad group had now reached the front of the audience. At their head strode a tall man wearing a helmet-like cowl styled to resemble a fierce canine visage. "Enough of this travesty!" he boomed, his headgear providing its own amplification. "I am the Knightwolf, and my Hounds and I are here to speak for the *true* mods, the gene-mods. The pure Striders who have seen our community attacked and eroded by pretenders, baseliner immigrants who rely on technology to give them strength and dare to call themselves mods!"

Emry had heard enough. Questioning her achievements was one thing, but this was sheer idiocy. As a teenage mod-gang leader, she'd fought against anti-mod bigots more than once and had seen their rhetoric of superiority for the craven pretense that it was. These Hounds may have been on the opposite side, but they sounded exactly the same. "Look, Huckleberry, you don't get to decide who's a mod and who isn't. The Belt was built by all kinds of people, cyborgs and baseliners as much as genetic mods."

"*We* speak for the people of the Belt! The Striders who value our traditional identity and resent seeing our way of life attacked as Earther immigrants flood our communities and use technology to compete with our natural advantages."

"What? You're not having your rights violated just because you have to share! That's just bein' part of a group. You should've learned that in preschool!" Hearing this kind of intolerance so brazenly expressed at ModCon, a celebration of the Striders' unity and diversity, was shocking and infuriating.

"You don't get to speak for my group, cyborg. You're the biggest traitor of all!" Knightwolf pointed a black-gloved finger. "You're a child of the Vanguard, the first true superhumans. You were born with the finest genetic advantages their science had engineered! And yet you chose to corrupt the perfection of your Vanguardian body by filling it with bionic crutches, like some pitiful Earther."

"My body is *still* perfect, pal, as I'm sure my fans would agree." That got a cheer. "And the only crutches are gonna be yours if you keep spewin' filth like that in my earshot! If I weren't a Troubleshooter, I'd have already—"

"The Troubleshooters," Knightwolf echoed with contempt. "A once-great organization, now hopelessly contaminated by cyborgs and base-liners in power suits."

"The Corps was *founded* by people like that, vackhead!"

"Lies! Revisionist history spread by Earth sympathizers, meant to erode our true heritage so the immigrants can legitimize their domi-nance. But then, your own mentor was one of those suit-users, wasn't he? No wonder you parrot their propaganda." A sneer was visible on his exposed lower face. "Getting him killed was the one heroic thing you've done."

That did it. She leapt off the stage with all her strength and tackled the rabble-rouser to the ground. He was ready for her and fought back fiercely, the force of his blows proving that his claims of mod status were at least genuine. But that was fine with Emry, because it meant she didn't have to hold back.

Before long, the local heroes converged on them and pulled them apart, with the con's NQPD security detail soon joining them to escort the Hounds to detention. "This isn't over!" Knightwolf cried on the way out. "It's not bigotry! It's about ethics in transhumanism!"

Seething with fury but ashamed by her loss of control, Emry stormed to the front of the hall, where Kelly intercepted her and led her off to the side. "Sorry. I'm sorry, Kel, I know I shouldn't have blown up like that."

"I don't think anyone will deny he deserved it," Kelly replied. "Still, you have to be more careful, Emry. This isn't a situation that calls for brute strength."

"You're right. You're… This is what he wanted. To make me mad, make me embarrass the Corps. Seems to be what I do best."

"Others have done a lot worse, kid. And you can still fix this, okay? You just need to make a good showing at the panels later on."

"You kidding? One wrong question from the audience and I'll tear apart the panel room."

"Look, the first panel isn't for three hours. Go enjoy the con, be a fan, get your head in a good space again, and you'll do fine."

"Yeah. Yeah, that sounds good."

"Just remember, it's a plainclothes sort of panel," the slender press agent said, "but wear something tasteful."

"I don't know the meaning of the word."

"This is my shocked face," Kelly replied in a complete deadpan. "Just check the options I loaded into your room's clothesfac."

"I still wanna be on that panel about real heroes in the movies."

"Not until you prove to me that you can have a conversation about *Blazing Banshee* without breaking things."

"It was one time!"

Emry took a quick shower to clear her head, declining her hotel room's offer to jam any motecams she might have tracked in. If she'd wanted privacy, she had a far more robust scrambler built into her skull. Besides, cameras were so ubiquitous these days that nudity taboos had become largely obsolete, while the popularity of voyeurism had plummeted in proportion. But people still liked to watch celebrities, so Emry belted out a loud and slightly off-key rendition of one of her favorite Roche Limit songs for the benefit of any spectators. As she toweled off, she got an eyetext from the band's drummer asking her to mangle Zodiacal Light's music next time.

Afterward, Emry began her walkabout on the convention floor, taking in the sights, sounds, and smells, the giant posters and screens and soligrams, the game booths and merchandise stalls, the cosplayers and body painters. Hoping to blend in (up to a point), she'd ditched her trademark green and black, wearing comfortable walking shoes, brief denim shorts, and a black cutoff t-shirt reading ROCHE LIMIT INNER BELT TOUR 2106. A TSC ball cap adorned her ponytailed head, and she carried a ModCon tote bag that soon became home to a commemorative Shashu the Archer collectible figure, an authentic replica prop of Annie Minute's Time Guitar, a *Blazing Banshee* poster for target practice, assorted gifts for her friends (a bonus Shashu figure for Arjun, a new Totoro doll for Tenshi's collection, a plush silver Pegasus to hang in *Zephyr*'s cockpit), and an Ephemeral Bare pinup autographed by the stunned and honored artist.

Emry's face and physique naturally got noticed, if not recognized, by the congoers around her. Aesthetics aside, a body with as much strength and training as hers moved with an undeniable power and poise, and the people around her instinctively felt that looming presence and took note of its passage. Many baseliners or low-level mods were intimidated by that power, others excited by it; but their first impulse was to give her space, and they didn't tend to approach her unless she acted approachable. Most of them understood that she was in fangirl mode, not superhero mode, so they let her be, often smiling and nodding or just staring, but respecting her status as one of them. She tried to extend them the same courtesy and not use either her strength or her fame to get in anyone else's way.

Not all the attendees were so polite, though. She noted several guests wearing t-shirts or buttons with slogans like PURE AND PROUD or FAKE MODS GO BACK TO EARTH. She tried to ignore them; there were a few vackheads at any con, and the security drones whirring overhead (a bit more numerous than usual following the earlier disruption) should discourage any outbursts. Or so she thought until she saw a group of purists openly harassing a cyborg couple, tugging at their bionic limbs and splashing them with hot coffee. "What? They're not a real part of you," one purist taunted, unconcerned with the drones' scrutiny. Emry recognized him and his allies from Knightwolf's group. How had they not been expelled already? Fearing someone might be hurt before convention security could arrive, Emry shifted her body language to Green Blaze and barreled forward to confront the purists. The cowards fled at her approach, hurling ineffectual taunts over their shoulders. Once the security personnel finally showed up, Emry stayed in Troubleshooter mode long enough to chastise their lax enforcement of the con's anti-harassment policy.

In time, Emry made her way back to the real-world side of the convention center and hooked up with Dr. Chaitra Varghese, the TSC's medical director, who was touring the modtech firms' promotional booths to check out the latest prototypes. According to the elegant, middle-aged doctor, the big thing this year was neural security, as multiple research firms investigated countermeasures to the cerebral and behavioral hacks used on the delegates at last year's conference. Emry listened with interest to the scientists' pitches; she'd mostly outgrown her youthful obsession with maximizing her power, but after last year, she would welcome some upgrades to her mental defenses. But once the scientists' questions about her own firsthand experience with those neural infiltration techniques grew too personal, Chaitra hurried Emry away to investigate some of the other presentations.

They were soon waylaid by a Nanodesics representative whom Chaitra introduced as Doctor Akar Lukman. The chubby-faced scientist seemed very excited about his latest breakthrough. "We have found a way to interrupt the power supply of bionic implants, which should allow law enforcement to more easily disable augmented criminals!"

"Is that feasible?" the TSC doctor challenged. "Bionics draw on so many different power sources. Body heat, ATP and sugars in the blood, piezoelectric nanofibers...."

"Ahh, but power *utilization* in nanosystems is far more standardized," Lukman replied. "That's dictated as much by physics as by economic practicality. And that's the Achilles heel. We've found a way to target a particular phase of the conversion process and disrupt it at a quantum level. It only works in direct physical contact at the moment, but we're trying to develop a longer-range application. If nothing else, it could be miniaturized to fit TSC and police dartguns."

Chaitra seemed intrigued, but Emry, so reliant on the bionics in her own body, was wary. "Couldn't this sort of thing backfire if it fell into the wrong hands?"

"Well, it's a very sophisticated technology, relying on proprietary metamaterials that are quite difficult to manufacture."

"I've met some pretty sophisticated wrong hands, Doc."

Lukman beamed and laughed. "And that diligence on your part is why I feel so safe, Ms. Blaze. How could our invention be safer than it is here, surrounded by heroes?"

An hour or so before the panels, Kelly roped Emerald into an impromptu autograph/Q&A session for the fans, to make up for Knightwolf's earlier interruption. It was comforting to feel the acceptance and approval of so many members of the public, though it got a bit bewildering when the Q&A degenerated into a debate over her sex life and which other Troubleshooter was her true, destined love. Sex among Troubleshooters was generally a relaxed, straightforward thing; they were in a solitary line of work, seventy-odd people spread out through the Belt and patrolling alone for weeks at a time between life-threatening rescues, so most of them freely took opportunities for pleasure and companionship with each other whenever they could. Yet fandom obsessed over their pairings, imagining them as epic and turbulent melodramas. One heavyset woman cosplaying as Tenshi, in a silver leotard and saffron-trimmed red *gi*, regaled her for some minutes with the plot outline of her epic Green Blaze/Tenshi erotic fanfic series—currently on its sixth volume—with such sincere ardor that Emry didn't have the heart to point out that they were just close friends. Finally, the Greenshi fan was shouted down by other shippers adamant about their own theories on her ideal love match, including several Troubleshooters she didn't even like, one confirmed asexual, and a couple who were actually dead.

Emry floundered at the first panel, whose focus was "Cultural Diversity and Peacekeeping Challenges in the Outers." She thought she had a good firsthand understanding of the issue, having spent most of her childhood and juvenile-delinquent years in the Outer Belt. But the other panelists' discussion of the cultural complexities of the more eccentric Outers communities, and the dynamic by which their isolationist and mod-purist tendencies were somehow becoming more widespread in the Belt as a reaction to increasing immigration from Earth, went way over her head. What did she know from politics and sociology? She was a lover and a fighter. She was able to fake it adequately when the panelists turned to her for comment, livening it up with some anecdotes and corny jokes, but she carried little of the discussion overall.

She gave a better showing on the next panel, a discussion of the advantages of various types of bionic mods in crimefighting. Since she more or less had one of everything, she was able to speak from experience about most of the technologies under discussion. A couple of audience members raised questions about her reaction to the earlier protest, but they showed no sympathy for the Hounds' agenda, belying Knightwolf's claim that he spoke for the majority of Striders. "It's a stupid distinction," Emerald summed up. "Gene mods are just as artificial as bionics. Just a hundred years ago, nobody had any of this stuff."

"Exactly," agreed Doctor DeMeter, a fellow panelist who was herself a genetic-bionic blend like Emry. "Mod culture is an ongoing invention of new definitions of humanity. Attempts to limit those definitions, to fall back into archaic patterns of exclusion and elite privilege, are the product of minds too small to face the unknown without fear." Emry applauded her words, wishing she had that kind of eloquence.

After the panels, Emry was pleased when the Decider—whose real name was Erwin Coleman, so "Decider" would do just fine—invited her to join him and the other local heroes for a night on the town. True to his championym, he insisted on choosing the venue, a cozy, private tavern on the far side of New Queens. It was a good opportunity to stroll through the midsized O'Neill cylinder—a pleasantly urban environment with plenty of open space and greenery growing on and between its many towering, elaborate skyscrapers and mini-arcologies, evoking the architectural styles of the Earth from which so many of the Sheaf's residents had immigrated. The view spinning past beyond the sun windows only added to the vista's sense of vastness and intricacy. The Ceres Sheaf was a massive complex of once-independent habitats scaffolded together into a unified whole. To someone as accustomed to empty space as Emry, the sheer number of habs ensconced in their mazelike matrix of sun mirrors, heat radiators, materials pipelines, and interway tubes felt almost claustrophobic—and dizzying, for the vast cylinders and smaller Bernal spheres that moved past the window as New Queens rotated were themselves spinning at various speeds in two different directions.

Beyond it all was the partial structure of the Band, a vast ring habitat that, upon its completion, would not only engird the Sheaf but more than double its total habitable area. The view reminded Emry of how swiftly the population of unmodded immigrants to the Belt was growing—an inexorable demographic shift that frightened many who still clung to the old idea of Striders being defined by their genetic augmentations, whether simple anti-radiation and bone-growth mods or the more elaborate improvements that her Vanguardian forebears had pioneered.

"So stupid." At the Decider's puzzled stare, Emry explained her thoughts. "Those Hounds just don't get it. Purity isn't strength—it never has been. It's when you mix things together that things get interesting. Hydrogen and oxygen. Iron and carbon. Chocolate and peanut butter. Pussies and cocks." She slapped Coleman's ass. "Genetics and bionics—it's a combo that's worked great for me. Great for the Corps, too."

"Well, sure," the Decider replied slowly. "But, you know, not all gene mods are like that. I'm one myself—born this way, no bionics. Nothing wrong with that."

"Of course not. But it's not about you. You're not the one tryin' to disrupt the con and trash the Corps's reputation."

"Well, as long as you remember we're not all like that."

"Yeah, I know!" She glared, irritated by his self-absorption. *Oh, well. It's not his personality I'm interested in anyway.*

Along the way, the group stopped to deal with a mugging in an alley whose surveillance had been scrambled. The others deferred to Doctor DeMeter on her home turf, but she invited them to assist, and the three assailants were disarmed and restrained in seconds. "Seriously, you try this during ModCon?" Emry asked them afterward while DeMeter made sure the victims were unharmed. "What, did you lose a bet?"

On reaching the tavern, the heroes mutually agreed to limit themselves to safe intoxicants that would not undermine their judgment or increase aggression; they wouldn't be good convention guests if they ended up trashing a local establishment. Besides, there were better forms of stimulation available. Emry had brought her Green Blaze gear in her bag, hoping to introduce the local heroes to the Troubleshooter tradition of full-costume strip poker—a game she routinely lost, both from lack of poker acumen and lack of motivation to keep her clothes on. The Decider, however, had other plans, inviting Emry to test her strength against his. "We can do that in the trials tomorrow," she demurred.

"Not all of us will get far enough to challenge you," replied Captain Coriolis, a leggy and sleekly powerful mahogany-skinned man with a sexy Hindi-English accent. Enough others joined in that Emry deferred to their wishes.

Finding a strength challenge that wouldn't damage bar property proved difficult. Arm wrestling worked for a while, but the table cracked when Emry defeated her fifth consecutive challenger. Lifting the pool tables worked, but it wasn't enough of a one-on-one challenge to satisfy the Decider. So the group finally retreated to the small courtyard behind the tavern for some full-on wrestling, which at least let Emry have some fun. Though the Decider seemed uninterested in turning their sweaty, bare-chested wrestling match into anything other than a wrestling match, at least not until he managed to beat her—which he persistently failed to do. He was too much of a bulldozer, pushing with all his strength and never letting himself yield or turn his opponent's strength to his advantage. It was part of the same competitive drive that made him unwilling to accept defeat and pursue a more fulfilling physical interaction. "Look, I love a friendly brawl as much as anyone," Emry said after pinning him for the fifth time, "but sometimes sharing's better than winning."

She tried to kiss him, but he pulled away and began challenging the others to test their strength against him. Soon he was wrestling with Oxosi, an up-and-coming peacekeeper from the Ijebu habitat around Davida. But though Emry found both men delightful to watch, she'd grown tired of letting the Decider's agenda dominate the whole group. Fortunately, there were others who proved eager to play with the Green Blaze in more intimate ways, including the giantess Kyojin and a bionic-legged man called Kinetyk. When Emry asked Captain Coriolis if he'd like to go for a spin with her too, he readily accepted, promising to alter her frame of reference.

Even the most secluded corner of the courtyard was still in view of the spectators who'd gathered to watch and record the wrestling matches — but superheroes were an exhibitionistic lot by nature, so having an audience only made Emry and her partners more enthusiastic. As they finished undressing one another, Emry noticed Doctor DeMeter exiting the tavern in full costume. "Doc!" Emry called out delightedly to the lovely Sheaver. "Come celebrate fertility with us!"

But DeMeter was all business, and Emry realized that Chaitra Varghese and Akar Lukman were behind her. "The party's over, Blaze," the New Queens heroine said, looking angry and embarrassed. "Someone broke into the convention center while we were indulging ourselves."

"What?" Emry stared. "When did this happen?"

"Half an hour ago," Chaitra told her. "We were going crazy trying to track you all down."

"Something in this tavern is jamming our comms," DeMeter added.

"Someone followed us here," the Decider said, panting hard from exertion. "They wanted us out of contact for the heist."

Emry stepped forward. "Hold on." Given who was accompanying DeMeter, there was only one conclusion. "Did they take—"

"Yes," Chaitra said, trying not to stare at the two naked men behind Emry. "They took the power disruptor prototypes from Nanodesics."

"Vack," Emry cursed. "Just the most potentially dangerous invention at the con. Do we have vid?" she asked as she pulled on her uniform trousers. "Are they still in the area?"

"They're gone, Blaze," DeMeter said. "In and out before anyone knew what was happening. NQPD tried to intercept and got plasma-walled for their trouble. Three cops are in hospital for burns and vision damage, and the thieves' trail is cold. They could be on their way to anywhere in the Sheaf by now."

Of course. A single hab could be locked down, ships prevented from launching; but closing off one component of the Sheaf from the intricate, bustling network it was connected to was a more difficult matter. It would be an enormous disruption that the New Queens authorities would not deem warranted for a nonlethal theft.

Emry gazed up at the small crowd that had gathered atop the courtyard walls, blushing at the gaze of so many eyes and lenses. Being watched having sex, sharing a thing of beauty and warmth and joy, troubled her not at all. But being watched as she let a personal indulgence distract her from her duties was deeply humiliating. She found herself transfixed by the look of disappointment and betrayal on Akar Lukman's face. He had thought his invention safe, surrounded as it was by heroes. And the Green Blaze was supposed to be the strongest hero here.

ModCon was turning out to be quite the learning experience after all. But what she was learning about herself wasn't pretty.

To add insult to injury, the assembled heroes and police had trouble even identifying a suspect in the theft. The perpetrators had jammed the convention center's security systems as well as the heroes' comms, and their forensic traces were lost amid those of thousands of conventiongoers. Emerald's suspicions naturally jumped to Knightwolf's Hounds, but Doctor DeMeter questioned whether they had the necessary skill or access, adding that there were plenty of far more formidable groups that would crave such a potentially weaponizable technology. Emry deferred to the more skilled detective, feeling doubly useless. What good was all her physical power if she didn't know who to hit?

Emerald's mood was lifted somewhat come Saturday morning, when she joined the rest of the Troubleshooter Corps delegation for a complimentary breakfast in the hotel's private dining room. She tried to pay attention while Kelly Hayashi-Chandler and assistant personnel director Anders Kopf discussed the potential recruitment prospects in the day's power trials, but she was distracted by all the delightful breakfast options. *Pumpkin-walnut muffins! Someone deserves a Nobel Prize for that.*

Still, her ears perked up (figuratively—that was one of the few mods she didn't have) when the conversation turned to the demonstrations the heroes had planned for the individual performance rounds in the power trials that afternoon. While the competitors would have to prove themselves against a range of shared obstacles, they could also propose individual tests to showcase their most distinctive mods and skills. The powerhouses like the Decider and Oxosi tended to go for the basics like lifting 800-kilo weights and bouncing high-velocity BBs off their chests, while more acrobatic types like Captain Coriolis and Slynx (a young, feline-modded Interamnian vigilante looking to go legit) went for obstacle courses to prove their speed and agility. "Look at Doctor DeMeter's presentation, though," Kelly said with interest. "Computing a complex orbital-dynamics equation out loud while escaping from a puzzle-box cage. That I'd like to see, if she can pull it off."

Emry flushed at the memory of DeMeter's accusing gaze the night before, but she put it aside, recognizing talent when she saw it—and still hoping to get naked with the lovely Sheaver at some point. "I'd say the Doc's given a better showing than the rest of us so far. Maybe we need a Troubleshooter like her to keep us honest."

Anders furrowed his brow. "Ekundayo DeMarais is definitely brilliant. She actually has two doctorates, and she's only twenty-nine. And she had the highest homicide clearance rate in the Sheaf last year. But the Corps depends on its reputation for neutrality. Heroes with strong nationalist identities aren't a good fit. Especially a Sheaver, given the recent political climate."

"Lots of recruits take new championyms when they become Troubleshooters. I did."

"Well, maybe in a couple of years, when tensions have eased." Emry felt that was probably an optimistic prediction, but then she took another bite of pumpkin-walnut muffin and forgot that anything else existed in the universe.

After breakfast, Emerald donned an abbreviated green sports bra and black shorts, tied her hair into a sloppy ponytail with a green scrunchie, and went out for a morning run around the circumference of New Queens, an easy twenty kilometers. Since she was on vacation,

Emry took it easy by running to antispinward, slightly reducing her angular velocity and thus the effective gravity she felt. She soon realized that a growing number of spectators stood along the sides of the path, no doubt wanting a look at the Green Blaze in scanty exercise attire. She waved and flexed her biceps at the crowd. But in addition to the usual cheers and wolf whistles, she heard a number of boos and taunts. "Sleeping on the job, Blaze?" "Some superhero!" "We wanted the Green Blaze, not the Scream Daze!" "The Hounds were right about you! Cyborg traitor!" "Half-Earther!"

Anger and humiliation burned within her, but she wasn't about to let herself lose her temper again—certainly not against civilians. Instead, she channeled her adrenaline into running, slipping on a pair of sunglasses to keep bugs and motecams out of her eyes and pushing herself to top speed. The jeers blurred together and Dopplered past into near-inaudibility as she soared past the crowd at over eighty klicks. She ran until it felt like flying and laughed at the wind pummeling her face.

The power trials were held outdoors in the park next to the hotel. Emry, of course, was not in competition with the locals, but would evaluate their performance alongside Anders and the other recruiters. Once the top performers had risen from the pack, though, they would have to face her as their climactic challenge. Naturally, she attended as the Green Blaze, in full light armor with her unruly hair braided for action.

First off came the costume competition, a fan-favorite portion of the trials. Per tradition, the locals started out by Clark Kenting—performing an onstage quick-change from civilian clothes into hero gear, either revealing it beneath their clothes, drawing it from a pack or case, or transforming their everyday wear into heroic attire. Since it was almost impossible to maintain a secret identity in an age of ubiquitous cameras and biometric sensors, the exercise was largely frivolous, an indulgence in nostalgia and mild titillation; but it did serve to demonstrate the heroes' preparedness, dexterity, and the like, as well as the practicality of their costumes. Generally, the more difficult the gear was to don, the greater the risk of error or malfunction in the field.

The Decider certainly had no problem in that regard, whatever other deficiencies his minimal attire may have had. He shed his business suit swiftly but with the panache of a stripper, and Emry and the audience whooped appropriately. Other competitors offered less primal but equally impressive costume-change techniques. Quicksylvia's street clothes flowed and morphed into her skintight silver catsuit, no doubt some kind of heavy-duty soligram gel. Spindizzy had somehow managed to perfect the classic Wonder Woman spin, her gyration triggering her business suit to vaporize in a flash of light and reveal her psychedelically patterned light-armor leotard—a spectacular performance, though surely impractical for everyday use.

As New Queens's resident hero, Doctor DeMeter had been scheduled to come last. Her Kenting was simple, swift, and practical, achieved simply by shedding her jacket, unrolling her bootlegs, and donning her headband and equipment belt, all in under eight seconds. The hometown audience gave her a standing ovation, and Emry leaned over to discuss the costume prize with Kelly and the other judges. As DeMeter took her place on stage with the other heroes, she glanced down in puzzlement at something beneath their feet.

But the emcee had a surprise announcement: One more competitor had been penciled in at the last minute. As the audience and the heroes murmured among themselves, a strong, lanky blond man with epicanthic eyes strode confidently onto the Kenting platform. "I am the Protector," he intoned in a voice Emry found familiar. "And you're in for a real show now."

"Hold on," DeMeter called out. "There's something—"

But the man on the platform worked a control that shifted his trousers and jacket to solid black, and his small backpack unfolded and clamped a black, helmet-like cowl around his head—a cowl styled like a snarling wolf. "Let's make this a fair fight!" Knightwolf cried.

Even as he spoke, a humming sound came from the platform beneath the heroes' feet. A few, like the Decider, Slynx, and Kyojin, seemed largely unaffected. But others including DeMeter, Coriolis, and Rammer screamed and clutched their heads. Spindizzy staggered and fell as if her equilibrium had failed her. Quicksylvia's costume melted into a pool on the stage, leaving her in panties. Oxosi and Kinetyk collapsed heavily, their bionic limbs twitching before falling utterly limp.

"Oh, no," Chaitra cried even as Emry charged forward. "It's the stolen power disruptors! Blaze, be careful!"

That was another word whose meaning Emry didn't know. She leapt onto the Kenting platform and grabbed Knightwolf by the front of his jacket, lifting him into the air with one hand. "You've been a bad doggie!"

Under his mask, Knightwolf smiled. "Like I said — I'm the Protector. Against people like you, who think your power entitles you to dictate to the rest of us."

"The rest of who, Baskervilles?"

"I'm glad you asked."

"Blaze, look out!" Kelly cried.

Emry spun, but it was too late. Powerful arms seized her, and she had just enough time to recognize the bare, bulging chest and flaxen hair of the Decider before he hurled her onto the power disruptor plates. She gave a banshee shriek as pain surged through her body. Feedback overwhelmed her vision and hearing, and her limbs and fingers convulsed. Error messages cascaded across her retinal HUD before it flickered and went blank, along with the near-subliminal somatic feedback in her brain.

When her senses cleared, Doctor DeMeter was holding her, stroking her hair. "Green Blaze. Emerald! Are you with us?" She looked odd at first, and Emry realized it was because she could no longer see the subtle glow of infrared light through DeMeter's skin.

"Yeah, I'm here, Doc. Ohh, but all of me hurts except my tits." She managed a faint grin. "Only part of me *without* implants."

"On the plus side, that is rather a lot of you." Emry glared at her. "Okay, I'll leave the jokes to you. Can you move?"

Emry realized she was better off than a lot of the cyborgs here. Even with just her native genetic mods, she had three or four times baseline strength for her weight class. She'd need it to fight off the Hounds, especially if the Decider was on their side.

But as she began to rise, she faced unexpected resistance. Her light armor was rigid and inflexible. She could bend her bare shoulders and elbows, but her own costume fought her attempts to move her legs and hands. Her jerkin, which had automatically sealed up to the neck and waist when she'd leapt into action, put enough pressure against her rib cage and diaphragm to inhibit her ability to take deep breaths. "Oh, no. My hard landing must've put it in rigid mode just as the power shut down. The microplates are locked together. My armor's not just dead, it's got vackin' rigor mortis!"

"Well, can we get it off you?" DeMeter tried pulling at the collar seam, with no effect.

"You're welcome to strip me anytime, gorgeous, but I'm afraid I'm sealed in for now." DeMeter shifted her efforts to one of Emry's gauntlets, but they had tightened too snugly about her wrists. *Just my luck I had to debut those here,* Emry thought.

The Decider loomed over them, laughing. "See, Green Blaze? I told you not to wear so much."

"Yeah, well, I'll try to get out of the habit!" The pun went over his head, of course, though DeMeter chuckled. "What the vack, Erwin?" Emry went on. "Weren't you the one saying you weren't like these losers?"

"He was with them the whole time," the Sheaver detective deduced. "He chose the tavern, remember. Got us away from the con, kept us distracted and our comms jammed." DeMeter's dark eyes skewered him. "I suppose you planted the disruptor plates on the stage while your accomplices led the police on a false trail. As one of the con guests, you would've had no trouble getting in."

"I had to," the Decider—Erwin—insisted. "It was the only way."

"Only way to do what, Mister Coleman?"

"To have a fair shot in the power trials! Did you know they've been won by cyborgs for the past four years running? This is the only way to make it fair again!"

The women stared. "You're muscle all the way up, aren't you?" DeMeter said.

Emry grimaced. "Now I'm glad I didn't fuck you."

Erwin pouted. "I'll show you both. Without your tech tricks, you've got no chance of winning." He strolled off with a self-satisfied grin.

Several burly Hounds were moving in to escort or carry the nullified heroes off the stage. "Doc, what powers you got without your bionics?" Emry whispered as the Hounds approached the two women.

DeMeter grimaced. "Just my brain and my senses."

Emry tried to swing at one of the Hounds as he picked her up, but she could get no leverage. She was able to force her legs to move somewhat against the armor's resistance, but her kicks were feeble and useless. The Hound dropped her unceremoniously back in her seat, and a terrified Kelly and Chaitra had to catch her shoulders to keep her from falling over. It was humiliating to feel so weak, so powerless. She was supposed to be the one protecting them.

Knightwolf strode forward to address the agitated crowd— which, Emry now saw, was being held at bay by a ring of Hounds surrounding the amphitheater. Though they would not have been able to bring weapons through security, many displayed claws, fangs, and other dangerous biomods, and it was safe to assume that the rest were as strong and aggressive as they looked. "Don't be alarmed, congoers," Knightwolf intoned. "The power trials will still proceed as scheduled. This… intervention… was necessary to ensure that they could be conducted fairly, in the true spirit of Strider heroes, unadulterated with false powers.

"Given that the pool of legitimate competitors has been slim these past few years, we Hounds have arranged our own slate of heroes to compete in this event. In addition to myself and the Decider, we have…" Several other Hounds of both sexes came onto the stage, some remaining in their black outfits, others stripping down to costumes or bare chests. Knightwolf introduced them with names Emry had never heard of.

"I recognize a couple of them," Anders Kopf murmured. "Starcules and Blue Nova. They washed out in the first round of the trials in '05 and '07." He shook his sandy head. "They wouldn't have made the cut with or without cyborgs."

Emry stared. "'Starcules'? Are you kidding me?"

Knightwolf continued. "And of course, the other pure mods already entered into the trials are free to remain. They're the only ones who got here fairly, after all."

"In your dreams," cried Slynx. "Don't drag me into your pathetic cause!" The diminutive vigilante leapt toward the Hounds, splaying her claws. Behind her, Kyojin hesitated, unsure what to do. Vestalia was the entertainment capital of the Belt, so the towering heroine's role involved more showpersonship than actual crimefighting. Would she play along with the Hounds if it gave her a chance at victory? Or would she hero up and join Slynx in the fray?

After a moment, though, Kyojin withdrew from the stage. "I'm sorry," she murmured. "I can't get involved with this kind of controversy." Yet the giantess winced as she watched Slynx fall beneath the blows of the Hounds.

"Hey!" Emry screamed over the sound of Slynx's bones breaking. Even the strength of her voice was impaired by her constrained breathing. "Leave her alone! You call this a fair fight?"

"We've made our point," Knightwolf said after a few more moments. He gave Slynx one last kick to topple her off the stage in front of Emry. "We have to be a united front. Those who don't see that are part of the problem." He spread his arms. "Now that we've dealt with the interruptions, let's get on with the power trials!"

The audience murmured angrily, but they were too cowed by the Hounds to do more. Chaitra moved to examine Slynx, and Captain Coriolis caught Emry's eyes. "What are we going to do, Blaze?"

"What can we do?" Oxosi rumbled despairingly.

Emry surveyed the other heroes around her. She was as helpless as any of them—more so than some, with her own wardrobe at war with her. More than anyone else here, she was defined by sheer overpowering strength, and now that strength had been taken from her. What else did she have to offer them?

Yet she was the one they all looked to for guidance and inspiration. She was the Troubleshooter. The guest of honor. They would follow where she led, whether she deserved it or not.

So she'd better vacking well deserve it.

With a supreme effort of sinew and will, the Green Blaze rose to her feet, waving off the others' attempts to help her. Stiffly, she turned to face the local heroes and the audience. "What we're gonna do," she said in as strong a voice as she could manage, "is stand up... and walk out of this place. Those who can't stand up, we carry." The mobile heroes wasted no time acting on her words, helping Kinetyk and Oxosi to their cybernetic feet. "If these bullies wanna hog the playground, let's leave them to it! Their own opinions are the only ones they care about anyway, right? So what's that vackin' gotta do with us?"

Her words heartened many, but the audience still hesitated. The Tenshi cosplayer spoke up tentatively. "But... what about the Hounds? They won't let us past."

"So what? We're stronger than they are."

"What? No, I—I'm not. It's just a costume."

"I said 'we,' honey. As in all of us, together. We outnumber them. We're the public they say they represent. But we're so much more than they think we are. Striders and immigrants, germliners and baseliners and cyborgs and suit-users. Heroes and fans, actors and artists, cosplayers and shippers. We are the Strider community. We're the superhero community. We're ModCon! They can't beat a whole convention! Come on! Room party in my suite, and you're all invited!"

She powered ahead slowly, step by straining step, but the TSC staffers and the local heroes and the audience moved with her, gathering at her back, helping her forward. "No!" Knightwolf cried. "Don't let her steal this from you! We're doing this for you! To get things back the way they used to be!"

"When?" demanded Chaitra, who remained at Slynx's side, and who was old enough to know firsthand how things used to be.

"And why?" Doctor DeMeter added. "None of us would even be here if our forebears hadn't chosen to change the way things were."

Emry grinned. "My people. Keep it coming!"

She stumbled, but hands caught both her arms. She glanced over and saw she was bracketed by Green Blaze cosplayers. "I knew I could count on me," she murmured to them.

The one on her left winked. "So did we," he said.

As the crowd surged toward the amphitheater's rear exits, the Hounds moved forward to block them. "Don't stop!" Emry cried. "Fear's only a weapon if you let it be! Make them blink first!"

True to form, most of the bullies fell into retreat when faced with real opposition. "No!" Knightwolf cried, rushing off the stage and charging at Emry.

But Kyojin surged forward and took him down with a single flashy kick. She turned to the crowd and shrugged. "Better late than never?" She knelt by Chaitra, carefully lifted the injured, unconscious Slynx into her arms, then turned to the remaining sentries at the exits. "So does anyone want to try to stop me from getting her to a doctor?"

With their leader felled, the rest of the Hounds scattered—save for the Decider, left decidedly alone upon the stage. "Aw, come on!" he called plaintively as the crowd surged out. "Now I'll never know if I would've won!"

"Don't worry about it," Emry called back as the police started to file in at last. "You'll have a whole jury to Decide that for you!"

Kelly caught up with her. "Should we try to get back to the trials?"

"We need to get our powers turned back on first," Emry said. "And get this damn suit off me—I really need to pee. Besides, I promised these folks a party, so they're gonna have a party." She smirked. "Which, come to think of it, is usually a surefire way to get my clothes off."

Come Sunday morning, Akar Lukman, Chaitra Varghese, and the various mod specialists attending the con had managed to reactivate all the disrupted power systems. With Knightwolf, the Hounds, and the

Decider all in NQPD custody for theft, assault, kidnapping, and so forth, the power trials were rescheduled for that afternoon. Knightwolf had turned out to be Hamish Oates, a wannabe who'd washed out humiliatingly in the power trials for three years running from 2102 to 2104, entering under a different championym each time. He was a mod by birth, but to Emry's complete lack of surprise, he turned out to have some unreported black-market muscle upgrades. Having used just such low-rent bionics in her teens, Emry wished him all the joy of the associated glitches and twinges of pain.

This time, the power trials went splendidly. Doctor DeMeter, Captain Coriolis, and Oxosi all made it to the final round, a mixed martial arts challenge against the Green Blaze herself. Pitting DeMeter and Coriolis against someone in a higher weight class wasn't exactly fair, but crimefighters were often outmatched and needed to learn to compensate with their own advantages. Emry overpowered Coriolis handily despite his speed and agility, and Oxosi's inexperience made him relatively easy to overcome, though his impressive physical prowess and determination could make him a real contender in the years ahead. But the Doctor used her wits and agility to lure Emry into a disadvantageous position and bind her arms behind her, besting superior strength with superior leverage and achieving a successful pin before Emry could break free. Her overall performance—both in the trials and otherwise—led Emry, the other judges, and the audience to vote DeMeter the hands-down winner of the event.

Emry insisted on being the one to tell her the good news that night over dinner—a quiet, private affair in civilian clothes, just Emry and Ekundayo at last in a cozy restaurant booth. "The Corps wants you, Doc. You've got it all—brains, strength, skill, charisma, a great body… and after this, the whole Belt respects you and trusts you."

"So my Sheaver ties won't be a problem?" DeMarais asked.

"No. We're all one community, after all. All heroes." Emerald took her hand. "And you're my hero, Ekundayo."

The other woman blushed. "One of many," she demurred. Still, she sidled around in the booth until her hip pressed against Emry's. "But if I'm the hero… does that mean I get the girl?"

Her kiss left Emry as transfixed as had her wrestling holds. For once, Emry was delighted to feel completely powerless.

Early Warning Systems

"I'll get right to the point," Agent Rashmi Pandit said to the badly injured woman in the hospital bed. "What century are you from?"

The patient—whose license identified her as Jacqueline Foreman of Dayton, Ohio, age 47—stared back at the federal agent in disbelief. Only the bleeping of the medical monitors filled the next several moments. Pandit had ordered the woman moved from the ICU to a private room for this conversation, over the protests of the hospital staff.

"I'm sorry," Foreman finally said. "I don't—" Pandit caught a trace of an unfamiliar accent in the woman's speech, as hard to pin down as her ethnically ambiguous features. But Foreman seemed to catch herself, the accent vanishing as she continued with a laugh. "I must be more sedated than I realized. Say that again?"

"Let's not beat around the bush," Pandit told her. "We may not have time, as you probably know quite well. I'll lay it out for you. You're the latest of several similar accident cases over the past few days. Pedestrians who, according to witnesses, stepped out brazenly in front of moving cars with no concern for their own safety."

"Ohh, don't rub it in," Foreman said. "It's my first time in D.C., I got caught up gawking at the sights—"

"You're the lucky one this time," Pandit told her. "The other four didn't survive."

Foreman winced. "That's terrible."

"Did you know them? Do you travel in groups, or are you all from different eras?"

The other woman stared. "You actually said that, didn't you? You think I'm a... *time traveler?*"

"It's not the first time we've seen a cluster of accidents like this. People carelessly stepping in front of moving cars. All with no known relatives, aside from whoever shows up to check them out of the hospital or claim their bodies — and none of those people can be tracked down again. Usually multiracial. All uncannily healthy prior to their accidents. Perfect vision, perfect hearing, no evidence of disease. Remarkably rapid healing, for the survivors. All clustered in the same area and within a few days or weeks of each other. Beijing, June 1989. New York City, September 2001. Darfur, February 2003. Tunisia, December 2010. Here in D.C., January 2021. Mumbai, August 2029. See the pattern?"

Foreman laughed weakly. "So you think time travelers are coming back to watch important historical events... and getting hit by cars? Why? Don't they have cars in the future? The past I could understand, but I don't think H.G. Wells put his time machine into mass production." She smirked. "Or are the drivers enemy time travelers trying to kill them? Would Terminators bother to make it look like an accident?"

"This is no joke from my side, Foreman," the agent insisted, her voice hardening. "And we're not as easy to outsmart as you and your... fellow travelers assume. Granted, it was a mystery to us for a long time. It took us a while to believe they could be time travelers at all, of course."

Pandit declined to mention how many of her own superiors were still skeptical of her theories — some from lack of imagination, others because they were fossils of older regimes and she was a daughter of Muslim immigrants. Jacqueline Foreman was her chance to prove them wrong, if she could get the woman to talk. So she wasn't about to admit the weakness of her position. She never would've gotten where she was if she'd let herself back down in the face of skepticism or mockery.

"But the autopsies were telling," Pandit went on. "None of their lungs or skeletons had accumulated the toxic residues that build up in our systems today, as if they'd grown up in a world without pollution. Some showed residual traces of body modifications or technological implants beyond anything currently known — removed so they'd blend into our era, no doubt, but leaving signs we could find once we got an idea what to look for. Some even showed mitochondrial mutations consistent with the genetic 'clock' advancing thousands of years.

"But the high rate of traffic accidents and fatalities — that confused us for just the reason you say. How could people from the future not understand the dangers posed by automobiles?"

Foreman glanced down at the casts encasing her legs. "Look, under other circumstances, I'd be amused, but this is in pretty poor taste, don't you think?"

"It's only in the past, ohh, fifteen years or so that we've started to understand," Pandit went on relentlessly. "That's about how long pedestrian detection and automatic emergency braking have been standard in nearly every new car sold in the United States. Unluckily for you, the average age of the American automobile is around twelve years, so nearly half the cars on the road still don't have crash avoidance systems, and Congress is still debating the bill that would require retrofitting them into older cars.

"A bill that would also authorize the development of a smart roadway system, by the way — allowing cars to communicate with a network of sensors and anticipate possible collisions well in advance. Bringing us closer to the time when all cars are autonomous, able to react far faster than any human driver.

"So, yes, they'll still have cars in the future — but they'll have cars they don't need to be afraid of. People will be able to step unthinkingly into traffic and know that the traffic will always give them a wide berth."

Foreman stared wordlessly for a few moments, then rallied herself. "That's very clever, Agent. But surely time travelers would know that older cars lacked avoidance systems, that traffic accidents were once common."

"Knowing is one thing. A lifetime of habit and reflex is another. The injured or killed time travelers we're seeing are probably just the small fraction who forgot their training and let their everyday habits take over for one distracted moment." The medical monitors showed a slight increase in pulse and blood pressure. Was that embarrassment in Foreman's eyes?

Pandit stepped forward, pressing her case. "Which means that there are probably a lot more travelers we don't find out about. That many time travelers at once? They must be gathering to witness something pivotal. Some major event that changes the course of history. We've never been able to prepare for it before, because we didn't fully understand what was going on. And as grisly as it sounds, once crash avoidance becomes mandatory, we'll lose the early warning system that careless time travelers provide us with.

"So this may be our one chance to get ahead of history. What's going to happen, Jacqueline? A terror attack? A natural disaster? Another coup attempt?"

Foreman laughed again, but the exertion caused her pain, so it faded into a sardonic sigh. She paused to catch her breath, the monitors' bleeping gradually slowing back to normal. "Even if I were what you say, would you really expect me to answer? If time travelers were allowed to prevent disasters — or able to — do you think you'd still have any memory of those disasters?"

Pandit controlled her irritation at the woman's condescension. "We both know that it doesn't work that way. My unit is advised by the leading theoretical physicists in the field, you know — today's field, at least. So I'm fully aware that there are only two physically valid ways time travel can work. One, the post-selection model: time travelers create a quantum correlation between the past and the future, so their very presence ensures the creation of the future they originally came from. Two, the probabilistic model: a time traveler will simultaneously follow all possible quantum paths, resulting in some timelines where the traveler's actions change history and others where they don't. Either way, the original timeline endures. It never gets 'erased' like in the movies. So those disasters may have been prevented — just not in our branch of history.

"But maybe that means we have a chance to create a branch that avoids the disaster, to make a better future for at least one version of ourselves. Maybe we're already on that branch *because* you survived the accident instead of dying." When that got no reaction, Pandit went on. "If nothing else, some forewarning might allow us to prepare, to reduce the impact — maybe prevent an even worse disaster than history records. Maybe that's your role in creating the history you know."

Foreman studied her for a long moment. "When I was, oh, thirteen or so," she finally said, "I convinced myself I'd figured out how to trisect an angle using only a compass and straightedge."

"What has that got to do with anything?"

"Oh, I was thrilled. Countless mathematicians had insisted it was impossible for centuries, but I'd finally cracked it. My name would go down in history! I ran downstairs and excitedly told my big sister all about my brilliant breakthrough.

"She just looked at me politely and said 'Oh, that's interesting.' Nothing more than that." Foreman smiled. "About an hour later,

I realized my mistake. The three sectors of the angle weren't equal at all. I'd mistaken three-eights of the angle for one-third, or something just as stupidly obvious in retrospect.

"I was embarrassed, of course… but I thanked my sister for letting me discover my own mistake. For *trusting* that I was smart enough to fix my mistakes without her help."

Foreman cocked her head. "So if I were some sort of time-traveling historian, or even just a tourist… why would I want to take away your right to fix your own mistakes? Wouldn't that be the whole thing I came back to watch you do?"

Pandit clenched her fists. "Nobody dies when you get a geometry problem wrong."

"They might if you're designing a bridge."

"You still think this is a joke. Maybe you can't appreciate what it's like to live in a time as screwed up as ours.

"You want to trade family anecdotes? Fine. I lost both my parents to the COVID pandemic in 2019. Because their employers trusted leaders who denied the crisis for their own petty reasons, my parents were forced to work in unsafe conditions. And when they both got sick, the hospitals were too overloaded with other patients to help them.

"An entirely preventable catastrophe killed my parents, and countless others, because of people who had the power to stop it and chose to do nothing. So don't expect me to show any sympathy for the idea of refusing to help when you *know* something terrible is coming."

Foreman's gaze had softened, grown sad. "I'm very sorry you had to go through that. But doesn't that just prove my point? It wouldn't matter if time travelers warned you about future crises if the people in charge weren't ready to listen… or willing to act. Societies only face their problems when they're ready to."

Pandit leaned forward urgently. "That's the whole reason for my division. We're the ones who *are* ready to listen."

Foreman held her gaze. "Then if you already have that willingness to look forward… you don't need time travelers."

The door opened, admitting Foreman's doctor, and Pandit fell silent. "You need to leave now," the older man said. "You're agitating my patient."

"This is important, Doctor. A possible matter of national security. I may not have another chance to talk to her."

"Believe me, this woman isn't going anywhere for at least a week."

"I have no doubt she'll be gone well before then. By which point it may be too late."

"Too late for what?"

Pandit had no reply.

"Look, your questioning won't do much good if she's in no shape to answer," the doctor told her. "You can post a guard if you have to, but you'll need to come back tomorrow."

Pandit was tempted to exploit the power that invoking "national security" would give her, the license to run roughshod over the rights of the few in the name of the many. But her superiors were less sanguine about such tactics than some of their predecessors under previous administrations. If she took such steps, she would be required to account for them. And her standing was tenuous enough as it was. If she were wrong about this woman, then any overreach could end Pandit's career.

It might be worth losing her job if she knew for certain that she would prevent a tragedy in the process. But what about the tragedy after that? Studying time had made her keenly aware of the long game.

"All right," she finally said. "But this room will be guarded at all times. And if anyone — *anyone* — comes asking about her, alert me before you do anything."

"Fine, as long as you go now."

"Just give me one more minute with her."

The doctor looked over at Foreman, who hesitated for a moment, then nodded. "One minute," he said. "That's firm."

Once he was gone, Pandit met Foreman's eyes. "Sleep on this: If time is immutable, you have nothing to lose by telling me the truth. If not, then you could save a lot of people in at least one reality.

"And you wouldn't be taking away our right to solve our own problems. You'd just be giving us a head start. After that, you could just sit back and watch to your heart's content."

The woman in the bed studied her for a moment. "All I can tell you," she finally replied, "is that you have all your answers already."

"Don't you understand? You have a chance to make a better future!"

Foreman pursed her lips. "No pollution. No disease. No pointless deaths in traffic. Ethnic harmony. Humans still thriving and evolving thousands of years from now. The future you think I came from sounds pretty incredible already. And yet all you can see when you look ahead is danger and disaster." Her gaze grew sympathetic. "I understand where that fear is coming from, Agent Pandalai. But do you really believe that a better future can be created from fear alone?"

"Pandit. My name is Pandit."

"I'm sorry, I must not have heard—" Foreman stared. "Rashmi Pandit? And… you said your department had top physicists advising it? On temporal physics?"

"That's correct. Why?"

"Oh… nothing."

The doctor re-entered, hectoring Pandit, and she had no choice but to relent and turn for the exit. But on her way out, Foreman's voice stopped her. "It's just… It's a privilege to have met you, Direc—Agent. I think you'll have a hell of a future… once you learn to look forward to it."

✳

Two days later, despite all of Pandit's precautions, Jacqueline Foreman vanished from the hospital without a trace. Five days after that, the president signed the mandatory crash avoidance bill into law. Shortly thereafter, the rash of exotic, unidentifiable people having careless traffic accidents subsided, as it always did in the wake of major historical events. The time travelers had gone back home. And Rashmi Pandit realized what Foreman had meant.

I had all my answers already. I told her about the bill. Surely tragedies and disasters were not the only world-changing events that would lure time travelers. Pandit had argued it herself: The denizens of the future must live with no fear of dying in traffic. The universal adoption of crash-avoiding cars, and autonomous cars after that, would save countless millions of lives for generations to come. Surely the beginning of that process was a moment in history worth witnessing.

Societies only face their problems when they're ready to.

And that explained why Foreman had refused to cooperate. The change she'd come to witness was already set in motion; nothing she said or did would have made a difference, for better or worse. She was a big sister, standing back and giving her juniors room to solve their own problems. Trusting them to get it right in the end.

In any case, Pandit's unit would need to think of some other way to anticipate imminent threats. Before long, there would never again be another spate of time travelers dying pointlessly in traffic.

And it embarrassed Pandit that she had trouble seeing that as a good thing.

The Monsters We Make

The convoy hit the landmines on the Lincoln Highway, about an hour's drive east of Pittsburgh. The mines must have been calibrated for high tonnage, given that the lead escort vehicles drove over them without difficulty. The Monster Truck was not so lucky.

"Don't call it that," Colonel Harold Darville said for the thirtieth time as he supervised the science team's inspection of the hobbled Mobile Heavy Containment Unit, which had swerved off the road and smashed through several dozen trees before finally coming to a halt. Strolling beside him, Ariana Vallejo smirked at his futile insistence upon solemn respect for the hazard it contained. *As if calling it anything other than a monster would achieve that,* she thought.

"They couldn't have known we were bringing this in, could they?" asked Kenji Hirata, one hand placed protectively on the shell of the enormous vehicle. Rumbles and bangs from within were audible even through thirty centimeters of armor, though the gray-haired xenobiologist didn't flinch.

Vallejo shook her raven-tressed head. "Even if someone out here could have gotten word, there's no way they would've had time." Sizing up the thickly wooded swells around them, she continued, "This is one of the few remaining passes through the Laurel Highlands. The mines are probably a general defense in case one comes through this way. I doubt they expected a captive one."

Darville doffed his cap to wipe his clean-shaven, dark brown scalp. "I'm more concerned that their actions might set it free. How well is the Unit holding up?"

Hirata finished his inspection. "Some increased torsional stresses on the armor, but well within tolerances. Internal restraints are loosened but holding. But there's damage to the drivetrain and the left forward tread is out of alignment."

"Do the Unit's self-repair capabilities extend to the undercarriage?"

"I prepared for every possibility, Colonel. Past capture attempts have failed due to overlooked weaknesses. Not this time." He sighed. "Still, self-repair will take at least ten hours. I don't see us reaching the outer Pittsburgh wall before morning."

The Monster Truck rumbled, and a bone-shakingly deep bellow resonated from within. Darville stared uneasily. "I don't suppose there's any chance its calls could attract other xenofauna?"

Again that insistence on proper terminology that Vallejo found oddly endearing. "Seismics and satellites don't show any other kaiju in range," she replied, using the term just to see him wince. "In any case, Tricerantulas aren't social animals. The cry is an intimidation behavior, not a call for help."

"I'm more concerned about it attracting a rival or predator. This thing's designed to keep them in, not out."

"I considered that contingency as well, Colonel," Hirata insisted. "Nothing short of a Ragnarex could breach the Unit."

"The weak link isn't the Truck, Harry, it's us," Vallejo said. "The injured drivers need proper attention, and we're down a medic." The capture operation had taken its toll, and the unit's doctor had been airlifted out with the wounded. "Plus, we're all exhausted from the capture and the long drive in. There must be a town nearby."

Darville frowned. "That's what concerns me, Ariana. Whoever planted these mines is probably local. And the people out here…"

"I know what they think of us, Harry. But that's all the more reason to investigate, surely. As long as we don't tell them what we're really doing…"

"You think that will make a difference to these people?" Hirata asked. "One look at us and—"

"We'll have the advantage in that case, Doctor," the colonel declared. "Even with diminished numbers, we're more than capable of handling a few backwoods ruffians. And Ariana's right—as long as we're stuck here, we need to know who and what we're dealing with."

The colonel ordered Major Hutchison and a full squad to accompany him and the scientists to the nearby town, leaving Sergeant Scislowski's squad with the convoy. It meant leaving the Monster Truck with an inadequate guard contingent, but Darville left them the full complement of patrol drones, and they could camouflage the MHCU with the broken wood and foliage that half-covered it already. It was worth the risk, since the unknowns awaiting them in the town might pose the greater danger at the moment.

The four-kilometer hike through the hilly woodlands was easy enough for the soldiers, and for Vallejo, whose love of such walks was one of the few positive things she'd derived from her rural childhood. But Hirata's age, and the injuries he'd accumulated over four decades of studying predatory alien megafauna larger than blue whales, made him a poor fit for strenuous field operations. Unluckily for him, his expertise made him indispensable.

It was perhaps inevitable that many of the leading kaijologists were Japanese, though not (well, not only) for the obvious reason. The spawning units crawled along the ocean floor to evade detection and to mine raw materials for bioprinting their eldritch offspring, so coastal regions had been hit the hardest, forcing mass migrations that had dwarfed the previous century's retreat from the rising oceans. But coastal and island states like Japan, with no inland to speak of, had no choice to but to stand and fight in order to survive as nations. The Chileans, the Sri Lankans, the Portuguese, and others were refugee peoples now, but Japan held on against the odds, perhaps because their whole history had been shaped by the battle against devastation from the sea and the forces of the earth below.

Even with satellite maps, it was hard to know what the team might find up ahead. Populations had shifted enormously in the eighty-odd years since Brigitte Lee had unknowingly brought the first spawning unit back to Earth. Countless smaller cities had died out from the loss of commerce and urban support, yet the masses of refugees had still needed places to live. Many, of course, would never go near a dense population center again, and had raised their children to feel likewise.

Thus, the landscape was littered with small, isolated towns like Laurel Shade, as the sign on the outskirts called the sparse scatter of farms and community buildings that hugged the west edge of the Laurel Highlands as if hunkering down to evade the notice of whatever might peer over them from the east. The kaiju were nowhere near that large or upright, of course—"more Baragon than Godzilla," as Hirata had been known to observe—but in Vallejo's youth in an Oregon community very much like this, the threat of the kaiju had loomed as large as the Rocky Mountains in the tales her older brothers had scared her with—and sometimes it had seemed they loomed no smaller in the adults' fears. Becoming an expert in kaiju behavior had helped diminish her fears to a more reasonable size, while honing them to a far sharper focus.

The town seemed vacant when the party arrived. The residents had no doubt retreated to their kaiju cellars upon hearing the mines detonate, hoping any xenofauna that survived the blast would pass them by. Kaiju didn't come this far inland very often, but the rate had been creeping upward despite the defenders' best efforts, and there was no human habitation left on Earth that was not shaped by awareness of the threat. The town's buildings were spread out widely, with plenty of walking room between for even the largest behemoth. Their construction was sturdy but simple, largely metal-free and easy to repair or rebuild. The livestock had evidently been set loose into the hills; better to risk losing a few strays than to have a whole penned herd consumed.

Soon enough, a small scouting party emerged from the dense woods to intercept Darville's troops on the edge of town. They were all male, and all pale, save only one brown, high-cheekboned face under a mop of straight black hair. They stared at Darville's more diverse party with surprise and wariness. Several reflexively raised their rifles, prompting the troops to do the same. Their leader, a robust, thirtyish man with wavy blond hair, raised a hand to hold his men back, then stepped forward with his rifle in a two-handed ready carry, not aimed but positioned for quick deployment. "Just move on," he said. "There's nothing for you city types here."

"We have injured," Vallejo said. She and Darville had already agreed that a civilian spokesperson would be less likely to provoke the townsfolk. "They need treatment, and we could all do with a rest."

"They can get what they need in Pittsburgh," the man countered, spitting the first syllable as if it preceded "of Hell." "We don't need you bringing your troubles down on us."

Darville spoke now. "The enclave is too far to reach on foot."

"Shoulda thought of that before you brought your machines through our lands," said the darker-complexioned man. "What were you carrying that was heavy enough to set off those mines?"

"Then you know about the mines." It was not a question.

The other man hesitated, trading a look with his fellows. The blond man answered. "Some folks mine the passes to keep the monsters from crossing. Everyone knows it. Except city folk who think they know everything."

"What were you carrying?" the black-haired man reiterated.

"Whoever set those mines made them too sensitive," Hirata bluffed. "They damaged our supply truck. Thousands in the enclave could die of disease or hunger if the refrigeration equipment is too badly compromised. Someone needs to be held ac—" Darville put up a hand to stop him. Vallejo approved; letting these townsfolk see the colonel as the calm, reasonable one might help counter some preconceptions.

She saw one man perk up as if about to deny the accusation of shoddy work, only to be held back by glances from his fellows. "The problems of the enclaves are no problems of ours," the blond man said, trying to reassert dominance. "Your kind sowed this disaster, so now you can reap it." He began to angle his rifle forward. "You'd best just be moving on before we—"

"Duane Patterson!" Vallejo turned to see an approaching group of townspeople, now emerged from their kaiju cellars and led by a formidable-looking middle-aged woman. "Just what do you think you're doing?" the woman went on. "These people obviously need a doctor. And a good meal too, I shouldn't wonder."

The blond man—Patterson—maintained his bluster, but with less confidence, his rifle sagging. "Brenda, they're city folk!"

"I can see where they're from, Duane. But where *we're* from, there's such a thing as basic hospitality. You don't turn away people in need. You certainly don't turn them out to wander the woods at night."

Her moral authority established, the gray-haired woman stepped forward and offered her hand. "I'm Brenda Barnes." Vallejo introduced herself and her party in turn, and Barnes continued. "I apologize for the boys. They're good folk, but they can get a hair too protective at times. Come along and we'll get your people fixed up."

The dinner in the community hall was predictably awkward. Laurel Shade's residents were very traditional; the preparation and serving of the meals was done exclusively by the women and the few girls, leaving the men and boys—those who weren't out retrieving the livestock—with plenty of free time to stare at the newcomers and mutter among themselves. Though the wives and mothers did their best to maintain civility, it was only a matter of time before one of the younger men could hold his tongue no longer. "What the hell you doin' with that thing, old man?" the curly-haired youth demanded of Hirata, who kept glancing at his handheld monitoring unit for the Monster Truck.

"Language, Hoyt," Brenda Barnes warned, her manner mild but resolute.

Hoyt threw back a sullen look. "He was bein' rude first, Brenda. Playin' with those machines at the table. They could bring a monster down on us!"

"There's nothing to worry about," Hirata replied in calm, professorial tones he no doubt believed to be reassuring. "Kaiju are attracted to urban areas because of the abundance of biomass and of the heavy metals they consume to fortify their skeletons and body armor. There's no reason they'd be drawn to the small amounts of metal we carry, even if there were any kaiju loose in the immediate vicinity." He pulled a satellite tracker from a vest pocket and held it up. "Which, I can assure you, there are not. The nearest ones are nesting in the ruins of Harrisburg."

"You people think you have it all figured out," Duane Patterson spoke up. "Same as the astronauts who brought the monsters back in the first place. 'Cause *of course* there ain't no harm in bringing a giant alien machine to Earth and pokin' at it."

"Yes, that happened," Hirata acknowledged. "But how do you think we're going to survive the consequences of that without science? By praying? By hunkering down and hoping the kaiju go away? The Makers engineered them to depopulate and modify entire planetary ecosystems for colonization. They won't stop until Earth is uninhabitable for humans. We suspect the Makers bred in some form of shutdown command for when the job was done, but the only chance we have of discerning it before it's too late is through research, through—"

"Doctor," said Darville, his own calmly implacable tone a mirror to Brenda's. Hirata finally took the hint and turned his attention to the food cooling on his plate.

Vallejo's eyes were on one of the girls sitting nearby. Her long black hair, her ruddy brown complexion, and her strong cheekbones marked her as the daughter of Patterson's colleague, whom Brenda had introduced as Jason George. The girl had been craning her neck to stare raptly at Hirata's devices, but guiltily lowering her eyes when she noted her father's gaze upon her. And yet she was the only one here who had reacted to Hirata's lecture with curiosity rather than resentment or fear.

For Vallejo, it was like looking back through time at her younger self.

After dinner, Darville received a call from Sergeant Scislowski and led the scientists aside to take it in private. *"The Tricer's broken free of the direct restraints and sedative lines,"* the sergeant advised. *"I'm surprised you can't hear it bellowing from there."*

Hirata retrieved the Monster Truck monitor and called up the interior feed. The Tricerantula was repeatedly striking its foremost horn against a single point near the base of the unit's shell wall. "Somehow it's identified the most vulnerable point in the seal," he reported, studying the telemetry. "The self-repair systems are compensating, but as long as it keeps striking there, they can't restore it completely."

"Is there a risk of a breach?" Darville asked.

"The seal should hold, assuming we set out promptly in the morning — and provided there's no further damage to the Truck. We'll have to proceed with extra caution tomorrow."

"That was a given in any case. Major Hutchison is already working on mine detection protocols. In the meantime, Sergeant, keep a close watch on that containment unit. I'll send a relief squad as soon as feasible."

"Yes, sir." Scislowski signed off.

The elderly kaijologist sighed. *"Yare, yare.* I was so sure I had every contingency planned for this time. I failed to consider the paranoia of the American redneck."

"They still offered us help and hospitality when we needed it," Vallejo said. "Our mission is to help them in turn, even if they don't approve of our efforts."

"Or our existence? How many anti-intellectual purges and genocides have there been worldwide since the kaiju came? How many ethnic purges?" He shook his head. "They blame us for bringing down the monsters, but we had plenty of our own monsters lying in wait." He glanced down at the display, where the Tricerantula was still pounding. "Taking advantage of any weakness, pushing until they broke through. Now they have free rein, out here beyond any civilized restraints. We could be dragged out of our beds and lynched for all we know."

"I'll keep enough guards here to ensure that doesn't happen," Darville assured him. "We've been making observations since we arrived, assessing their numbers and their armaments. And we'll all move out as soon as the wounded are ready." He clasped Hirata's shoulder. "Go get some rest, Doctor. I'll make it an order if I must."

"Leave the monitor with me," Vallejo said. "Maybe I can figure out how the Tricer identified that weak spot." In truth, she was just trying to stop Hirata from obsessing over the monitor all night. But the doctor nodded and handed her the unit as he said good night.

Once he had left, Vallejo noticed the dark-haired girl lurking in the doorway. "I... I'm here to show you to your room," the lanky teenager said.

Vallejo started to protest, but the colonel caught her eye. "What I said applies to you too. Rest while you can."

After a long day and a hearty meal, the offer was irresistible. "Show the way," she said to the girl, smiling. "Sorry, I didn't catch your name."

"Jess. Jessica George."

"Hello, Jess. I'm Ariana." She pronounced it with its true accent. The girl seemed intrigued.

Once they reached the guest room, Jess lingered to get Vallejo extra blankets and run hot water for the bath. She offered to make up a cot for "Miss Lopez," but Vallejo assured her the corporal would be fine outside.

Finally, the girl got up the nerve to ask, "You're really a scientist?"

"Yes, really. It was all I ever wanted, growing up in a town a lot like this one. To learn all I could so I could help protect my people. But it wasn't something my parents or my brothers thought I should be doing."

Jess nodded in clear understanding. "They say science is what doomed the world. That the monsters are God's punishment for worshipping metal and machines."

"And for the sinful ways of the city folk," Vallejo agreed. "So everything that reminds them of cities is to be shunned. Everything."

The girl understood. "I've never seen so many different kinds of people as in your group. Went to a town of black folks once—they keep apart, they get left alone, usually." Vallejo winced at the implication, but Jess didn't seem happy about it either. "Folks around here are okay with Indians like my dad and me, though. Because we're supposed to have lived pure as part of nature." She rolled her eyes. "Like we never had Cahokia or the Pueblos, like we just ran grunting through the woods for fifteen thousand years. But we play along so they accept us."

"I remember that kind of 'acceptance,'" Vallejo said as she helped the girl make up the bed. "You're tolerated as long as you don't step outside the boundaries they set. Like trying to learn about science and the way the world used to be."

"Or just looking the wrong way," Jess said. "Or... liking other girls. Let's say."

Vallejo smiled. "You know, the colonel has a husband. That's fine in the cities. We're all in this fight together, after all. We can't afford to reject anyone with value to offer."

"Try telling Duane or Hoyt or even Brenda. Living mixed, living in sin, they'll have no part of it. It's what city folk do, and cities brought the monsters."

"Those attitudes were around long before the kaiju came." She smirked. "The irony is, society had been growing more urban for centuries. Rural communities feared the loss of their way of life and grew more resistant to change. But being so heavily urbanized made us more vulnerable when the kaiju came—creatures engineered to target and destroy large population centers. Returning to a dispersed, rural existence was a necessary survival response, but it works against the sharing of ideas and resources that helps us fight back. Which is why we still need the cities that survive."

Jess stepped closer. "The old Japanese man said the monsters were paving the way for colonization. Is that what will happen?"

Vallejo shook her head. "The spawning unit that Brigitte Lee brought back was knocked off course thousands of years ago and drifted into our system. The Makers don't even know it's here, if they still exist at all. We're accidental casualties of someone else's war."

"Is that how monsters that big don't get crushed under their own weight? Because they were made?"

"Partly. We think their ancestors evolved naturally on a superterrestrial planet with abundant heavy metals to strengthen their skeletons. Our lower gravity probably lets them grow larger than they could have on their own world—though not much bigger than the largest whales, since they're still subject to physics. But they're clearly bioengineered, enhanced with nanotechnology. And of course, the spawning units manufacture their juvenile forms, just as the original unit manufactured duplicates of itself once its power recharged."

"Why did Lee even bring it down to Earth, though?"

"She didn't. The unit reactivated while under study at an orbital space station. It tore free and wrecked the station—half of Lee's team was killed. It followed its programming to splash down in the ocean and begin replicating more spawning units. The juveniles need to start out in the ocean until they gain the strength to support their mass on land."

A mind like Jess's was a rare find in a place like this—and Vallejo knew from experience how stifled it must be. So she fed Jess's hungry curiosity, hoping to offer a glimpse of the broader horizons that Vallejo had been denied in her own youth—and, with luck, to give the cities a future scientist to carry on the fight.

Jason George looked across the fields at the community hall for the umpteenth time, wondering if the light in the guest bedroom would ever go out. He and Duane Patterson had spent the past twenty minutes patrolling the town, watching out to make sure the soldiers didn't get too close to anything they shouldn't find. It ought to have been plenty of time. Walking next to him, Duane caught his glance and said much the same thing Jason was thinking. "Your girl's spending too much time talkin' to that lady egghead."

"Jess is smart," Jason told him. "She knows the rules."

Duane spat. "Smart's the whole problem with that girl. Thinks she knows better than the rules. If she was my kid steppin' outta line, I'd whup her ass till it was twice as red as the rest of her."

Jason bristled. "I'll raise my girl the way I want." He usually let Duane's casual slurs roll over him, but nobody got to talk about hurting Jess, let alone tell him to do it. A father's job was to keep his kids from getting hurt.

"Just sayin'. You can't trust those scientists. Like Ol' Squinty-eyes, fiddling with his machines all through dinner. He was way too nervous for someone just worried about a supply truck."

"You think they're hiding something more out there?"

"City folk are always up to something bad. Inventions, experiments... I bet they're out here to test some new weapon. They never learn—all their machines do is draw down more of God's wrath. Too smart for their own good, just like your girl." He shook his head. "I can't believe Brenda's letting 'em stay here! They'll bring the monsters right down on our heads, just like they did to the world." He seethed. "What I should do, Jace, I should go in there when they're asleep and pop a coupla shells right in those big brains. It's what their kind deserves."

"They got a lot of friends with guns, Duane. And a whole city of soldiers to avenge them. Plus you'd have to get past Brenda."

A sigh. "You're right," Duane said, making it somewhat easier for Jason to convince himself that the younger man was only considering the safety of the town. "Besides, we keep watching 'em, maybe we can find out what they really got out there. Stop whatever they're doing before it brings down hellfire on Laurel Shade."

"That's smart thinking, Duane." Jason tried not to sound surprised.

The younger man shook his blond head. "But I tell you, Jace — the minute I hear roaring or stomping headed this way, I'll drag them all out of bed and drop 'em right in the beast's path. Maybe it'll be satisfied with a sacrifice." He grinned darkly. "I know I will be."

Jason threw another look at the lighted window. Jess could take care of herself a while longer. He needed to stay with Duane and keep him from doing anything stupid — or else be ready to back him up if it came to a fight anyway.

Jess is smart. She knows the rules.

Vallejo and Jess sat on the bed and talked for more than an hour as the biologist ran through the list of kaiju she'd personally seen — Thormadillos, Tiamantises, Baku Genbu, Montium Typhons, even the occasional Ragnarex, the rarest but mightiest breed. She explained the anatomy that made their size and power possible: The semi-metallic skeletons with hollow construction and carbon fiber reinforcement, the muscular circulatory vessels that used collective peristalsis to pump blood higher and faster than a single heart and could pinch shut at any point to stem blood loss. She explained how the heavy metals in their waste and the gases in their exhalations were gradually altering the Earth's environment to something presumably more amenable to the colonizers.

"Abandoning cities would only be a stopgap. In no more than a century, at the current rate, humans will no longer be able to survive outside the enclaves. But the enclaves themselves would become unsustainable within another century after that."

"Then how can we hope to stop them?" Jess asked.

"Through understanding them and finding their weaknesses. If we can identify whatever behavioral responses the Makers built in for controlling the kaiju, or even the shutdown command that Doctor Hirata mentioned, then we can use that to contain or destroy them."

Jess stared. "But you'd have to catch one first. Experiment on it. If you think it's behavioral… then you'd need a live one." Vallejo grinned, continuing to be impressed by the girl's raw brilliance. "Nobody's ever caught a live one."

Vallejo decided to take a chance. A mind like Jess's was worth recruiting by any means. Drawing out the monitor, she called up the live feed of the Tricerantula, still methodically pounding away at the weak point. The girl stared in wonder and terror.

"The specimen is… being held nearby. Don't worry, it won't get free." *Probably. I hope.* "We've already learned so much from the sensors in the Mon—the containment unit." Jess's fear gave way to fascination as her eyes roved over the image of the kaiju, surely the first she'd seen in such detail. "We call this one a Tricerantula, because of the horns and the shape of the legs. See, the five long, angled outer legs give it greater leverage for locomotion, while the three stubby ones underneath support its weight."

"How did you catch it?"

"Largely by luck. We found it battling a Thormadillo over the ruins of a steel mill in the Philadelphia wastelands."

She called up the battle footage recorded by the aerial drones. The girl observed the gruesome fight clinically, showing neither disgust nor glee as the Tricerantula's vicious horns struck through the gaps between the Thormadillo's armor plates and drew spurts of thick brown blood, or as the giant living tank lumbered about and rammed its broad hammerhead into the other behemoth's arched forelimb with a bonesplitting crack and a sputtering static discharge. The longer-limbed kaiju suffered from the other's forceful blows and electric shocks, but in time, it managed to wedge its horns beneath the Thormadillo's armor skirt and lever it up enough to skewer its underbelly, driving it into a limping retreat.

"The 'dillo shouldn't have been hurt that bad," Jess said. "What you told me about their organs, their healing…"

Vallejo nodded. "Exactly. We suspect the horns may contain some sort of toxin for use against other kaiju. Perhaps a muscle paralyzer to stop the blood vessels from stanching a wound. If we could isolate the compound—"

"We'd have a weapon againt them."

"It could be the breakthrough we need. Luckily, the fight weakened the Tricerantula enough for us to capture it."

"Show me that. The capture."

Vallejo hesitated. She'd bent the rules enough already. Revealing the Monster Truck to Jess would be a step too far. "I'm sorry, Jess—some things are only for authorized personnel. But tell you what—if you come join us when you're a little older, I'd be happy to teach you everything I know."

The intense absorption on Jess's face as she left assured Vallejo that she had the girl hooked.

Vallejo's sleep was restless, her dreams replaying the tension and violence of the capture operation. The relived memories were largely procedural, the well-rehearsed steps of the capture burned into her mind, but screams and blood and terror intruded upon them as well. She had seen many colleagues, soldiers, and civilians killed by kaiju over the years, yet for all the emotional calluses she had formed by necessity, she had never entirely stopped reliving their deaths in her dreams, usually with herself in their place. In tonight's dreams, as in so many others, the fear that engulfed her along with the Tricerantula's maw was not that she would die, but that all her efforts would make no difference to the world she left behind.

When a mighty thunderclap shocked her to alertness, it took a moment to realize it had been no dream. Her pulse racing, she shot out of bed and contacted the colonel. *"Looks like a munitions cache on the outskirts went up,"* Darville said. *"This might be a diversion, but we have to check it out. You and Hirata stay put."*

Hirata joined her a few moments later, and they settled in to wait. After their fourth check of the Monster Truck's monitor in fifteen minutes, Vallejo heard a scuffle and a cry outside her door. A moment later, the door burst open and Brenda Barnes strode in, leveling a shotgun at the two scientists. Behind them, Lopez lay wounded on the floor, another villager binding her wrists.

Vallejo looked on in concern, not blaming the corporal for her failure. The soldiers were trained primarily to fight kaiju and protect civilians. The townsfolk, conversely, had probably spent most of their lives preparing for conflict with the urban military.

Hirata attempted to speak placatingly. "Mrs. Barnes, please try to understand. What your men intend to do—"

"Don't try to lecture me, city man. Not after you brought that abomination to our very doorstep."

"The kaiju would've been safely contained in the enclave by now if your people hadn't mined the road!" Hirata countered. "Your unthinking recourse to violence is no solution to anything!"

"You think we're so stupid, don't you? Didn't think that once we knew you had one 'nearby,' we couldn't figure out what set off the mines."

Vallejo spotted Jess lurking in the doorway, flushing at Barnes's words, and she knew how the townsfolk had found out. Seeing her realization, the girl winced. "I'm sorry. I had to tell my dad."

"Don't apologize for anything to these people, Jess," Brenda said. "You proved your value to this town. You owe them nothing."

"What do you plan to do with us?" Vallejo asked, holding her eyes.

"You're going to take us out to where it's hidden. Then you'll be hostages, to keep your soldiers in line.

"And then… we're gonna kill that damned monster."

In theory, the Allied Defense Forces had the training to deal with a guerrilla attack as well as a kaiju attack. Even outnumbered and fatigued, even outflanked by foes who knew the local turf far more intimately than they did, Sergeant Scislowski's squad should have been able to hold their own, especially with drone support. But the hostages changed the game. Patterson's men used the cover of the trees to avoid sniper fire from the drones, ordering Scislowski to shut them down if she wanted the scientists to live.

Vallejo saw the calculation in Scislowski's eyes as the sergeant stood her forces down. The townsfolk had moved quickly thanks to their knowledge of the woods, but it wouldn't be long before Darville, Hutchison, and the rest caught up with them. It was simply a matter of stalling until then.

The Tricerantula was not so patient. As the townsmen shouted and threatened the soldiers, ordering them to disarm, the Tricer intensified its frenzied pounding in response to the noise. "Good God," Jason George gasped. "Jess was right. You lunatics got one of the beasts inside that thing!"

"Go get the bombs," Duane Patterson ordered.

"You're insane!" Hirata cried. "The containment seals are already degraded. Inflicting further damage will only —"

"Shut up!" Patterson raised his rifle to silence Hirata.

Vallejo watched helplessly as the townsfolk tried to breach the Monster Truck's seal in order to hurl their firebombs inside. Jess's father led another group to set fire to the broken branches and leaves beneath and atop the Truck, perhaps hoping to roast the kaiju if they couldn't break in to burn it directly. "They're just making it angrier!" Hirata hissed as the pounding from within intensified.

"Harry will be here in minutes."

"We don't have minutes."

Vallejo turned to Brenda Barnes, who stood guard over the two scientists at a theoretically safe remove. "Please, Brenda. None of their weapons will be enough to kill a kaiju. Even if they could blow it apart, its neural nodes are distributed. A severed limb can potentially grow into a new kaiju. Far from killing the Tricer, they could multiply it."

"Not soon enough that we couldn't burn the parts," Barnes told her. "We know how the monsters grow. We're not as stupid as you think."

"Then prove it. Don't let them blow the door. At least it's safely contained for now."

"Until you get it back to your godforsaken city. Who knows what you'll do with it then? How can we trust people who hide behind walls?"

Any further arguments Vallejo could offer were rendered moot as the charges went off. The Tricerantula roared as if in imminent triumph, and moments later, its three-meter horns finally burst through the Monster Truck's blast-weakened shell. The townsmen threw their firebombs, but the creature was unaffected by the flames as it squeezed the rest of its body out through the rift.

"Get back!" Vallejo cried. Barnes didn't object this time, retreating into the trees with the two scientists. They watched from cover as Patterson rallied his men to hold their ground and open fire.

But the townsmen were far too inexperienced with kaiju to realize how swiftly the enormous creature could move—or how useless their guns would be against it. They'd never faced a living creature so vast before, never learned to cope with the sheer cognitive dissonance of it. Many froze in terror, and the kaiju's horns threshed them like wheat. Their fearless leader Patterson screamed like a child and ran, abandoning them to die. He did some good, though, for his shrieks attracted the creature. The time it spent chasing down and devouring Patterson gave the few surviving townsmen a chance to limp away.

Heavier fire began to strike the Tricer's flank; Darville's reinforcements had finally arrived. Scislowski's people moved to join up with them, as did the townsmen, now led by Jason George. The colonel looked them over and issued orders as if they'd been a united force all along. "We need to reach the heavy weapons in the IMVs before it does. Come on!"

But the fatigued, ravenous Tricer had finished feeding on the townsfolk and was already making its way for the largest infantry mobility vehicle, instinctively driven to replenish its metals as well. It smashed into the IMV with its horns, then took a sizeable bite out of its armored side, setting off some of the more unstable ordnance. The explosions did no more than annoy it, provoking it to back away and turn for the other escort vehicle.

Major Hutchison turned to the colonel. "If we can get to that IMV, rig a high-powered charge, maybe we could knock it out."

"At least drive the damned thing off," Jason George added.

Darville shook his smooth head. "No time. It'd be a suicide mission."

"I don't take your orders," George said, starting to run for the vehicle. "And I've got a daughter to protect!"

Hutchison started to run after him, but Darville stopped her. "No time. Let him try." Hutchison nodded and tapped the IMV's access code into her wrist unit, unlocking it.

George reached the IMV before the Tricer and climbed inside, but Vallejo could already see that he'd have no time to rig any kind of high explosive. She could only think of Jess as the Tricer's horns tore into the vehicle moments later. The kaiju shook it around like a dog with a bone, and when it slid free, the central horn was slicked with blood. The explosions that went off within the truck were too small to harm the monster.

Vallejo retained the presence of mind to relieve a stunned Brenda Barnes of the shotgun that had sagged in the matriarch's limp grasp. "We need to get back to town," she advised. "Get your people to safety."

The reminder of the women and children who still depended on Barnes was enough to cut through her shock and snap her back into matriarch mode, and she led the scientists back at a brisk pace. Vallejo focused on helping Hirata navigate the dark woods, a distraction from the burning question of what she would tell Jess about her father's futile sacrifice.

Yet the girl's resourcefulness had taken the decision out of Vallejo's hands. Back in town, she and Barnes found Jess still holding the monitor unit, on which she had watched the entire massacre as it happened. When the matriarch reached toward her, the girl finally broke down and buried her head in Barnes's chest, wailing.

Recovering the monitor that had fallen from Jess's hands, Vallejo replayed the drone footage, watching as the Tricerantula charged the surviving troops. Its engineered brain had entered full conflict mode, driving it to attack relentlessly. Darville had been forced to call a retreat, but he informed Vallejo that the kaiju had already found the scent trails that both the townsfolk and the soldiers had previously laid. It was heading straight for Laurel Shade.

Barnes rallied the women and children to get to safety in the kaiju cellars, except for a few who insisted on setting the livestock free once again. Vallejo and Hirata were allowed to go below while Darville and his people attempted to draw the beast away from the town. The surviving drones were lost in one of their first attempts, so Vallejo and the others were left only with darkness and the thunderous sounds of battle and destruction up above.

By the time it was over, the enraged Tricerantula had destroyed the barns that the townsfolk had not been able to empty in time, consuming numerous cattle and horses and sickening the surviving ones with its toxic exhalations. Two more townsfolk had been killed as well—as had Major Hutchison in the effort to save several others.

And then there was the part that the old kaiju movies had rarely addressed. The Tricerantula had excreted upon the town's fields, contaminating their soil and groundwater with heavy metals and alien toxins. The whole area would have needed to be evacuated anyway; a rampaging kaiju within 150 kilometers of the Pittsburgh enclave was an unacceptable contingency, the response to which had been predetermined as part of the original capture plan. Darville and his troops were given barely enough time to load the townsfolk onto an evac quadrotor before the missiles were unleashed.

Vallejo and Hirata could only watch with grim acceptance as half a dozen massive thermobaric explosions engulfed the Tricer, immolating it beyond what even a kaiju could regenerate from. The bombardment would save lives in the short term, but the blast waves and seismic effects took their toll on what was left of Laurel Shade. The town was a lost cause, and the death of history's first captive kaiju would set back the behavioral modification research by months, if not years. There was no telling how many more people—and communities—would die as a result.

"*Shimatta*," Hirata said, his frustration as tightly contained as the Tricer had been before Laurel Shade. "Well… back to the drawing board."

After the other evacuees had debarked at the relocation center, Vallejo found Jess sitting alone, staring out the quadrotor's side window at the inside of the Pittsburgh wall. Or rather, staring through it to the home she would never see again. "It's all my fault," the girl sobbed without preamble. "I told my dad, and…"

Sitting beside her, Vallejo gently stroked the girl's hair. "No, Jess. I should never have put you in that position. I saw my younger self in you, but I didn't realize that… that my image of who I used to be has been pared down to fit my present narrative."

The girl frowned up at her. "What's that mean?"

"It means I remembered how eager I was at your age to escape the restrictions of my upbringing… but I forgot how strong the ties of community and family can be in spite of it all. I should've realized that you don't have that luxury to look back from the outside. Laurel Shade was still your home, your family. You couldn't ignore the obligations that still governed your whole world. Nobody can blame you for that."

"I can," Jess said. "I blame the whole damn town for it, me included."

"And I blame myself for trying to recruit you as an asset before you were ready to make that choice. I pushed you into it."

"*I* pushed *you*. I wanted to know everything. If you'd tried to keep me out, I wouldn'ta let you."

"But I still blame myself. And you know what? Hirata blames himself too, for not making the Monster Truck robust enough. And Darville blames himself for not calling in reinforcements from Pittsburgh.

"No one person in this carries the blame alone, Jess. We all acted as we thought best, to protect our communities, our families. But our choices are shaped and limited by forces larger than ourselves. By our circumstances… by our past. It's hard to step far enough outside those to see the bigger picture, to know what we must do. Sometimes only history can decide that."

"No," Jess said resolutely. "We could figure it out ourselves if we tried. We all see different pieces of it — but we don't listen to each other long enough to add them up. We should all be working together! Why is that so hard for everyone to see?"

After a moment's thought, Vallejo replied, "Because we already have our own monsters. The ones we make for ourselves. And when real monsters come along, we mistake them for the ones we made, and we keep fighting the same old fights against the wrong enemies."

Jess leaned against her. "We never learn. Maybe we're not worth saving."

Vallejo smiled down at her. "The things you just said, Jess — the things you figured out all on your own — are what prove to me that we are. That we have it in us to make more than just monsters."

After a while, the lanky girl looked up at the scientist. "Do you think I'll like living in the enclave? The others can find different towns to take them, but…"

"Jess, I think you know you wouldn't be any happier in another town like that. People like you and me need something bigger. Something that lets us shape the future rather than hiding from it. You deserve that chance — although you didn't deserve to get it in this way."

"I still feel it's my fault."

"You always will," Vallejo said. "Because you're very much like me. And that's why I know you'll never stop fighting to keep this from happening to others."

The girl stared into her eyes for a long moment, realizing how much they shared. After a lengthy silence and a few sniffles, the girl stood. "Okay, then let's go."

"Now?"

"The world's still ending, ain't it? So we're on the clock."

As Vallejo followed her out into the city, the girl kept talking. "I was thinking. You were trying to find a kill switch to shut these things down. Maybe it'd be easier just to redirect what they already do. Like, against each other."

"'Let them fight?' Seriously?"

"More like, train some guard dogs. You city folk are smart and all, but you have a lot to learn about wrangling animals…"

Legacy Hero

The Green Blaze and Jackknife stood back-to-back, hemmed in by their foes. Jackknife morphed his forearms into blades, parrying the swift strikes of Leigong's shock batons. Blaze's knees buckled as she blocked a piledriver blow from Bellatrix's power-armored fist.

Ekundayo DeMarais merely watched, unable to come to her fellow Troubleshooters' aid, for she struggled with a far more challenging conundrum.

"Give me a crime scene to analyze, a missing person to track down, and I'm in my element," she told Lydia Muchangi. "But picking a new superhero name..."

Kunda rose from the bleachers and leaned against the clear partition, gazing out at the vividly costumed champions sparring on the combat training floor. "It was my mother who picked 'Doctor DeMeter' for me. She was so proud of my doctorates, and very loyal to Ceres."

The Troubleshooter Corps's director studied her with a cool but sympathetic gaze. "You're reluctant to let go of the championym she gave you."

Kunda nodded. "I understand the need." The manifesto of the Corps's founder Yukio Villareal echoed in her mind: *Troubleshooters serve no state, no corporation, no ideology, no master — only the cause of peace and justice.* "Still, this will be my public persona for the rest of my career, most likely. It should be... personal. But my whole life has been in the Sheaf. What else carries equal meaning for me?"

Muchangi's lips quirked upward. "Would you allow a suggestion?"

"I'd welcome it."

"How about Lodestar?"

Kunda's eyes went wide. "Take *your* name? I couldn't!"

The elegant, shaven-headed Martian stood and came alongside her. "I never felt that title belonged to me, Kunda. I understand the publicity merits of the Corps's superheroic conceit, and I play along for the sake of the Troubleshooters and civilians who value it. But I've never been comfortable being treated as a superhero. I'm a detective, that's all. Now I'm an administrator and a teacher, and I'm happy with that."

The director looked out at the training floor, where Leigong had shorted out one of Jackknife's bionic legs, while the Green Blaze lifted Bellatrix over her head and slammed her to the floor, making the lights on her armor flicker.

"Still, I have studied the traditions of superhero lore, and there is one that the Troubleshooters have rarely exercised: the legacy hero. The identity passed down from one bearer to another, making it a generational tradition that can outlive any one person."

Kunda's head spun. Her eyes were moist as she said, "You think I'm worthy to inherit your mantle as Lodestar?"

Muchangi laughed, stroking her shoulder. "Who better, Kunda? We're both detectives, whether private or police. We both rely on mental and sensory mods more than strength or speed. And I like the idea of the name staying with a woman of African heritage, though resemblance has rarely been a requirement for a legacy hero."

Kunda glanced at the director's smooth, gracefully curved scalp. "Would I have to shave my head?"

"I wouldn't dream of asking you to lose those lovely braids."

Muchangi looked her in the eyes, resting her hands on the younger woman's wrists. "I don't want you to copy me, Kunda. I want you to surpass me."

She flushed. "I'm honored, Director. I shall try to reach that level one day."

"Actually, I was hoping it would be rather sooner."

"Director?"

Out on the floor, Jackknife had morphed his forelimbs into cables and pinned Leigong's arms to his sides. Bellatrix had tapped out, but Blaze was now under paintball fire from Quetzal, who soared overhead with her jetwing drone strapped to her back, her bright green-gold ponytail whipping in the wind.

Muchangi began to pace slowly before the bleachers. "To win swift acceptance as the new Lodestar, you need a dramatic debut. A victory that no one can deny. And I hope that in the process, you can resolve the old Lodestar's one remaining loose end."

Kunda jerked back as if pushed. "The Moros case?"

"Exactly. The Eurekans have worked hard to put the old regime's corruption behind them, but until they can finally prosecute Gao Meihui's murderer, that wound remains open. Perhaps the case needs fresh eyes. Someone who can spot the one clue I have always missed."

Kunda shifted her weight. "I'm humbled by your faith in me, Lydia. But if I should fail..."

Muchangi shrugged as she returned to her seat. "Then you'll go on to solve many more notable crimes. Don't worry—you won't taint the Lodestar name." She sighed. "After all, I've borne this stain for six years, and it survived."

Ekundayo pondered, watching the fight. Blaze had leapt four meters straight up to grab Quetzal's slender leg and was pulling her to the floor. Jackknife, though, was struggling in a tangleweb fired by some unseen adversary, a vague shimmer even to Kunda's enhanced vision.

Finally, she nodded. "Then I guess I'm off to Eureka. I haven't been assigned a ship yet, but—"

"Don't get ahead of yourself, Lodestar." The director chuckled. "It sounds nicer on someone else. But there's no rush. We still need to arrange your coming-out party to satisfy the Troubleshooters and the press. Schedule a uniform design meeting with Kelly—I tipped her off an hour ago, so I'm sure she has at least four options drawn up already.

"After that, since we waived the usual apprenticeship period, it would be proper to assign a partner for your first few missions."

"Of course." It didn't offend her. As an established local superhero, she'd needed less training than a raw recruit; but she respected how seriously the Troubleshooter Corps enforced its qualifications and ethical guidelines, a safeguard to ensure that the corruption that had crept in under Lydia's predecessor would not be allowed to return. That commitment to integrity meant everything to her.

On the floor, Jackknife had conceded defeat to his nigh-invisible foe, who dropped her camouflage to reveal a tall woman completely cloaked in black. Kunda nodded toward her. "Hijab might have unique insights on the case..."

Lydia shook her head. "Maryam has tried on my behalf, with no more success." She smiled. "I was thinking more along the lines of the Green Blaze."

Kunda was running out of ways to react to surprises, though this was a pleasant one. "Are you sure? As... stimulating as I find Emry's companionship, surely this is more an intellectual challenge than a physical one."

Both women contemplated the Green Blaze, whose powerful form was convulsing on the floor, reduced to helpless paroxysms of laughter by a tickle attack from the diminutive Quetzal. Lydia sighed. "That's the idea. Emerald has a superb mind, but she still tends to assume she can muscle her way through any problem. I've had limited success persuading her to cultivate her detective skills. Knowing Blaze, perhaps encouragement from a lover could motivate her better."

Muchangi rested her chin on her hand. "Besides, she's a former juvenile delinquent. Maybe she'll have some insight into this particular game of three-card monte."

"So what do we call you now, Doc?" Emerald Blair lay naked on her stomach atop her rumpled bedsheets, kicking her muscular calves in the air as she gazed admiringly at Ekundayo DeMarais's new Troubleshooter uniform. "Lodestar Junior? Silver Age Lodestar? Doctor Lodestar?" She snapped her fingers and pointed. "Lodestarlet!"

"You know my bionic upgrades mean I can hurt you now, right?"

"Promises, promises." Emry's smile grew sultrier as her vast green eyes roved up and down Kunda's body. She tilted her head forward just enough to let a turbulent cataract of autumn-red hair fall alluringly across the alabaster face that was the only dainty thing about her. "Just wear that while you do it, honey."

It felt strange for Emerald to approve of her wearing anything substantial when they were together — let alone to ask her to put it back on after their excited lovemaking in the wake of the new Lodestar's debut party. Kunda turned to study herself in the mirror once more.

The form-fitting light-armor bodysuit had some lines in common with her old Doctor DeMeter gear, but in Lodestar's trademark red-brown hues rather than cornstalk green. She'd kept her old utility belt, containing a mix of TSC-issue gear and her own custom-made forensic tools, but with Lodestar's emblem on the buckle, a guiding star casting a spreading beam of light below. A long black coat, shorter and glossier than Muchangi's iconic duster, completed the ensemble.

"I'm glad you like it," she told Emry. "I still feel like something of a fraud in this. I haven't earned it yet."

Emry leapt off the bed and snuggled up behind her, arms around her waist. "If you hadn't earned it, we wouldn't have recruited you, dummy. And if anyone can harpoon Lydia's white whale, it's you, Lodestarlet."

"It's *us*. It'll be reassuring to have a veteran Troubleshooter along."

A rude noise passed through Emry's exquisite lips. "An eighteen-month veteran. You've been a superhero longer than I have. And I'm no detective, no matter how hard Lydia tries. You should take Maryam or Ravi."

"I don't need another detective. But I could use a Watson. A trusted sounding board... and moral support."

"I'll be more nervous than you will, Doc. I get silly when I'm nervous. As a Watson, I'd be strictly Nigel Bruce." Her eyes widened. "Oh, hold on. I want to see how we look together in costume." She started searching the bedroom for the far-flung pieces of her Green Blaze gear.

Kunda chuckled. "Fine, then you can get them off their guard for me. Besides, I've never operated outside the Sheaf. You've been everywhere."

Emry shrugged. "Closest I ever got to the Mars Trojans was Phobos, maybe nine years ago. My early runaway phase, before the gang. A lot of it's kind of a blur now, but I guess I knew enough about Eureka to stay the vack away."

"Were you aware of Moros?"

"Heard a thing or two. He was just getting started around then." With her flame-patterned green-and-black light armor now donned, she pulled on one green boot, then spotted the other lying atop the dresser and hopped toward it. Kunda resisted pointing out that it would have been more sensible to collect them both beforehand. "Or 'they,' I guess. Weren't there three of him?"

"More than that," Kunda told her. "Moros was a fiction constructed by the Eurekan police state. An armored vigilante operating outside the law, inflicting violent, often lethal punishment on criminals who had eluded justice. Unstoppable, unkillable, a mythic bogeyman to strike terror in the hearts of evildoers.

"Or, in truth, a cover to allow the regime to inflict tactics too brutal to commit openly without sparking revolt. The state publicly condemned Moros, putting on a show of concern for due process and civil rights, while their online bots praised him for taking down criminals who had escaped a legal system hidebound by those very principles.

"Several men were suspected of being Moros, and the police made a show of investigating them, but each theory was discredited due to a solid alibi or conflicting evidence, since, of course—"

"—they were *all* Spartacus."

"So to speak. A secret police hit squad consisting of men with the same height and build, wearing the Moros armor interchangeably."

"What, they couldn't find anyone of another gender who'd fit?"

"I doubt it occurred to them to look."

"Point taken."

Now dressed again, Emry posed alongside Kunda, admiring both of their figures in the mirror. "Which is why Lydia never caught the one who killed Gao Meihui."

"See? You're not so bad at this."

Gao's murder had been the incident so shocking that it had finally broken the regime's iron grip. While confronting Andrei Narayan, a political reformist falsely accused of being a Martian war criminal, the man in the Moros symbot armor had fired indiscriminately outside a campaign meeting, striking Gao, the sixteen-year-old daughter of another activist. When Narayan had surrendered and begged him to call an ambulance drone, Moros had refused and forced him to watch the girl die, telling him it was his own fault. The killing had been so cruel and arbitrary that a conscience-stricken member of the regime had finally leaked the truth about Moros to Eureka's social net. After the resultant upheavals had carried the reformists to victory, they had prosecuted the old regime's crimes, but this case had remained unsolved. Eventually, they had called on Solsys's most celebrated detective, Troubleshooter Lodestar.

"The planners behind Moros went to extraordinary lengths to hide his identity," Ekundayo continued. "Not only was the symbot all-concealing and airtight, but its servos altered the wearer's gait and body language. Combat tactics and targeting were software-enhanced to even out differences in skill or training. The voice was synthesized, repeating the wearer's words but not his accent, rhythm, or intonation. The wearers were even trained to choose their words similarly, with heads-up prompting as necessary to ensure consistency."

"Vack. Even Maryam doesn't go that far."

Kunda nodded. "Hijab maintains a secret identity to protect her family, not herself. But Moros was designed specifically to shield its operators from accountability." She grimaced. "That's what burns me up. They *knew* what they did was wrong. They wanted license to do it anyway."

Emry stroked her braids soothingly. "What about alibis? Tracking the suspects' whereabouts or their social activity?"

Kunda smiled. Despite her protestations, Emry was invested in working the problem now. "That was how Lydia narrowed it down to Travis Feng, Jayant Khan, and Aaron Macklin. But all their movements put them in the same vicinity that evening, out of range of any surveillance for the duration. She believed it was part of the anti-identification protocols."

"No inconsistencies in their stories? None of them knew a detail the others didn't, or showed more guilt than the others?"

"Lydia interviewed them all, studied their microexpressions, sampled the hormones in their sweat, got a warrant for the data in their neural interfaces, you name it. All their data connected to Moros operations was wiped. And they closed ranks, kept their stories straight to cover each other."

"Then charge them all with conspiracy. Obstruction of justice."

"Since it was their superiors who ordered their silence, they have an entrapment defense for conspiracy to obstruct. They've avoided mutual contact since then, which gives them a withdrawal defense. And we can't prove they're lying under questioning without verifying the facts. There's no proof that the other two even *know* who the killer is, though Lydia's certain they do.

"More importantly, a lesser conviction wouldn't bring Gao's family the closure they need. They deserve to know what really happened that day."

She clenched her jaw. "For six years, Lydia has hoped that one of the three would grow remorseful enough to break ranks. Yet they haven't wavered. They care more about protecting their fellow enforcers than protecting civilians."

Emerald laid a gentle hand on Kunda's fist, which she realized was painfully clenched. "That really vacks you off, huh?"

She relaxed her fist and let Emry stroke her fingers. "It's not so unlike the culture my mom and dad worked to change in the Sheaf."

Emry nodded in understanding. When the Ceres Sheaf had been assembled, the challenge of physically connecting and balancing so many formerly separate habitats had proven simple next to balancing their cultures and laws. The older habs, with their easily disrupted ecosystems, had demanded a strictly regimented existence and an emphasis on the good of the habitat over individual liberties. It had been easy for such authoritarian control to become an end in itself, even as the habs' biospheres had been upgraded to become more self-correcting. Older Sheaf members like New Queens had resisted the liberal ways of their new neighbors, growing even more repressive in reaction. Their partisans had gained influence in the interstate council and pushed for stricter policing Sheaf-wide.

"My mom was NQPD down to the bone. My dad was from Piazz-iville, a police-free hab with community-driven restorative justice—at least until the post-merger crackdowns began. They both saw the dangerous turn law enforcement was taking, but Mom tried to reform the system from within, while Dad followed the example of the early Troubleshooters, becoming a masked vigilante called Silhouette to provide a more populist peacekeeping alternative—and to shield civilians from police excesses."

"Ooh. Awkward..."

"You don't know the half of it. The first time Mom encountered Silhouette face-to-mask, she promptly recognized Dad by the tilt of his head, the rhythm of his voice through its filter. He could've fooled a stranger, and his dance training let him trick gait analysis, but she knew his every move and mannerism intimately. She was easily able to confirm it by social tracking, and by connecting an alleged racquet-ball injury of Dad's with a fight Silhouette had been in at the time."

Emry stared. "They were already married?"

Kunda nodded. "I was five."

"Vack. So did she turn him in?"

"She couldn't. Her integrity demanded it, but she knew the force would judge her guilty by association and she'd lose the influence she needed to push for reform. Not to mention what she feared it would do to me."

She sat on the edge of the bed. Emry followed suit, putting a powerful arm around her shoulders. "Although their fights when they thought I was asleep hurt me enough," Kunda went on. "I was afraid they'd break up."

"They didn't, did they?"

Kunda smiled, easing her suspense. "Eventually they realized they were fighting for the same goal and could achieve more working together, one within the system and one without."

"Aww, it's like you're the daughter of Batman and Commissioner Gordon! I always thought those two would make a cute couple."

"Let's just say they found a synthesis of their respective methods and helped bring it about throughout the Sheaf, allowing Silhouette to unmask and become the Cerean States' first official costumed reservist. I grew up seeing superheroes as an extension of the police, and the police as champions of the people. That's the legacy of both my parents—one I was proud to inherit.

"So to see what Moros did, the mockery they made of law and justice, makes me furious. They degrade everything I grew up believing."

Emry pulled her head down and kissed her. "Maybe that anger is what you need to crack this case. The extra push Lydia never had. She likes telling me to use my brain more, and I should... but it's the heart that fuels the brain." She smiled. "I guess I better come along after all— to remind you of that."

Ekundayo kissed her back, cherishing her warmth and unexpected wisdom. Emry's affections were not exclusively hers, of course; the Troubleshooters' hazardous, largely solitary life selected for personalities that could thrive without committed relationships. But beneath her defensive layers of toughness and snark, Emerald Blair had a bottomless reservoir of love to share. Kunda was glad to make the most of it while she could, hoping it would armor her against the ugliness that lay ahead.

Once past her initial reluctance, Emry had thrown herself into her new detective role with her usual juggernaut enthusiasm. Just before setting out for the Martian L5 Trojans in her scout ship *Zephyr*, Emry had accessorized her Green Blaze light armor with an emerald-green trench coat and matching fedora—which Kunda found a bit ridiculous but undeniably gorgeous on her. En route, Emry wore the hat and coat (and often nothing else) whenever the two Troubleshooters studied the massive evidence packet Lydia had uploaded to the shipmind's memory, hoping the cosplay might help her cultivate a deductive state of mind.

Yet Kunda could tell how difficult it was for the younger Troubleshooter to review the footage of Gao Meihui's murder. A decade ago, the thirteen-year-old Emry had seen her own mother gunned down by a criminal in a symbot not dissimilar to the Moros armor. Still, Emerald controlled herself tightly during their study periods, burning off her rage and pain afterward in ferocious sparring matches that tested the new Lodestar's combat mods and light armor to their limits. Once, Emry used *Zephyr*'s soligram stage to form a simulacrum of Moros that she assaulted violently, ripping off its death's-head mask and black armor with her bare hands and beating the anonymous figure inside until its smart-matter gel lost cohesion and melted back into the stage. It was frightening to see her unleash her full strength, but Kunda had faith that she was burning off her rage now so that she would not take it out on the real Feng, Khan, or Macklin.

The record had been compiled from several selfone videos taken at the campaign meeting, as well as surveillance recordings from greater distances, those that had survived the outgoing authorities' purge of the government servers. Lydia Muchangi had done everything she could to reconstruct Moros's movements and speech from the tiniest scattered photon traces and decayed echoes captured in non-line-of-sight footage recorded nearby, but there was no clear, unambiguous audio until the confrontation with Narayan was already underway, as other participants emerged into the street and began recording. Soon, the two Troubleshooters had every word and gesture memorized.

"*—aught up with you, Narayan! You can't escape!*"

"*Is that Moros? Why is he after—*"

"*Please, not here! There are innocent people—*"

"*The innocent don't run!*"

"*Andrei didn't do anything! You have the wrong person!*"

"*Mei, get out of—*"

"*My God! Oh, my God, Mei!*"

"*That should have been you, Narayan!*"

"*Help her! I surrender, okay? Anything, just call an ambulance, please!*"

"*What lesson would that teach you? Actions have consequences, hull-punker.*"

"Enough!" This time it was Kunda who stopped the playback in disgust and leapt into motion, crossing *Zephyr*'s residential deck to the dining nook. After a few deep breaths, she was calm enough to ask, "Zephyr, some herbal tea, please?"

"Of course, Kunda," the cyber replied, his Art Deco winged-horse avatar bowing to her from the nook's menu screen. "My most relaxing blend. I have plenty to spare; Emry rarely partakes of any brew without ample caffeine, redundant as that is for her."

She let Zephyr's soothing baritone calm her, then accepted the hot tisane with thanks. As she sipped, Emry came over and put an arm around her. "You holdin' up, Doc?"

"How are we going to catch him? I'm seeing nothing Lodesta—Lydia hasn't already accounted for. She was incredibly thorough. Gait and kinetic analysis, thermal penetration, semantic extrapolation... Plus she examined that symbot from top to bottom, scanned every molecule of its surface, sifted every byte of its memory for anything that hadn't been wiped."

"I've been running simulations based on her records of its coding and neural network construction," Zephyr put in. "I've evolved some promising new algorithms for extracting metabolic and neurological data about the wearer from EM resonance patterns inferred from its diagnostic logs."

"Didn't Lydia try that last year, with inconclusive results?"

"I believe I can take the technique a few steps further. I admit I'm seeking hope in diminishing returns, but that's essentially our current mission statement."

"I wish I could disagree, Zeph." Kunda sighed. "Lord knows, I can't think of anything else she didn't cover. She even looked for a connection to the Gao family, on the theory that it was premeditated murder disguised as a random slaying. But the Moros users were recruited from off-hab so they'd have no ties to the community."

She sipped the tea, but it made little dent in her frustration. "How can I possibly fill Lodestar's shoes, Emry? Her methods are flawless, meticulous, relentless. She spent six years examining this case from every conceivable angle."

"Hey. Vack the techie stuff. Lydia didn't expect you to find any new clues that way. That's why we're going there to question the suspects, look 'em in the eye. Facts don't change, but people do. Sooner or later one of the punkers will slip up. We just have to catch them doing it. Or make them do it. The same way you did with a hundred bad guys back on New Queens."

Emry clutched her shoulders. "Stop worrying about being Lodestar. The image is for other people's benefit. Just be Doc. Do what you do. That's what Lydia wanted when she picked you."

Kunda took a deep, cleansing breath. "You're right." She kissed Emry deeply, then headed back to the table with her teacup. "Zephyr, no more playback. Give us the suspects' files. I want to know everything about these three excuses for men by the time we arrive, down to the number of hairs on their asses."

Emry stared, wrinkling her nose. "That reminds me. We need to find you a decent catchphrase."

"I wish I *had* fired that shot." Aaron Macklin's steely eyes darted back and forth between Lodestar and the Green Blaze, as if challenging the two Troubleshooters to hate him. "Those radicals needed a good hard slap in the face, and I'm proud of my brother who delivered it, whoever he was. It wasn't his fault they didn't take the lesson. It was the fault of those reckless fools who didn't understand how things had to work out here and conspired to overthrow the system I swore to defend with my life."

"With *somebody's* lives," Emerald muttered.

The burly, gray-haired man stared at her. "It was about protecting every life on Eureka. That takes order, discipline. Things have gone to shit since the radicals took power. Voluntary work details. No public gathering protocols. No regulation of movement between segments. No behavior monitoring to predict subversion."

"And yet the habitat's ecosystem has not collapsed," Ekundayo pointed out, sitting calmly while Emry paced behind her. "There is no chaos in the streets. No epidemics have burned through the population. The people have taken care of their habitat and their community without needing to be coerced and intimidated."

"The homicide rate's plummeted since they dissolved your little undercover death squad," Emry added. "Now why do you think that could be?"

"Propaganda. You believe those statistics? We stood for the *real* truth."

"From behind a mask," Kunda countered. "Hiding your names. Incinerating and replacing the interior components of the symbot after every kill to eradicate any evidence of the killer's identity. Hardly the behavior of people proud of their actions."

"That anonymity was for our protection. How many of you Troubleshooters have been hunted down and killed by your enemies?"

Macklin sneered at their colorful outfits. "Muchangi acted like she was above it, but she played the same game as the rest of you. Posing and preening for the cameras, worrying about public outreach and community engagement. Throwing conventions, modeling for toys and calendars. This is war!"

Kunda shot to her feet. "Police are not soldiers! We protect and we serve. That means the public, not just ourselves."

She felt Emry's fleeting touch on her arm, calming her. *Role reversal.* There was tightly controlled rage in the Green Blaze's voice as she spoke, though. "Almost every Troubleshooter who's died on the job has done it fighting to save people. And it's worth it when you don't see the people as enemies to terrorize."

Macklin idly picked up his beer can, countering their emotion with cool smugness. "Sheepdogs don't see the sheep as their prey. But they're effective because the sheep see them as wolves." He took a final draft and crushed the can. "I wouldn't expect you outsiders to understand that."

"You're an outsider yourself," Lodestar reminded him. She gestured at the paraphernalia on his apartment walls: the iconic Samuel Dinh painting of Olympus Mons, the models of the first colony ships, the unit flag of Amazonia's long-dissolved corporate enforcement division. "Clearly proud of your Martian roots."

"I was — until radicals and insurrectionists defied company rule and declared independence. Their chaos is everywhere. I came here to get away from it, but it followed me."

"There are still surviving company states on Mars. Why come out to Eureka instead?"

"Because Eureka needed discipline. They needed experienced soldiers who'd put down insurrections before, who knew how to get the job done."

Emry loomed over him. "You're proud of being a killer."

He rose to face her. "I'm a warrior, child. An ugly job, but society can't survive without it."

"If you think killing a sixteen-year-old bystander was so punking heroic, then why hide who fired the shot? If it was you, why not boast about it? If it was Feng or Khan, why not give credit where it's due?"

"Even if I knew, I wouldn't defy operational security. It's by order and discipline that a unit survives. You cosplayers can't understand that." His eyes roved up and down Blaze's vividly attired figure, lingering on her breasts. "I shouldn't have to tell the Troubleshooter who got *two* of her mentors killed within months of each other."

A second later, Macklin was dangling in midair, suspended by Emry's fingers clutching his shirt collar and the chest hairs underneath. "You wanna go? Fine. Let's see how tough you are out of your shell!"

"Blaze!" Kunda called sharply to get her attention but sent the rest subvocally. <He wants you to lose control. Remember, brains over brawn.>

A moment later, Emry hissed sharply, let Macklin drop, and stroked the brim of her fedora. "Just be glad I don't want to get blood on my flarin' new hat."

Kunda's heightened senses could hear his heart racing, smell the terror in his sweat—although the open fear on his face rendered those perceptions redundant. Clearly he hadn't realized just how strong the Green Blaze truly was.

After a moment, Macklin caught himself and regained his bluster, brushing past Emry with feigned nonchalance and heading to his kitchen for another beer. "You little girls haven't said a single thing Muchangi didn't try on me years ago. At least she was Martian once. If you're the best she could find to replace her, then God help the Troubleshooter Corps."

Kunda should have been able to dismiss his words as the empty bluster of a weak man. It would have been easier if they hadn't echoed her own thoughts.

"Whoa. Now, this is a collection!"

Ekundayo wasn't sure whether Emerald's admiration of Travis Feng's action figure collection was genuine or part of a ploy to win his trust. Kunda knew that fandom could be a compelling bond between people—at least when it wasn't driving intense feuds—so the Green Blaze might be able to forge a link here that the original Lodestar never could.

Then again, Emry might simply be lost in awe of Feng's roomful of collectible figures lovingly preserved in their unopened boxes. "Damn, you've got some rare stuff here. Gold Series Sunblaze and Nighteye. The *Gods of Olympus* Theomachy set. Henshin Edition Sam Murai, Private Eye! Another fedora connoisseur." She chuckled as the action figure reacted to her touch, its hat and trench coat morphing into overly elaborate samurai armor inside the packaging while an aggressive techno-jazz cue played tinnily.

"Ooh, Doc, look here!" She picked up a mint-condition Lodestar figure and held it out so Kunda could see Lydia's signature on the box.

Feng rubbed the back of his head in embarrassment. "Lodestar—the *first* Lodestar," the lean-faced, bearded man amended with a nod toward the new model, "gave me that in our third interview. I was tempted to throw it out, let her know I wouldn't be bribed, but how could I pass it up? Despite all this, she's always been one of my favorite Troubleshooters. That duster, those boots—the lady had style."

Kunda took the opening. "Then I hope you appreciate that I'm here with her blessing, to complete the work she began. Whatever respect you had for her, I hope you'll—"

"I don't see it."

"Mister Feng?"

He looked her over skeptically. "You think *you* can be Lodestar?" He scoffed. "You're just a kid. You're not Martian, just some Sheaver upstart. Hell, you aren't even bald!"

Kunda kept her cool. "I know I have much to prove as a Troubleshooter. I don't pretend to be as worthy to wear the coat as Lydia Muchangi, but she chose me to represent her, and I take that obligation seriously."

"And *about* that coat. Too slick, too short, too modern. Pandering to the brats who don't know classic style when they see it." He gave a mean chuckle. "They should call you 'Lodestarlet.'"

Emry blushed fiercely and cleared her throat, developing an intense renewed interest in Feng's collection. "Vack me sideways! You even have Fate Chaser!"

Feng stared in shock. "You've actually *heard* of her?"

Emry lovingly fondled one of the boxed figures. "I was on Phobos for the five minutes the series was out."

The Phobian native shook his head. "So unfair that they killed it. She deserved far more than seven episodes."

"So rageous to meet another fan! What was that cool catchphrase she had? 'Fate has caught you up?' No—"

"*As* I was saying," Kunda interposed loudly. Emry fell silent and threw her an apologetic look, realizing she'd gotten carried away again.

Turning back to Feng, Kunda tried to regain control of the conversation. "Whatever uniform I wear now, I'm still a cop at heart. So I understand the loyalty you feel to your fellows in the Moros unit. But I hope you can understand how your superiors abused that loyalty to make you complicit in their cruelty. You owe that greater system no loyalty. Denying justice to Gao Meihui's family only keeps the scars it inflicted from healing."

Feng returned her gaze with sadness. "That's what you still don't understand. Even the real Lodestar didn't get it. You're all looking for one murderer to blame. There is no individual killer here. As Moros, we were subsumed by the system. We rode in the machine, but the machine took the lead. It guided our steps, shaped our words, steadied our aim. We weren't individuals, just extensions of the mechanism."

"How convenient," Emry sneered. "You and I both know that's not how it worked. It made sure you hit what you aimed at, but you picked the target. You *chose* to fire when Meihui was in your sights."

"*One* of us did."

"You just said it didn't matter who it was."

"But it does matter why. The Gaos were part of the anti-government movement."

"You mean the reformist coalition," Kunda countered.

"To us, according to our orders, they were a threat to the security of Eureka. And we were conditioned to deal with threats ruthlessly, to allow no hesitation or qualms. Anyone who got in our sights had only themselves to blame for the consequences."

"So you feel no remorse?"

Feng glared at her. "Of course I feel remorse that a girl died. Just as I would if she'd been caught in a solar flare or a construction accident. But you're looking for a person to pin a murder on. It wasn't a murder. It was just the system operating. A harsh system, yes. Prioritizing the state over individual lives. But that was the way it was designed to work."

He sighed. "I wish I hadn't been part of those deaths. I thought they were necessary and right at the time, but I took no joy in them. But there's nothing to be gained from singling out a scapegoat—one person to blame for the entire system. None of us deserve that.

"Moros is dead. The system he killed for is dead. So justice has already been done. Please leave it at that."

The four-year-old gazed up at the Green Blaze with her eyes wide and round. "Can I wear your hat?"

"Of course!" Emerald crouched down to Rajya Khan's level and transferred the verdant fedora to the girl's head, where it sank down over her eyes and ears. "Oh, you look gorgeous! There's just something about long-haired girls in fedoras."

"She's good with kids," Giselle Khan said to Ekundayo, holding her husband's hand as they sat together on their couch. She had insisted on remaining with Jayant Khan throughout the interview, showing a protectiveness Kunda would have admired had the cause been different.

Kunda chuckled as Emry lay prone on the carpet and challenged the tiny girl to arm-wrestle. "It helps that she never stopped being one." The girl threw herself bodily upon the forearm that had effortlessly lifted an 85-kilo man the day before, making Emry roar in mock agony.

"Maybe we should talk in the dining room," Giselle said.

The Troubleshooter nodded and followed the Khans into the next room, leaving Emry at the mercy of the girl she had allowed to force her arm down to the carpet. "Ohh, I'm done for! Never fight a woman in a hat!"

Once seated at the kitchen table, Jayant Khan stared at his delighted daughter for a long moment before speaking. "I think about it every night, you know. What if it had been my kid in those sights?"

Giselle grimaced. "Jay."

He clasped her hand. "I know, I'm sorry. But I want Lodestar—both of them—to know. I'm not happy about my part in all this. I understand exactly how Gao's fathers feel."

He held Kunda's gaze evenly. "What we did as Moros was wrong. I didn't understand that until I married Giselle and had Rajya. I thought only the fraternity mattered.

"I was a loser back on Vestalia—I failed at wrestling, couldn't even keep a job as a bouncer. The Eurekans offered me the chance to be a superhero. More—they let me belong to something. Maybe that's what you Troubleshooters feel in the Corps. But it turned out more like a cult. I see now how we were indoctrinated, conditioned to think we were the masters and the people were ours to control. They brainwashed us to be ready to kill for the state." He winced. "Some of us looked forward to it. Like Macklin. But I won't say I never felt the same."

Jayant sighed. "If it had been me... and if I didn't have Rajya to take care of... I'd confess. I don't expect you to believe that, but I would. But as it is..." He shook his head. "If I told you the murderer's name, the other one would close ranks with him and they'd both accuse me. In their minds, I'd be a traitor to the fraternity—the only real crime."

Kunda leaned forward. "Then you do know who it was."

"We all know. We never said it in as many words, but we knew from the start. I won't lie about that. But I can't tell you the truth either. It'd be their word against mine, and I'd have no way to prove they were lying."

"That's the best case," Giselle added. "That coward Macklin wouldn't hesitate to threaten Rajya, or me, if he thought it served his twisted idea of order. And Feng blames it all on the 'system,' on forces beyond his control, so he wouldn't have the will to defy Macklin."

Kunda studied her vivid gray eyes. "Then you're convinced your husband wasn't the killer? Has he told you who it was?"

"He's tried, but I refused to let him. I'm content to have faith in my husband's goodness. I don't need to know the truth, and I respect his need to keep it hidden. It's safest for all of us just to leave it in the past."

Giselle looked over Kunda's outfit. "You took Lodestar's name, her mantle. You want to close the case she couldn't. You think that'll prove you worthy of the legacy." She shook her head. "That's the same bullshit Jay was dragged into—the role above the person, the cause above anyone's life or safety.

"Please... don't fall into that trap. Don't sacrifice my girl to a name and a cause like Moros did."

"So who gets your vote, Doc?" Emry asked back on *Zephyr* as she retrieved her fedora from his cleaning unit, checking to make sure none of the grape jelly stains remained. "Please say Macklin. I so want it to be Macklin."

Kunda sighed. "I just don't know. All their reactions to the murder are different, but not in a way that lets me differentiate their microexpressions or thermal readings. The way they were conditioned to see themselves as a single unit, to share responsibility for all of Moros's actions, means they all feel equally as if they pulled that trigger—regardless of whether that fills them with pride, detachment, or remorse."

She groaned, rubbing her fingers across her scalp between her braids, which were tied loosely back while the ship was in free fall at

Eureka's docking hub. "Am I making the same mistake, like Giselle said? Have I been so caught up in the legacy, in matching my wits against Lydia's, that I forgot about the lives at stake?"

"Hey. I get how Rajya's mom felt, but it came from fear. That's how people like Moros win—by making people afraid to stand up to them. Because they know that if we do stand up and stop them..." Emry donned the fedora for dramatic effect. "...then there'll be nothing more to fear."

Kunda smiled her thanks. "Right, then. Back to work." She glanced over at the foldout lab module next to the medbed, where the Moros armor rested in a web of sensor probes and contacts. "Zephyr, have you made any headway with the symbot?"

"I finally broke its operator lock," the cyber replied. "But it relied on a standardized tag implanted in every user, so it's no help in determining which user was inside that day."

"Have you had a chance to review our own buffer playbacks? Could you spot any tells we missed?"

"I had no more luck than you, Kunda. As far as I can discern, you drew forth no information or reactions that Lydia hasn't already elicited in prior interviews."

"So much for fresh eyes. Some Lodestar I'm turning out to be."

"Here." Emry drifted over and plonked her hat onto Kunda's head. "Maybe it'll do you more good than me." Her expression became sultry. "Wow. I was right about women in fedoras."

"Don't distract me," Kunda said, but laughed and kissed her anyway. They spent a few comforting minutes at that, but only long enough for Kunda to clear her head and refocus on the problem. While Emry chased after the hat that had floated away, Kunda got another cup of herbal tea, sipping on the tapering lip that concentrated the liquid through its surface tension.

"The frustrating thing is that I think I have a plan to elicit a confession. What the Khans said gave me the idea, and—"

"That's great, Doc!" Emry pushed the hat back onto her head, floating upside-down relative to Kunda. "Why is that frustrating?"

"Because it'll only work on the real killer. If I tried it on the wrong man, he'd know I was bluffing, and he'd warn the others. Plus, of course, the last thing I want is to pressure a false confession. This has to be above board."

"Oh. So you have to know who it is before you can prove who it is."

"I need something, *anything*, that can identify the killer. Any detail we've all missed, no matter how trivial."

Emry went quiet for a long moment, biting thoughtfully on a knuckle. "What?" Kunda asked.

"I *may* have something... No. It's too dumb."

"Emry, I'm desperate."

Rotating back upright, Emry took a reluctant breath and explained her hypothesis. Kunda was initially skeptical, but the more she heard, the more convinced she became. A few questions to Zephyr provided corroborating data. "By the vack, Emry, I think you've cracked it!"

"I have? You don't think it's too much of a reach?"

"It fits. It holds together, as bizarre as it sounds." She laughed, pushing off a stanchion to collide with Emry and knock her into a roll, kissing her as they spun together. "And it's something only the Green Blaze could have thought of!"

"Are you sure you don't want legal counsel present?" Ekundayo asked, studying the man who sat across the table in the interrogation room. Emerald stood behind her in hat and trench coat, carefully positioned so that the overhead light would shadow her face in the most noirish way she could manage.

"Why should I?" Travis Feng crossed his arms, meeting her gaze with defiance. "Because you dragged me down to police HQ this time? Just another bluff. You've got no new moves, no leverage that the real Lodestar and all these cops haven't already tried." He glanced down at her attire. "All the closet cosplay in Solsys won't change that."

Lodestar steepled her fingers. "Oh, I think there's one costume that could change your mind, Travis." She turned her head and nodded to the observers on the other side of the one-way mirror on her left. A moment later, it turned transparent. Feng nearly fell out of his chair as the ebony death's-head mask of Moros stared back at him through the pane. The hulking symbot stepped forward to confirm it was occupied. Eureka's police captain stood behind it, watching it warily.

Feng panted, trying to gather himself. "No. It's impossible. It's a replica, a soligram. You'd never get the real one moving."

"Not without an authorized user inside," Kunda agreed. "Test it for yourself. I'm sure your interface still works. Ping the symbot."

The bearded man tentatively stepped up to the window, and the Moros armor moved closer in response. Kunda watched Feng as he engaged the long-dormant protocols still hard-wired into his neural interface implants, eyes widening at the responses projected onto his retinal HUD. "It... it's real. I can still feel... oh, that surge of power..."

He shook himself. His gaze hardened as he faced the mask. "It's you, Khan, isn't it? Trying to protect your family from finding the real truth."

"You tell us," the Green Blaze said. "Is it? Can't you tell?"

Feng glared at her. "You know the suit protects its wearer's identity, even through the interface. But Macklin would never break."

"Can you be so sure? Come on. Tough guy like that, all bluster and rage? You know as well as we do he's a coward underneath."

Kunda rose and joined Emry in facing down Feng. "You talk of your loyalty, your fraternity, but we know how the game really works. You know that if either Khan or Macklin named you as the killer, you'd close ranks with the other and accuse him in turn—or threaten him. So they were both too afraid to come forward. Macklin hid behind a mask of unrepentance, Khan behind a mask of contrition. But you must know that either one would welcome the chance to escape the threat of prosecution that hangs over you all. You know it because you feel it too.

"But Moros was all about anonymity, wasn't he? So that's the way out. The way to make the accusation without fear of retaliation, while making it clear to the accused that it's no hoax.

"You didn't think I had anything new to offer, anything that made me worthy of the name Lodestar. There have been times when I felt the same. But it turns out that just being granted that name gave me something new, Travis. It got me to think about the potential of a shared identity. About the way the very anonymity that protected the killer for six years could be turned around to expose him.

"Perhaps it would've occurred to you too, in time... if you hadn't already known you were the killer."

Feng was shaking his head, staring at the armor, but Kunda could tell his disbelief was yet another mask. She continued relentlessly. "Now you're thinking you don't know which one of them you can still trust. You don't know which one you can side with to preserve reasonable doubt. So your strategy will no longer work. You're all alone, Travis."

She glanced at the police captain, who nodded back. "But you can still get ahead of it. Cooperate with us. Tell the truth." She took a step closer. "You say you regret what the system made you do, Travis. Prove it to me. Don't let the system win."

Feng took a shuddering breath, let it out. He threw one more glance at the death's-head, then spun away. "Get rid of *that*," he said. "I'll tell you."

Kunda felt a surge of relief. But the rules still held. "I advise you to contact your attorney before—"

"No... I waive counsel. What's the point anymore?"

Emry tapped on the window, and a moment later it was a mirror again. Feng was no more willing to confront his own reflection than the face he had worn when he had killed Gao Meihui. He sat at the table, looking down at his hands.

"I fired the shot. I killed the girl.

"I believed in the system, in the need to keep the people controlled through fear. I didn't feel culpable for anything I did; I was just a cog in the machine, carrying out its bidding. I followed the orders sent to me on the suit's display, acted on its prompts without hesitation. I trusted it to think for me.

"I was sent to kill Andrei Narayan, for the good of the system. He was a villain, deserving to be hunted down, terrorized, broken before he was allowed to die. And anyone in his orbit was just as guilty. When that girl stepped into my sights... when that courageous child unhesitatingly shielded my quarry from the monster I was inside... I got no prompts ruling her out as a target. The suit was just as willing to end her as Narayan, and so I ended her. I could've stopped myself, could've called that ambulance after, but I decided that letting the girl die as Narayan watched would be a good way to punish him. My role was to punish, not to save, so a single life was not a priority. They weren't individuals to me, any more than I was in the suit. They were both part of the same threat to the system, so that made the girl fair game."

Feng was weeping now. It was several moments before he could speak. "I tell myself I'm not that man anymore. That I left that indoctrination behind. But saying the words just now... So help me, it still feels right. I'm still trapped inside that suit."

He met both Troubleshooters' eyes, holding their gaze with sorrow and relief. "I'm grateful to you both for stopping me. I guess... there's more than one way to be Lodestar after all.

"But I want to know who else I have to thank. Now that you have my confession on record... can you tell me which one turned me in? I promise I won't retract, won't retaliate." He lowered his head. "Though I can't expect you to believe that. I'm sorry, I shouldn't have —"

"Oh, no problem," Emry shrugged, tapping on the window again. "We've got nothing to hide, have we, pal?"

The mirror turned transparent again, and Feng stared in confusion as the Moros armor unlocked and unfolded to reveal... a soligram of a blank humanoid shape.

"Travis Feng," Emry went on, "meet my shipmind, Zephyr. We forgot to tell you he figured out how to replicate your authorization tags and unlock the armor. And in Lodestar's defense, she never actually said one of the others had talked. She just let you assume that. Sorry — we don't like to trick people into confessing, but you guys left us no other way. He who lives by the mask, et cetera.

"So do you still want to thank us?"

Lydia Muchangi beamed with pride as she studied the two Troubleshooters seated before her desk. "I am so proud of you both. With Feng's guilty plea, you have finally brought peace to Gao Meihui's family... and let me close my last case as Lodestar once and for all."

"It was a privilege to be entrusted with it," Ekundayo told her.

Lydia met her eyes. "But what tipped you off? Your report was vague on what led you to identify Feng as the real killer."

Kunda smiled. "That's because I wanted Emry to get to tell you in person."

The director turned to the other woman in delighted surprise. "Blaze? *You* found the answer?"

"Well..." Emry pulled off the fedora she'd worn all the way back to Demetria and kneaded it in her hands. "I kinda stumbled into the answer."

"Don't be so modest," Kunda said. "You saw the crucial clue and deduced what it meant. That's a huge part of detective work."

"Well, don't keep me in suspense," Lydia pleaded.

Emry cleared her throat. "See, I'd been wondering. The first thing we heard on the video, over and over again, was Moros saying 'caught up with you.' Why would he say that when he wasn't chasing Narayan, when he just cornered him outside the meeting?"

Lydia nodded. "I wondered that myself. He could have been saying that his sins had caught up with him, perhaps. But it didn't point toward any one of the three. It wasn't outside the normal range of vocabulary and phrasing for Moros."

"Which is probably why it didn't get pegged as an identifiable phrase," Kunda replied. "Or more likely, the symbot's programmers would never have been able to recognize it as such, any more than you or I could."

At Lydia's clueless look, the quivering Emry finally burst forth, "It was Fate Chaser!"

The director stared. "Excuse me? You inflect that like a personal name."

"It's a character in a show. Also the title. It was this obscure Colonial they ran on Phobos when I was there nine years ago, but it was an alt-history with trappings of the American Old West, and there was an ancient Martian demonic curse involved... It was weird and dumb and incredibly violent, and nobody got it and it only lasted seven episodes. But you know me, I love anything trashy, plus I was fourteen, so—"

"Blaze."

"Okay. Fate Chaser was a bounty hunter. Every episode, she'd go up against some mass murderer or corporate embezzler, she'd blow away, like, half the population of Phobos hunting them down, and then at the end, just before she killed the bad guy, she'd say, 'Fate has caught up with you.'"

Lydia blinked, then turned to Ekundayo, who explained. "When we interviewed Travis Feng, Emry recognized a Fate Chaser action figure in his collection."

"Can you believe it?" Emry asked. "Even I've never been able to track one down in mint condition. He must've been one of the seventeen people in all Solsys who've even *seen* the show, let alone liked it."

"So you realized Feng was the only one of the three who would know that catchphrase." Lydia frowned. "It's tenuous."

"By itself, perhaps," Kunda said. "Once we had the clue, Zephyr searched through the entire runs of the other series and franchises represented in Feng's collection. He found occurrences of 'The innocent don't run' and "Actions have consequences' as notable phrases in two of the more obscure or critically reviled ones. Not rare in themselves—"

"But the probability of all three being used coincidentally is minuscule. Only a dedicated fan would know them all, or consider using them in such a context. Perhaps subsuming himself in fantasy personae made it easier to detach himself from the act of homicide."

Lydia shook her head in disbelief. "Finally, after six years, you found the one personal detail that Moros's designers and programmers failed to expunge. The one clue I would never have caught on to if I'd searched for the rest of my life."

Kunda nodded. "After all... you have taste." Emry glared and punched her in the arm.

Lydia laughed with warmth and relief. "I owe you an apology, Blaze. All these months, I thought that to develop your detective skills, you had to learn to think more like me. But you surpassed me at an intellectual puzzle in a way that was still uniquely Emerald Blair. I am so proud of you."

Kunda fidgeted. "I suppose I wasn't the right Troubleshooter for this case after all, then."

Lydia reached over and clasped her hand. "Of course you were. Blaze had the insight, but you were the one who trusted it and used it to close the case.

"No, you didn't do it alone, but that's never been a requirement. I was never Lodestar until I joined the Corps—until I became part of a larger team. Not subsumed to a cult mindset like Moros, of course, but balancing my individual strengths with others'. I let Yukio saddle me with that name because, as frustrating as he could be with his love of costumes and championyms and his swashbuckling vanity, I trusted his wisdom and his commitment to justice."

She met their eyes in turn, smiling warmly. "You have both proven that the new generation of heroes has the Corps's legacy well in hand. You wear the Lodestar name well, Kunda. I know you'll continue to do it proud."

"Great!" Emry stood and shrugged out of her trench coat and hat. "Now I can hang these up until my next murder mystery."

Kunda frowned. "I thought you loved them."

"I love the way they *look*. But you know how hot my metabolism runs. There's a reason my costume's sleeveless." She shook her head briskly. "And I could do without the hat hair."

Though Worlds Divide Us

Miranda Ayodele glowered at the not-quite-human being slumped on the rear bench of her rover. "I should have left you to die."

Wide, dark eyes with cybernetic irises gazed back. Slender fingers lowered the rover's oxymask from an androgynous, amber-skinned face. "I and my people have done you no harm."

That placid arrogance made Miranda wonder again why she'd bothered to rescue the Dijuno she'd found staggering through the Tharsis lowlands without breathing gear. "No harm? You've doomed life on Mars!"

The genderless Dijuno—they had given the name Teshien Ri—tilted their red-blond head to examine her. "Please explain."

"What are you even doing here?" she demanded instead. "What interest does your kind have in space travel? You jump between worlds as easy as riding an elevator. A million parallel Earths with almost-human natives you can study, trade with, or screw without consequences. Why risk yourselves on long, hard trips to barren rocks you actually have to *earn* a life on?"

"Ah." Ri nodded. "You blame transbrane contact for the cutbacks to Martian colonization initiatives."

"Damn right I do."

"However, human scientists had already confirmed the transmission of gravity between brane universes, causing equal-sized planetary masses to form in corresponding spaces, undergoing convergent evolution due to identical impact and flare events, tectonic—"

"I don't care about all that!"

"You would have achieved the breakthrough soon enough, and contact was accelerated due to the Irddru incurs—"

"We were building a life here on Mars! Building a nation of our own, through hard work and sacrifice!"

"If fewer lives are sacrificed, is that not good?"

"It's wrong to sacrifice a *way* of life!"

"That will be humanity's choice if it happens." Those unnatural eyes held hers evenly. "Do you believe sacrificing me will have any effect upon it?"

She refused to feel guilty. "Don't you care what happens to you, Dijuno?"

"Certainly. But we channel our emotions into seeking solutions." Ri's head tilted abstractedly, their hands working unseen threads. "Ah. Miranda Ayodele. First-generation colonist, resident of Robinson City for twenty-eight Martian years. Son Bernard born in second year."

Miranda bristled. "You have a file on me?"

"You have a large footprint in this planet's public network. Though the connection is tenuous here, the network poorly maintained."

"And whose fault is that?"

Their fingers danced. "Many Martian citizens' online posts blame us, while others blame those who abandoned Mars to explore or colonize Earth's transbrane counterparts." Ri's eyes narrowed. "Such as Bernard Ayodele, who returned to Earth nine months ago to join the exploration program. To pursue the unearned life, as you put it."

"Don't try to analyze me, cyborg."

"I have a scion too. One I hope to rejoin, if you assist me in repairing my transbrane capsule."

"Now you're trying to win my sympathy. You just want to visit your kid? No. That doesn't explain your people making the effort to cross space to a lifeless world. Only we did that, because you didn't think we were worth contacting and left us to fend for ourselves. We had to reach other worlds the hard way, with our own wits and struggle.

"And as soon as we got good at it, you showed up with your quick and easy magic portals and lured our best and brightest away. Like you were afraid of us achieving something you hadn't, so you had to seduce our children before they achieved something even greater!"

Miranda lunged out of her seat and grabbed the smaller humanoid by the front of their coverall. "No, you're gonna tell me the real reason you came here, Dijuno. To spy on those of us who still think the rest of the Solar System is worth our attention and effort? To undermine what few colonies and outposts we have left? To steal the kids you haven't already taken?"

Ri looked down at Miranda's hands with curiosity, as if her threat of violence were merely a social behavior observed from outside. After a moment, Ri said, "The best way to discern your answers is to examine my capsule. Please take me back there."

"So you can get a weapon, or activate whatever you…" She shook her head. "I'm not a fool."

"If my capsule is indeed a threat, is it wise to abandon it? There are few left in authority, or you would have summoned them already. You feel responsible for maintaining the colony yourself. Or for protecting it. That, I surmise, is why you declined to join your son."

Miranda resented Ri for knowing how to hit so close to home. Bernard had begged her to come with him, to explore not-quite-Earthly biospheres and civilizations together, insisting it was just as worthy a challenge as conquering Mars. Miranda had reminded him angrily how much she'd suffered and bled for Mars, how many friends and mentors had died for it. It had to mean something. How could Bernard be so ungrateful for all she'd done to build him a home here? How could he just throw it away?

How could he have let those be the last words they exchanged?

But Ri's assessment was accurate. For Mars's sake, she had to examine the capsule for herself.

Miranda left Teshien Ri in the rover and suited up to investigate the damaged transbrane capsule. She approached the spherical device with care, examining the intricate crystalline lattices embedded in its surface, though she realized she had no way to recognize any threat they posed.

The one clear thing was that the capsule was dented and lying on its side, at the bottom of a trail of depressions in the desert soil and dust, starting midway up a gentle slope. Glints of crystalline debris punctuated the tale the depressions told.

Leaning through the open hatch, its handle dark with Ri's dried blood, Miranda saw unfamiliar symbols flashing, some kind of universal pictograms for brane travelers — clear enough that even she could decipher them. *Malfunction. Off course. Contact lost.*

Back in the rover, Miranda studied Ri for a long moment.

"You weren't coming here."

"No."

"What went wrong?"

"To be determined."

"So you were going to a different Mar—a different fourth planet."

"It is called Guzae. My scion is a researcher there."

Miranda sighed. "Your capsule… it fell. From a few dozen meters up."

The Dijuno squeezed their large eyes shut. "Yes. It was very painful."

"But transbrane travel… it's always to the matching point in space."

"Yes."

"And every corresponding braneworld has the same size, the same topography."

"Essentially identical to those in relative proximity, except when altered by intelligent effort."

"So you were aiming for a destination at the same coordinates… the same elevation."

"Yes."

"But we're in an open plain. The only way you could have *two* capsule stations at the same height…" Ri simply waited for her to finish. "Is if they were both in tall buildings."

"Hence my lack of breathing equipment. Although Guzae has been terraformed, possessing a robust atmosphere and beautiful forests."

Miranda struggled to take it in. "*Why?* With countless Earthlike worlds an instant's jump away, why would *two* civilizations colonize space?"

Ri smiled—very slightly, but even that was beyond what Miranda had believed Dijuno capable of. "When the people of Guzae's brane discovered transbrane travel, they neglected space for a generation or more. So did the Dijuno's ancestors, far earlier. But once the novelty wore off, they remembered there was much to learn from the system's other planets. That the challenge of reaching them was no less worthwhile. Many others have done the same. Often they have even found life on the fourth world or the outer moons."

Miranda blinked away tears. "So Mars… it won't be abandoned?"

"It may be for a time. But on countless braneworlds, the species that thrive and build civilization are the ones compelled to colonize new environments, even ones unsuitable for their survival needs. This lets the species spread widely enough to survive local cataclysms, and the need to adapt to hostile conditions promotes technological innovation."

Another smile. "Humans are unlikely to lose that drive. Mars will be a home to humanity one day, with or without you, Miranda Ayodele. So you are free to find your son, make amends, and discover another new world alongside him."

The tears came more freely now. "Your capsule's trashed. You knew that."

"You had to see for yourself to believe."

"You don't deserve to be apart from your kid."

"If you will help me reach Earth, I can cross branes from there and reunite with my scion." Ri studied her again, and she now saw it as sincere interest, not cold detachment. "Might you do the same?"

Miranda thought of that last argument with Bernard, the fierce temper they shared, the things they'd said—no—the things *she'd* said that drove him away. "Some divides are harder to bridge than others."

Ri gave her a knowing smile. "Those are the ones most worth the effort."

Nilly's Choice

R'nilinnath had grown up feeling as if the whole of Shilirrlal revolved around them — and not just the way it literally did when they played in the free-fall park at the habitat's axis.

For the last two-thirds of their brief lifetime, R'nilinnath had been the only child in their estate's crèche, and the youngest Chirrn in Shilirrlal by half that span. They had been the last of an allotment of births authorized to rebalance the population after a prominent Zenith female had chosen to migrate off the habitat with her harem and attendants. The Shilirrlaln had called in specialists from the Vhethil habitat's childcare collegium, which sent out task forces as needed to habitats throughout the Void Alliance, to tend to the new generation of children. But R'nilinnath's conception had been substantially delayed due to their gestating parent's administrative responsibilities and indecision in selecting a suitable donor parent. Thus, once their elder crèche-mate had matured, R'nilinnath had become the exclusive focus of the educators and caregivers within their estate crèche. No one else in the entire habitat was as privileged, as protected, as catered to.

It wasn't long before R'nilinnath realized how boring that was.

To be sure, Educator Thavheth and Counselor Eshudj encouraged R'nilinnath to explore whatever they wished, to expand their horizons and learn about every estate, guild, and collegium in Chirrn society, every habitat where they might one day migrate. The possibilities seemed endless. But in time, R'nilinnath realized that once they matured and acquired their first gender, they would be expected to apprentice to an existing guild, to incorporate its consensus knowledge base and decision protocols into their own mind, and to live out their life according to the norms that billions of other Chirrn had lived by for four *yanarrach*, more than eight-cubed times as long as their entire childhood would last. All the freedom they were given now was merely to introduce them to the finite range of options that would be available to them as an adult.

Moreover, on those occasions when R'nilinnath did get to play with the older children from other crèches, they came to realize that each crèche's educational program was tailored toward a career within that particular estate—social management in R'nilinnath's case, with options such as government, regulatory enforcement, jurisprudence, mediation, inclusion counseling, and the like. In theory, they would be free to migrate from one guild, one habitat, one life to another, to reinvent their identity and way of thinking from time to time, the better to maintain dynamism and growth throughout the very long lifetime ahead of them. This, they were told, was as natural and expected as transitioning from female to male and back again. So why, R'nilinnath wondered, were the children of Shilirrlal raised in different crèches with curriculums tailored to the estates of their birth? With so few children, wouldn't it be simpler to raise them all in the same crèche, where they could better learn the full range of possibilities open to them, and where they could play together all the time?

Their gestator parent R'havhithi objected to that idea, saying that he and R'nilinnath's other estate-kin would not wish to be separated from their cherished child, nor would the members of any other estate. R'nilinnath appreciated that, but while being the only child in that expansive family made them feel special, it could be stifling as well. Even when they did play with the older children, the others often had little interest in spending time with R'nilinnath, due to their differences in age and estate. R'nilinnath was able to win some appreciation by being silly and mischievous, but it felt more like a performance than genuine bonding.

In time, R'nilinnath decided to take pride in their uniqueness rather than lamenting it. They enjoyed being the exception, the outsider, the one out of sync. But their education still guided them toward a future of conformity. Even their periodic changes of gender and guild would be part of the expected routine of an adult Chirrn's existence. They could migrate beyond the Chirrn's standardized cylindrical habitats, take up residence in a Zenith Star Palace or a Thesshish helix shell or some other nation within the Void Alliance; yet even then, they would still be immersed in the structures and conventions of established civilization. There was a whole galaxy beyond the Alliance, to be sure, but

R'nilinnath's education had driven home that a Chirrn would find little welcome out there.

So where in all the galaxy could they find a way to do something truly *new*?

R'nilinnath found ways to indulge these rebellious thoughts by sneaking into parts of Shilirrlal's physical and digital structures they weren't supposed to enter. They found a passage into the quarter inhabited by the enigmatic Ryohoch, observing the nine-legged giants' mysterious, slow-paced behaviors with a mix of fascination and tedium. They challenged the younger Zenith to dominance games, scandalizing the scintillating avians by not caring whether they won or lost. They pursued the study of feral, planet-dwelling sophonts with lurid fascination, intrigued by their wild, unfettered existence and amused by the elder Chirrn's shock and disgust when R'nilinnath raised the taboo subject of planetary living, with its concomitant filth, savagery, and death.

Still, R'nilinnath was aware that even their transgressions were part of Thavheth's carefully designed educational regimen, a permitted degree of rebellion within the limits of what society would tolerate. In the educator's view, it was better to let them indulge it now and burn it off harmlessly before the time came to take on adult responsibilities.

Indeed, by the time R'nilinnath's sex hormones started to surge, causing their mane to start growing in and their skin mottling to start fading, they had put aside their lurid fascination with feral sophonts and come to terms with the realities of adult responsibility. They understood that all Chirrn, Zenith, Ryohoch, and other habitat residents were part of a larger whole, that their survival depended on its healthy, stable equilibrium, and that they all had a responsibility to contribute usefully to that balance, to give something back in exchange for what they gained. R'nilinnath may have grown up feeling indulged, but that had made them grateful to the estate that had nurtured them and eager to repay its many kindnesses through their service as an adult.

So they would have to settle for finding novelty where they could — for instance, by declining to preselect their first gender. Yet that would be a minor surprise at best. The differences between a Chirrn's male and female phases were subtle, not at all like the Zenith, whose genders were permanent and all-important in defining their roles in life. The reproductive changes would be strictly internal, the tongue unaltered except when aroused, its pores secreting in male phase and absorbing in female.

"It's hard to explain before you've experienced it," Counselor Eshudj told them. She could have shared her memories directly through the cloud, but she insisted the perceptions would mean little to R'nilinnath until they had developed their own neurological baseline for understanding. Young minds that simply absorbed others' consensus knowledge and thought patterns would not develop fully on their own, any more than R'nilinnath would have developed her impressive hopping speed by riding on adults' backs.

"Naturally, the changes in your tongue chemistry affect your sense of taste," Eshudj explained. "I enjoy much spicier, bolder flavors when I'm female. Though I'm much more interested in cooking when I'm male, inconveniently."

"That's it?" R'nilinnath asked. "Sex and food?"

"The hormonal shifts influence our behavior and attitudes as well, not unlike adopting a different guild consensus, only more subtle. I tend to feel more withdrawn and contemplative as a male, more outgoing and optimistic as a female. Yet some are more assertive and confident as males, more cautious and protective as females. Hormones interact with neurology in complex ways, different for each individual. Now, isn't that an adventure worth anticipating?"

It soon became clear that R'nilinnath was turning female — the more probable first gender, and thus not a very exciting outcome. They — no, *she* — found herself starting to enjoy foods she'd disliked before. As for her personality and perspective, though, R'nilinnath noted little change. If anything, her surging hormones only intensified her existing feelings — both her eagerness to find a useful role in society and her lingering frustration at the lack of novelty in Chirrn experience.

Plus, of course, she had a sex drive now, reacting in surprisingly turbulent ways to the scent and movements of other Chirrn, the flexing of their powerful tail muscles, the rippling of their muzzle bristles as they breathed, the occasional brief glimpses of their tongues as they spoke or ate. It was exciting, yet also lonely. The other children had all matured and taken partners by now, while she was in that awkward phase where she was sexually mature but still looked childish. Until her mane grew out fully and her skin turned solid blue, she was unlikely to attract any older females. Or males, for that matter; she was nowhere near ready to consider procreation, but recreational sex with the opposite gender was not unheard of. However, that required contraceptive treatments not recommended for a Chirrn in first-stage maturation, for fear of disrupting the development of her reproductive organs. So it seemed she would have little opportunity to actually *use* her capability for sexual relations.

Then again, there must be females close to her age somewhere in the Alliance. There were few habitats in this lonely part of the Central Void, but R'nilinnath reached out through the wormhole network, seeking fellow young Chirrn with similar interests and outlooks. The nearest was a Lesshchin named Zhayetha, whom R'nilinnath found agreeable enough in their exchanges. They were still immature, at least a *narranl* from developing a gender, but R'nilinnath cultivated a friendship and gently encouraged them to go female when the time came. It would be a while, but R'nilinnath strove to be patient. After all, as her elders had always assured her, life in Chirrn habitats was measured, deliberate, and enduring, without the desperate haste of fleeting, planet-dwelling ferals trapped within the primitive cycle of birth and death. There would be plenty of time.

There was, of course, one question of vital importance that R'nilinnath had to wrestle with in her early *narrenn* of adulthood: Now that her mane was growing out, what color should she dye it? She simulated a range of different color and style options, posted them on her cloud journal, and polled the reactions of her followers… then just went with the glistening silver dye she'd liked most all along, feeling that it went best with the cerulean blue that increasingly dominated her skin as her mottling faded. Pleased with the final result, she posted a sensory record on her journal and awaited the reactions, particularly those from Zhayetha and her other mating prospects.

Yet the replies never came. Instead, the whole of consensus was flooded by shocking, bewildering news: Lesshchi had been murdered.

Initial reports were confused and chaotic, but a picture soon emerged: A primitive starship launched by feral planet-dwellers had fired a barrage of relativistic projectiles at Shilirrlal's sibling habitat without warning, tearing a vast gash through its outer shell and killing nearly one in six of its inhabitants in a matter of moments. Lesshchi's ships had promptly hunted down and captured the tiny, tenuous wisp of a starship that had done such disproportionate damage, but the habitat itself was fatally wounded and would have to be abandoned, its shattered mind euthanized and its survivors evacuated to Shilirrlal, Vhethil, and more distant habitats. Not only had countless Lesshchin been physically killed, most of them irreversibly, but Lesshchi's cloud had been mortally disrupted by electromagnetic pulse effects, the bulk of its data lost or corrupted, including the consensus memories of the majority of the Lesshchin. Most of the survivors had lost the cloud-based side of their minds and personalities, leaving them incomplete and cut off from their communal identities. And the backup memories of most of the dead had been lost along with their physical bodies, leaving nothing of themselves behind.

R'nilinnath had a hard time understanding what any of this meant. She knew of the concept of violent death from history, and from what she had learned of life on feral worlds. But no one she had ever known had died, and hardly any of her kin or acquaintances knew anyone who had died—certainly not without leaving memories and personality imprints in consensus to live on in others. The idea of anyone simply being gone forever was difficult to grasp.

It became no easier once it was finally confirmed that Zhayetha was among the dead.

R'nilinnath understood in the abstract what that meant. Her friend was gone from her life for good. She would never find out if they liked R'nilinnath's mane color, or have the chance to try out sex with them or beat them in a race, or even just to meet them in the flesh or real-time consensus. But it was a distant, barely tangible loss, for Zhayetha had not been a close friend, merely one of the few available. R'nilinnath felt bad that she didn't care more deeply, but she had a hard time understanding what she *should* feel in a situation like this. The adults around her didn't seem to have any more idea than she did.

As for the Lesshchin, judging from what they shared through consensus, they mainly felt rage and contempt toward the ferals that had killed their home. To R'nilinnath's shock, some crew members of the vessel escorting the captured ferals to Shilirrlal for their tribunal had already attempted to kill them. Their captain, Rillial, had stopped them barely in time, insisting that civilized beings had to be better, to resist being dragged down into the dirt in which planet-dwellers crawled. But there was a startling amount of sympathy in the public network for the aspiring killers, and not only among the surviving Lesshchin. The attackers' memories of their violence even found their way into the back channels of the cloud despite being officially censored, though R'nilinnath was too repulsed by her brief taste to experience them in full. The ugliness she perceived in the consensus dialogues only worsened her confusion about the meaning of death. If it was such a horrible thing, why would so many be willing to inflict it on others?

When the refugee fleet reached Shilirrlal, R'nilinnath joined the large crowd that gathered as the captured ferals were paraded through the streets. The augreality feeds displayed a continuous loop of the extensive, largely symbolic decontamination and medical examination process they had been subjected to upon arrival, both to assuage the public's fears of planetary disease and as a ritual humiliation. The adults around her showed revulsion toward the primitive, destructive creatures, but R'nilinnath watched the feeds eagerly, intrigued by the anatomy of this new species, who called themselves "Hhyumhan" or something close to it. In some respects, they were surprisingly like Chirrn, with two arms, two legs, and relatively smooth-skinned bodies with discrete manes, although those manes had been shaved to the scalp by the decon ritual. Yet their skin came mostly in bland shades of brown or pale orange, their faces were flat-muzzled with a strange, tiny respiratory protrusion in the middle (how could they breathe adequately with only two nares?), and their eyes were beady and for-ward-facing, incapable of swiveling independently, so that they could look in only one direction at a time. They had no counterbalancing tails, yet somehow managed to teeter along vertically like Zenith in constant display posture. Also like Zenith, they had two distinct, permanent sexes, with genitalia between the legs; their tongues were used purely for eating and speech, with no apparent sexual function. The males' genitalia were external and surprisingly vulnerable, the evolutionary benefit of which eluded R'nilinnath. They looked quite silly, like tiny, limp tails on the wrong side of their legs. But the fatty glands atop the females' pectoral muscles were even more hilarious, as if they had oversized Chirrn eyes peering out from their chests. Altogether, they were the most awkward and ridiculous sapient creatures R'nilinnath had ever seen, which made it impossible for her to fear or reject them the way the adults did.

"Why are the Hhyumhan being held for tribunal?" R'nilinnath asked Educator Thavheth later on. "I thought they were all in hibernation when their ship destroyed Lesshchi. So how can they be held responsible for their shipmind's actions?"

Thavheth answered evenly, as though he had anticipated the question. "Arachne's duty, like that of Lesshchi's consciousness which she slew, was to nurture and protect the living beings within her. It was in service to that duty that she bombarded Lesshchi, which she had mistaken for an asteroid in the ship's path. Does that not make it the responsibility of the crew that placed her in that position?"

R'nilinnath flicked her eyes around uncertainly. "I don't think so. It was Arachne's choice, and it seems like an honest mistake. As terrible as it was, there was no malice behind it."

"Perhaps, R'nilinnath. But by Void Alliance law and Chirrn tradition, those responsible for a loss are obligated to give something in return, to contribute constructively to society to balance out the loss they have inflicted. That includes Arachne, yes, but she cannot do it alone. Lives lost must be compensated for with lives gained."

"Only six eights of lives are hardly enough."

"But those six eights intended to build an entire colony, and they have more than eight-cubed fertilized embryos in storage to begin that process. They may begin to balance the loss by building that colony here, among us. But first they must repent for their offense, renounce their planetary ties, and accept inclusion into Chirrn society. Also, the anger and mistrust of the Chirrn must be appeased before that process of inclusion can begin. Thus, it is the judgment of the Mediators' guild that the humans must undergo remedial transition. They will face an ordeal of atonement to break down their existing allegiances and values, and to persuade them of the need to seek inclusion in Chirrn society and devote themselves to restitution. It is similar to the transition process between guilds or collegia, but necessarily more strenuous given the resistance of the subjects. The ritual cleansing was the first stage of this ordeal; the tribunal shall be the second."

R'nilinnath was startled. "That's it? All the deaths they caused, and they just get to join us?"

"Many have voiced that same sentiment. But dealing with outsiders is the Mediators' responsibility, so we must accept their judgment.

"Of course, it will take much time and work for the humans to forge new identities that may earn inclusion. But we are not ferals who meet destruction with destruction. That would merely worsen the imbalance. You have seen this in your studies of planetary history, the cycles of war and vengeance that amplify hostilities to the point of mass devastation. Here in space, we understand the need for balance above all. What is lost must be restored, in any way possible.

"Besides, though it is difficult for the Lesshchin to see this through their grief, you are wise to recognize that Arachne did not act from malice. Her action resulted from the humans' recklessness, their irresponsible haste in traveling from one planet to another, rather than transitioning to a habitat-based existence as civilized sophonts eventually do. It was a crime of ignorance, and so it calls for their education. We must treat them as juveniles and raise them to become contributing members of Chirrn society." Thaveth tousled R'nilinnath's short silver mane. "Much like we have done with you, little one."

Thaveth's words intrigued R'nilinnath. Thinking of the humans as children changed everything. Finally, there would be others on Shilirrlal close to her own age and status, others who would share experiences like her own. Even better: they would be younger than she was, in status if not chronology. She would finally get to be the one passing down the wisdom of her experience to her juniors.

Best of all: they were something *new*. Something totally beyond the staid, civilized confines of the Void Alliance. Something primitive and feral and alarming to proper Chirrn adults.

They were the very thing she had been seeking for nearly her whole life.

Senior Mediator L'chellin turned his head to the side to peer more closely at R'nilinnath with his dominant eye. The cobalt-blue Chirrn grasped the edges of his vest and clicked his tongue as he contemplated her request.

Finally, he turned to Educator Thaveth. "I am reluctant," L'chellin said.

Thaveth looked surprised. "I understood that the Mediators' guild usually prefers to recruit young apprentices with no prior guild alignment. And she is from your estate, so the broader foundations of thought are already there."

"That is generally true; our specialty requires adaptability between modes of thought, and a fresh mind that has not previously been imprinted with any single guild's consensus perspective and habits is ideal for that. But that is for mediation between different guilds or factions within the Alliance, or in the case of this collegium, between the Alliance and other societies. Interaction with ferals is a far more perilous and delicate undertaking."

"But the Arachnen have renounced their planetary allegiance. They have shown repentance and accepted provisional inclusion. Indeed, they did so more swiftly than anticipated."

"The majority of them, yes. The remainder, though, have been motivated to assert their planetary allegiance and refusal to repent more forcefully, even knowing that it prolongs their confinement. No doubt a range of intermediate attitudes exist within both the Arachnen and the Unrenounced. They are simply too unpredictable for me to be comfortable risking Shilirrlal's only remaining child in their presence."

R'nilinnath snorted rudely through her nares, drawing a startled look from both elders. "First, I'm not a child anymore. As you can smell for yourself, I'm female and out of crèche. And second, what risk? They're even smaller than I am, and they don't have tails or talons or mandibles or stings or anything to defend themselves with. They even have soft glands *outside* their bodies, incredibly vulnerable to pain! I don't know how they managed to survive this long!"

L'chellin looked her over clinically with one eye. "They survived by learning to compensate for their vulnerabilities through great inventiveness, particularly with regard to weapons. They are both feral and highly creative, which makes them unpredictable and dangerous."

"And we aren't? It was Chirrn who almost beat the humans to death just after their capture. It was Chirrn who ran riot in the tribunal hall, and the humans who had to be taken away for their own safety."

"I was there, child."

R'nilinnath held her ground. "But did you really understand how it must have felt to them? How long has it been, Senior Mediator, since *you* were a child? Do you even remember what it was like? To be surrounded by people who were all bigger than you, who all understood the world better than you, who all had a sense of belonging and purpose that you didn't have yet?" Her voice shook with passion. "That's what it's like for the humans now—not just the Unrenounced, but the Arachnen too. Even though they may want to belong, they're still small and helpless and alone, afraid that they'll never truly achieve inclusion.

"And I'm the only Chirrn on Shilirrlal who still understands what that feels like."

Both L'chellin and Thaveth gazed at her in stunned silence for a time. Then they traded a long look, and R'nilinnath could not tell whether what passed between them was cloud communication or some more primal, fundamental thing.

Finally, L'chellin twitched his eyes and puffed out a breath. "Well. That was an impressive display of the mediator's skill—to open another's mind to a different point of view. I believe I have underestimated you, chi—R'nilinnath. Perhaps the words you spawn may indeed be able to form a connection with the Arachnen. And… perhaps it could be beneficial to you as well as to them."

R'nilinnath straightened, swiveling her eyes in surprised satisfaction. "Then… I can apprentice with you?"

"Provisionally," L'chellin cautioned. "And only in interaction with the Arachnen. Dealings with the Unrenounced are more delicate and hazardous, requiring expert supervision."

"That's fine. I know I have a lot to learn."

L'chellin tilted his head, shaking his cornrowed, yellow-white mane ever so slightly, the first hint of warmth she'd seen in his body language. "Indeed, young R'nilinnath. You have reminded me that there is always more to learn."

Once R'nilinnath had been formally apprenticed to the Intersocietal collegium of the Mediators' guild, been granted entry-level access to its consensus knowledge base, and had time to assimilate its insights—including a working acquaintance with human language, physical expression, and psychology—L'chellin eased her into interactions with the Arachnen. At first, these meetings took place in the administrative offices of the compound where the Arachnen resided in relative isolation until they had earned fuller inclusion, and were limited to those Arachnen that L'chellin deemed least threatening. These included the Arachnen's leader Stephen Jacobs-Wong, who had shown himself to be the one most committed to atonement and reconciliation; Kweli Ndege, the kindly female who served as the group's physician; and Oyama Kazuko, one of the human's administrators, who had not only proven gentle-natured and reasonable, but was one of the group's smallest, least physically imposing members.

Soon enough, R'nilinnath was granted permission to move out into the Arachnen compound and mingle more freely with its inhabitants.

But L'chellin advised her to steer clear of one Arachnen, Diana Thorne. The youngest yet largest of the group, matching R'nilinnath in size and mass, she was a member of a genetically modified human subspecies called Vanguardians, far stronger and faster than the others. According to her psychological profile, she was aggressive, prideful, and vain, the one Arachnen most inclined to chafe at the limitations imposed on the group, pushing for greater liberties and lacking the patience to earn them through the appropriate, gradual process. By a fluke, Diana had been one of the few crew members of Arachne to suffer medical difficulties upon revival from the ship's crude hibernation system, which offended her pride in her physical robustness and drove her to seek to prove it through other means — which included repeatedly yet futilely challenging the group's Chirrn and Zenith guardians to contests such as wrestling or climbing. L'chellin insisted that Diana was still far too feral and erratic for a young apprentice to approach safely.

Naturally, therefore, R'nilinnath decided that Diana was the one she most wanted to befriend.

She found Diana swimming in the pool in the lower level of the Arachnen's recreation center, cutting through the water with powerful strokes. Spotting R'nilinnath, the young human female swam toward her and pulled herself out of the pool in a single forceful move. A number of the other Arachnen present, mostly the males, stared at Diana's unclothed form with marked interest, and her body language suggested (if R'nilinnath interpreted the consensus data correctly) that she welcomed and encouraged their scrutiny. She did indeed stand out among the humans, the longest-limbed and most muscular of them all with the richest brown skin, topped by a vivid bronze mane that seemed to be growing out faster than the others'. Yet she also had the largest, most bulbous pair of "eyes" on her chest, which jiggled comedically as she padded toward R'nilinnath with the strange, one-foot-at-a-time gait of her species. It was all R'nilinnath could do to restrain her toes from drumming loudly at the hilarious sight.

"Well, hi," Diana said, pulling back her lips to bare straight, bright teeth in what R'nilinnath had learned to recognize as an expression of pleasure, approval, or friendliness. "You're the new kid, right? Rillanath?" She extended a hand.

"R'nilinnath," the apprentice corrected, returning the "hand-shake" in the human way.

"Ra-nilla-nath."

"Close enough. I am pleased to meet you. You swim well for a human."

"I do *everything* well for a human. I bet I can outdo a Chirrn too. I hear you guys are great swimmers, but nobody's agreed to take me on. You up for a race?"

"Always!" R'nilinnath shed her vest and leggings and began to stretch, which Diana watched with interest. "Just try to catch me!"

Diana made the pant-hoot sound that humans used for social bonding and to express amusement. "Finally, a Chirrn who doesn't have a stick up their ass! I think I'm gonna like you, Little Girl Blue."

R'nilinnath snorted. "You're the children now, remember. And I am here to educate you."

She stepped up to the edge of the pool, but Diana sidled up alongside her, draping an arm over her neck and speaking softly. "Oh, no doubt. The older kids always have the best lessons. Like the things the grown-ups don't want you to know, right? I bet you know a way to sneak me out of this place, show me around all the fun parts of Shilirrlal."

R'nilinnath hesitated. "L'chellin says you're not ready for that yet."

"Come on, what harm could it do? Unless he thinks *you're* not ready. I mean, you're so young, and this hab is so big. Really, how much of it have you had a chance to see? I bet they don't even *let* you into all the best places."

R'nilinnath bristled. "I have my ways! I can get in anywhere I want."

Diana ruffled R'nilinnath's mane with one hand. "That's the spirit. Tell you what—if I win this race, you have to take me with you."

The apprentice pondered, remembering Educator Thaveth's policy of allowing a reasonable degree of transgression as part of the learning process. It would certainly be more fun than L'chellin's orderly remedial program.

"Agreed," R'nilinnath said, resolving to let Diana win—just barely. She crouched on the edge of the pool, tensing her legs for the dive.

"Great!" Diana did the same above the adjacent lane. "Nilly, I think this is the beginning of a beautiful friendship!"

Nilly? R'nilinnath was distracted enough to be left behind when Diana launched herself into the water. Hastening to follow, she swam hard, abandoning her plan to let the human win. If Diana wanted her help pushing past the boundaries, she would have to earn it.

Still, this was the most fun she'd had in a long time. At last, Nilly had found someone her own age to play with.

Growth Industry

My name is Dorbit. I'm one of a horde of biomechanoid monsters currently invading the Earth in the name of the interdimensional Vandral Empire. And I am surrounded by idiots.

Half an hour ago, I was engaged in my usual routine. Empress Vandrala had unleashed her latest Vandrabeast, a hybrid scorpion-backhoe concoction called Scoopion, in order to undermine the foundations of Airy Harbor's major buildings. Inevitably, the first couple of collapsing skyscrapers (which, by an astonishing coincidence, had both been completely unoccupied) had brought the Hyper Sentry Jet Force to the scene, and now those multicolored jellybeans were engaged in their usual acrobatic but inefficient combat tactics against Scoopion—supposedly an advanced form of tech-assisted martial arts, but to me it always looked more like interpretive dance with fireworks.

Yet it was more effective than it looked. Even though the Hyper Sentries insisted on calling out their every attack by name ahead of time, Scoopion was taking a lot of avoidable hits. All because the empress insisted on sending in every new Vandrabeast alone as soon as it was completed, with no backup except a dozen or so mindless Fodderoids whose attacks the Sentries treated more as a workout than a threat. After all, any single Vandrabeast was worth any fifty humans, as the empress insisted no matter how many times reality argued otherwise. I knew it would only be a matter of time before the Sentries combined their individualized, color-coded weapons into the Scramjet Cannon and delivered the *coup de grace* to Scoopion, just as they had to all his predecessors.

That was where I would come in. As the prototype of the empress's Vandrabeasts, I'm too small and feeble to engage in combat; I'm little more than a furry soccer ball with a face, stubby limbs, and leathery wings. But I can flit around quite fast when I need to, and the empress's beastmaker imbued me with a unique power: I can inject other Vandrabeasts with Gargantuator Venom, kicking their growth process into high gear. Not only does this let them regenerate from mortal injuries, but by drawing mass from our home dimension, they can shoot up to giant size in a matter of seconds, large enough to tear down buildings with their bare hands.

And all thanks to little Dorbit. This invasion would be nowhere without me.

But despite my unequaled contribution to the fight, we're barely holding our own against the Hyper Sentries. Whenever I Gargantuate a fallen Vandrabeast, the jellybeans take advantage of its initial moments of disorientation to call in their Jet Mechs and combine them into the giant robot they call the Jetfire Megaknight. Week after week, monster after monster, they Megaknight up, unleash an ever-growing arsenal of superweapons, and blast our brave Vandrabeasts to bio-mechanical scrap one by one. Unfortunately, I can only produce enough venom for one injection a week, so once the beasts die a second time, they stay dead. At least I can take comfort in the property damage the giant battles cause, and the continuing drain they inflict on Airy Harbor's economy. If we can't destroy the city with fire, maybe we can bankrupt it. (Come to think of it, that's probably why there are so many empty skyscrapers.)

I keep telling General Malevolar that we should just *start* by Gargantuating the beast, so it's good and ready to trample the Hyper Sentries as soon as they show up. Or bide our time and build up a whole army of Vandrabeasts to unleash all at once. But does the mighty Malevolar, Scourge of Three Hundred and Two Worlds, listen to a furry winged soccer ball? Of course not. He has his martial pride to consider. Hard experience has taught me that questioning the orders of the empress and the general just gets me swatted aside or shocked with an energy blast. And so I keep lying in wait while my brother (and occasional sister) Vandrabeasts battle the Hyper Sentries, ready to spring forth when they fall.

At least, I did until half an hour ago, when a comical little robot shot me in the back.

Once the shock and pain faded, I looked up from the filthy pavement to see a large white quadrotor drone descending to block the exit from the alley where I was hiding. Just before touching down, the drone unfolded into a goofy-looking bipedal robot, the rotors folding back behind its limbs yet still sticking out in what looked like an unwieldy configuration. The Jet Force's arrowhead logo was outlined in LEDs on its upper chest.

"Just so you know," the robot said in a squeaky, childlike voice, "I've injected you with antivenom nanites designed to shut down your Gargantuator gland permanently."

"Don't make me laugh," I fired back, but the high-pitched timbre of my own voice made it sound less than intimidating. Despite my bravado, I attempted to deploy my stinger as an experiment, but nothing happened. I strained harder, but there was nothing, only a numbness deep inside me. I was… impotent.

"What have you done?" I cried, lunging at my ambusher. But I was still weak from the shock, and I fell flat on my face.

"What someone should have done months ago," the robot squeaked. "It didn't take me long to notice the pattern. You aren't exactly subtle about it. Every time a Vandrabeast is destroyed, you spring out of hiding to Gargantuate it."

I scoffed. "I hardly have to be subtle against those imbeciles you're working with. Every time they shoot down a Vandrabeast, they're always *just so surprised* when I shoot past them and inject my venom. I do it every single time, but they never see it coming!"

"I know, right?" said the robot. "I've tried to tell the Sentries and Professor Ishinomori time and time again. 'Dorbit is the key. Watch for him. You can avoid the whole Megaknight battle, and every one after it, if you just blast Dorbit before he can inject any more beasts.'"

"Oh, thanks a lot!"

"But because the professor made me with this thrice-damned goofy voice, they just laugh it off. They don't even listen to what I say, just pat me on the head for how adorably I say it. 'Oh, look, Whirlygig thinks she can be a Sentry like us, ha-ha-ha!"

I snorted a laugh. "Your name is Whirlygig?"

She glared back. "Your name is Dorbit."

"Fair point."

"And you're one to talk about being slow on the uptake, Vandradweeb. You're the one who always waits to inject your venom until *after* the battle. Why not just *start* with the giant form?"

If I were human, I would have blushed. That's the creepiest thing about humans, if you ask me—those nauseatingly flexible faces that move when they talk and show emotion. They're also one of the only species in the universe who don't explode when they die. They just lie there. It's deeply unnerving.

Rather than confess my embarrassment, I fired back, "Oh yeah? Well, why don't *you* just start by calling out your Megaknight? Why send puny humans after a monster when you could just stomp it with a giant metal foot?"

"Are you kidding? Do you have any idea how much it costs every time we have to deploy the Jet Mechs? And who do you suppose has to fix the damn things after every battle? Me, that's who!" She made an adorable bleeping sound that she somehow made obscene-sounding. "I'm surrounded by idiots."

"You too, huh? I suppose that's what you get when the Earth's leading line of defense is a half-dozen high school students recruited by a renegade inventor to wield a prototype technology powered by a mystical ancient gem."

Whirlygig stared. "So you *do* know their secret identities after all! Given all the Vandrabeasts that have tried to put them under evil spells or ruin their school trips, it stood to reason."

"Oh, Empress Vandrala sussed that out right off with her paradimensional scrying window."

"So why don't—No. I shouldn't suggest it."

"Why don't we kidnap their families? Expose their identities and leave them open to endless lawsuits for all the property damage they do? Or just send a giant Vandrabeast to stomp on their houses in their sleep?" Whirlygig's optic shutters widened in surprised confirmation. I sighed. "The empress's warrior pride would never allow it. The imperial court built their reputation on the ruthless conquest of a thousand worlds across the dimensions. Any perceived sign of weakness or cowardice would open them up to overthrow by their backstabbing relatives back home."

The robot nodded sagely. "Of course," she said. "That must be why your forces keep attacking *this* city, instead of all the others that don't have Hyper Sentries. Empress Vandrala needs to avenge her pride against her nemeses. It explains a lot."

"Honestly, we've wondered why you haven't just given the Sentry tech to your nation's military." I couldn't resist gloating a bit. "What's left of it after our first attack, that is."

"With our president? Are you kidding? He'd just use it to invade Mexico or something. We're in the middle of an alien invasion and he still says the real threat is illegal border crossings. Why do you think they've only quarantined Airy Harbor instead of sending in the armed forces to defend it?"

"Tell you what," I said. "Help us beat the Sentries and we'll take care of your president problem, permanently."

"Tempting, but no." She chuckled. Were we... bonding?

"It's the same problem everywhere, isn't it?" Whirlygig asked, leaning against the brick wall beside her. "A few big, loud people decide they know what's best and refuse to consider what the little people have to say."

"Exactly," I replied, nodding my whole body. "It's the curse of being tiny and adorable. No matter how wise your counsel, everything you say gets dismissed as comic relief, if not ignored outright. No matter how much destruction you have the power to unleash, even the city's defenders resolutely fail to notice you as a threat."

"Or to listen when I urge them to notice you as a threat."

"Yes! You understand. I have tried time and again to convince Malevolar of the need to adopt new strategies. Sure, sometimes we upgrade the Vandrabeasts' destructive power, but it's an incremental improvement. You're always able to match it with a new weapon, a new armor upgrade, or a new Megaknight combination."

"Oh, the professor loves designing those. Jetfire Megaknight, Bomber Megaknight, Armada Megaknight..." Her bleep sounded like a sigh this time. "You throw more brute force at us, we throw more brute force at you—it's a vicious cycle. A formula that repeats week after week and never really changes."

I nodded again. "Neither side can win this war unless someone breaks the pattern."

Whirlygig looked at me pointedly. "Like, say... if someone permanently neutralized your ability to Gargantuate Vandrabeasts."

I was very quiet for a moment. "Yes."

"Like... I just did."

"Yes," I said through gritted teeth. To be honest, though, I grudgingly respected her for taking the kind of initiative that I'd never had the guts to take. Though maybe that was because her superiors were less likely to blow her to bits for it.

"So we have a chance to end the war, don't we?" she asked.

"In your favor."

"Not entirely." The robot advanced on me with a cute, mincing gait. "Here's what I propose. You sneak me into your Vandrabase. Once there, I'll signal the Hyper Sentries, claiming that I'm being held prisoner by the empress, and that the only way to save me is to attack with all our Megaknights. You will *not* inform your superiors of your… incapacity. Once the Sentries come, your forces will be taken off guard, unable to Gargantuate, and the Megaknights will make short work of them."

"They've never tried attacking the Vandrabase before."

"Oh, but if your forces threaten adorable, helpless little Whirlygig, they'll be furious and they'll come in guns blazing. Oh, better idea: we'll arrange to fake my death when I call them for help. They'll raze the Vandrabase to the ground to avenge me, and I can always reveal my miraculous survival afterward. The Vandral threat will be ended once and for all. But since you're small and harmless, they'll overlook you — and you can slip away as the lone survivor."

I scoffed. "No wonder the jellybeans don't take you seriously. Those spinning rotors must've made you loopy."

"Have they?" Whirlygig turned to look outside the alley. I followed her gaze just in time to see Scoopion struck head-on by the rainbow energy bolt from the Scramjet Cannon. The bolt went right through the poor beast's body, and he stood there frozen in agony long enough for the Sentries to turn away and strike a heroic group pose while Scoopion fell slowly to the ground and then exploded.

I lunged forward, reflexively trying to come to my fellow Vandrabeast's aid, but I was still weak, and Whirlygig spread her limbs and rotors to block my path. Once the impulse passed, I realized it would've been useless anyway. My venom gland was neutralized, my stinger unable to deploy. Before much longer, Scoopion's burning remains would disintegrate too fully to be regenerated. I could only stand by helplessly and watch it happen.

After a few moments, the Sentries' helmeted heads began to look around and tilt inquisitively. It was starting to sink into their hormone-addled teenage brains that something had disrupted their routine. But soon they laughed it off, powered down their nanomystical armor to reveal stylish street clothes in the corresponding colors, and wandered off together to celebrate their victory at the pizza parlor that somehow happened to be the center of the city's entire social scene. Still, their jubilation seemed a bit forced to me, as if they were disappointed to miss a chance to pilot their giant fighting robot. I supposed that chance would be a long time coming now.

Whirlygig turned back to me. "Pretty soon, your general and your empress are going to start asking why you failed to show up to Gargantuate that Vandrabeast. Once they find out that you can never Gargantuate anything again, what do you imagine they'll do to you?"

"I have other uses to the Empire!" I insisted.

"Like what?"

"I... I provide valued counsel! I can... They rely on..." I sighed. "You're right. Let's face it—I'm their court jester. They mock me, ignore me, slap me aside when it pleases them. They experimented on me, mutilated me to put this venom gland in me, and I let them because it finally made me feel useful. Like I could really accomplish something for a change."

She held my gaze in sympathy, then asked, "And have you?"

"No. I just give my sibling beasts a chance to get blown up a second time in a matter of minutes. It's cruel, really."

"This war between our makers is a pointless, repetitive cycle," Whirlygig said. "It's too much of an ingrained habit for either side to break." She stepped forward and put a stubby-fingered plastic hand on my arm. "But we can end it today, you and I. We can take the decisive action in this war all by ourselves, and nobody will see it coming— *because* we're the ones that everyone overlooks."

I held her cybernetic gaze. "I do love how devious your plan is," I admitted. "And... it means a lot just to be able to talk to someone on my own level."

"For me, too."

"Still... you're asking me to help save your world. Whatever my frustrations, I *am* still evil. And I like it that way."

"I know." Her head took on a devious tilt. "But what could be more evil than betraying your own empress?"

The more I considered her words, the more excited I became. "Yes. Yes, just imagine the feeling of power, to be the one who'd single-handedly brought down the entire Vandral royal family through one mighty act of treachery!"

"'Single-handedly'?"

"True, it would mean the end of our thousand-year war of interdimensional conquest."

"Oh, such a shame."

"But let's be honest—such a massive operation doesn't leave much opportunity for a squirt like me to do any real evil. At least until I had the damn gland installed, and that just made me a slave to the gland."

"Sounds like someone deserves to be punished for that."

"Sure, but *after* that… the internecine squabbling back home, the jockeying for power among the remaining nobles, the black market that would thrive in the ensuing chaos…"

"I see what you mean. Those are places where a small, clever, seemingly unthreatening monster might find numerous opportunities for evildoing and personal gain."

I hesitated. "As long as none of Vandrala's surviving loyalists back home found out about it. Sure, they'd probably fall fast in the ensuing civil war. There's a lot of disaffection over the resources being wasted on this stalled invasion. But a few loyalists might last long enough to assassinate the empress's betrayer."

Whirlygig chuckled. "They'd have to know who that was first. Sounds to me like, for once, there might be advantages to being overlooked."

I stared at her. "Like how you were able to stay overlooked long enough to trap me."

"Not unlike that."

I would've grinned wickedly if I had facial expressions. "All right," I told Whirlygig, waving my hand to summon a dimensional warphole back to the Vandrabase. "Let's do this."

The robot brandished her weapon. "No tricks, remember. I can do worse things to you than neutralize your venom gland."

963.understands me."

Whirlygig's eye shutters irised wider. "Me too. It's such a relief to get all of this off my fuselage at last."

"Whirly," I said as we stepped into the warphole, "this could be the start of a beautiful—"

"Don't push it."

Aleyara's Descent

— From *The Ballad of Aleyara's Descent*,
attr. to Baralihu Narrayo Lya
(trans. by Madeleine Kamakau)

Aleyara leapt with sure-footed abandon along the tightly woven branches of the ground. Energized by curiosity, her leaps grew longer, faster, shaking off the moisture that had condensed upon her bright magenta scales. She spread her arms for balance, stretching out the mantelets that extended from her elbows to her hips, and turned her body sideways so the membranes would not slow her as they caught the airy body of Skyfather Halai. Still, the brilliantly patterned mantelets fluttered in the wind, as did the open-sided triangular garment she wore to accommodate them. Tickled by wind and enthusiasm, Aleyara inflated her neckpouch and let out a ululating cry of pleasure. The others shushed her, fearful of being caught, but Yara doubted the laugh of one Biauru would stand out in the clamor of the rainforest.

Still, as they neared the place where the body of Rulai grew thin, the youngsters heard the distant cries of hunter-scouts echoing through the fog. The children spread their mantelets to brake their forward rush, their long toes grasping the branches to stabilize them. "We *have* come far," said orange-scaled Mirele, the eldest of the group. "Those accents are not of Diurailya Village." All scouts shared the distance-language, concise in words and long on vowels to carry through the canopy's din; but each province or solitary village had its own near-language that tinged the timbre of the vowels. Mirele tilted her head, listening. "They must be from Raubyelinyu Province, across the Rift."

From closer by, they heard an answering cry as another scout relayed the news toward Diurailya, then an echo of the same as the next scout called the news back home. "We're two whole calling-lengths away!" exclaimed Rinutela, the youngest, most timid male. "They must be missing us by now."

"Don't worry, we're almost there," Mirele hissed. "Can't you hear Eloro's Roar?"

Over the endless cackling and chirping of the canopy, Aleyara could now hear a distant roar like heavy rain. She shuddered; it was the voice of Eloro, Lord of the Under, bellowing in envy of Rulai and Halai and the glories of life they had created. Ever covetous, Eloro pulled constantly on all living things, dragging them down toward the Under so He could make them His own. Only the firm wooden body of Mother Rulai held the Biauru against Eloro's pull, until finally their bodies tired of the fight and died, and their souls descended to the Under.

Now the children had reached the place where lifeless bodies were delivered to the Under to be reunited with their souls. Here the woven body of Rulai was thin, with gaps unfilled by the soil and vivid green foliage that covered most of the canopy. Through the gaps, the children could see the dense infrastructure that supported the world: an intricate network of massive wooden buttresses and trusses, all growing outward from the huge pillars that bore the canopy's weight, descending infinitely into the Under. Aleyara peered down, seeking a glimpse of one of the mighty columns, even though she knew they were found only at the thickest parts of the canopy. The village of Diurailya had been shaped within and around the upper part of one such pillar, and Aleyara had been raised in its shadow. Still, she couldn't help looking for one as she gazed into the roaring darkness below.

Mirele noted Yara's fascination and laughed sharply, her neckpouch convulsing. "I dare you to climb down there."

Yara's muzzle tightened in annoyance, but she kept it from her body language. She thrust her streamlined head defiantly at Mirele. "Don't you think I'd do it?"

"What? Pampered Aleyara? Lovely daughter of Orihinu Resinsmith? Precious of all the boys, that they'll do anything for?"

Yara pulled her head back and shook it distastefully. "Boys? I'm not interested in them."

"You will be soon enough. And they're mad for those exotic blue scales of yours."

"I'm not blue," Yara said, fidgeting. "Just purple."

"Blue enough for them."

"You shouldn't be jealous," Aleyara assured her. "Your crests are filling out big and dark." Self-consciously, Yara stroked her own twin dorsal crests, paling next to Mirele's, which flared out wide and comely atop her lacertilian head and joined at the base of her spine in a sharp and shapely tail.

"Oh, I bet yours will too, any month now," Mirele countered. "And then what males will crow for my attention?"

Nervous at this talk of sex, Aleyara retreated to the safer subject of the afterlife. "Whatever may come, there's a challenge been offered. You dare me to climb down and spy the face of Death? Well, I'll do you better—I'll call at old Eloro's door and ask Him to come out and play. You can have your boys, Mirele; I prefer the gods for my dance partners."

Aleyara leapt forward with an insouciant somersault and landed on one of the thick branches stretching out into the Rift. She let her momentum flip her forward and hung upside-down, tilting her head at her alarmed clanmates. "No worries, friends," she called. "I'll be down and back quicker than Motai can steal the fruit from the Dragon King's table!" She let herself fall, doing a showy flip around two axes before catching a lower branch. "Oh, yes," she called up, hanging cavalierly by one four-fingered hand, her thumb-claw digging into the wood to anchor her. "I could do with the lantern down here. With Miyuro in the day sky playing the moon, the Under will have no sun to light my way."

Rinutela carefully tossed her the lantern, and Yara caught it by its rope. She wrapped the line around her wrist and held the lantern in her right hand as she proceeded into the latticework of the Rift, using her other three limbs to hold on. The lantern was of her own family's manufacture: a wooden frame coated in hard flame-resistant resin, with clear resin walls around the sides to hold in the fire and openings in the top to let it breathe. Inside, the flame flickered in surprise, shaken by Aleyara's acrobatics, so she sang to it soothingly. "Burn steady, little Eiroai," she cooed. "Surely a child of the Sun need not fear the darkness."

She sang as much to comfort herself as the captive flame she carried. The misty light from above grew distant, the commotion of the greenwood becoming faint. New sounds came to Yara's ears, sounds of burrowing and crawling. She caught glimpses of some of the creatures that dwelt among the canopy's branches, those that dared the open spaces of the Rift: pale, huge-eyed lizards; sinuous serpents with dozens of tiny legs; and those odd, furred beasties that skittered around comically under the soil. And of course countless insects, like everywhere else. Aleyara caught an unfamiliar kind of crawler in her toes and brought it up to her mouth; it was surprisingly tasty.

Soon Rulai's limbs grew sparser as Eloro's Roar grew louder. Yara could see pure blackness beyond the few Tree limbs below. She thrilled; here was the very Under itself, the realm few Biauru had ever glimpsed and lived to sing of. As she stared upon it, frozen with awe, she began to feel as though it were gazing back....

But the feeling was not from below, she realized. Her dorsal crests tingled, sensing subtle movements in the air behind her. She spun — and beheld an apparition just a few armlengths away. It was Biauru-like, but pale and colorless, with huge, dark eyes. It had to be an *elobyeru*, a departed soul reunited with its body. She gasped.

The ghost reacted with a squeal, leaping away.

Aleyara jumped, startled, losing her grip.

The ghost spread its limbs and fell away on full-grown gliding mantles, the kind every Biauru dreamed of, and Yara felt a twinge of envy —

— as she plummeted toward the darkness that had no end.

Aleyara had barely begun her prayer for Eloro's favor when she jerked to a stop. The lantern broke free of its tether, and she watched absently, frozen in shock, as it plummeted downward, downward —

— and smashed against something solid and distant, no doubt a tree limb very far down. Bright sparks flew out just before the fire fell dead.

After long moments gazing at the darkness, Aleyara pulled her wits together and looked up. Wrapped tightly around a branch were the three front toes and the clawed hind toe of her own left foot. Her brachiator's instincts had served her well, catching her on the last branch she could possibly have caught.

Aleyara let out a crow of relief. "Thank you, foot!" she cried breathlessly. "Your quick thinking is immensely appreciated, and I promise to be very nice to you from this day on!"

As Aleyara scrambled back toward the bright, living surface, damning Mirele for the dare and herself for taking it, her mind traveled back to what she had seen. The Biauru eye was keen, as it must be to sift through the visual chaos of the rainforest; but there had been only one thing for Yara to see when that lantern had met its end, and as she reviewed it, the details came vividly. Those hadn't been sparks that had flown from the branch when the lantern hit.

They had been birds.

Orihinu Meraliya Diu ruffled her neckpouch in disapproval. "Young lady, you're in trouble enough already without adding lies to the mix." The low-hanging sun shone severely through the blood-red wall of resin behind her, giving her a fearsome aspect.

"It's not a lie, Mama," Aleyara insisted nonetheless. "They were birds! As certain as those hanging there for dinner are birds!" She gestured to the two *herutihui* over the washbasin, for which older brother Reyalihe was singing thanks to Tihui'iuri the Feathered Queen before he plucked them.

"Nothing lives in the Under, Yara, any babe knows that. If you saw anything, you saw ghosts. The ghosts of birds, perhaps, or dragonets."

"Well, what of the *elobyeru* I saw? That was no spirit."

Reyalihe laughed. "Silly girl," he cawed. "How is a ghost not a ghost?" He stood in the light from a green resin panel, giving him an annoyingly numinous air. The Orihinu house, like the Diu clan-house of which it was a branch, was built similarly to the lamented lantern, a framework shaped from the living branches of Rulai and the treelets that grew atop Her, filled in with multihued panels of the firm, translucent resin which the Orihinu family crafted from Her blood.

"Get back to your prayer," Meraliya warned her son. "We don't disrespect the gods in this household." She turned back to Aleyara. "And that includes Eloro."

"It breathed, it spoke, and I heard its mantles flapping in the wind! I was as close to it as I am to Reyalihe, and it was as alive as he! Maybe more," she amended, drawing a glare from her sibling.

"You say it glided," her mother scoffed. "No Biauru has glided since Aeli'inaru lost Eloro's Wager to Motai."

"Save those who refused to join her in her exile on the ground."

"And Halai cursed them for their disloyalty to their matriarch, shrinking their bodies and minds to those of glider-lizards."

"Well, maybe he changed some to *elobyeru* too."

Reyalihe, now finished with his prayer, croaked in disdain and tossed some feathers at his sister. "Don't you know any of the songs? The *elobyeru* are the dead, the glider-lizards are the cursed. That's basic."

"I know the songs better than you, Lihe!"

"Then you know I'm right."

Aleyara didn't know how to respond. Finally, her mother sighed and stroked her daughter's head-crests. "You had a shock, dear one. No wonder your senses were addled. I blame you none for being frightened and confused. I was just angry out of fear for your safety. So let us turn our minds from this and back to our dinner, where they belong."

"Very well, Mother," Aleyara said, subdued.

"Good. Do me a favor, will you, and chew some *leirra* fruits for your baby sister?"

> In days to come, her mind turned back to ordinary chores.
> She spoke not of the Under, for no others wished to hear,
> And no girl's panicked sights could outshout all ancestral songs.
> But she remembered, and she wondered still....

> Each year the heavens' dragons soared across the sky by night
> To mark the days they triumphed o'er the fiery comet-snake.
> Four times the fulgent cavalcade had lit Nurairo's realm
> When golden wings descended from the sky.

> To Aleyara's eyes it seemed the vast celestial drake
> Which bore the bright sunfruit across the sky was flying down.
> But then who raised the sun from the red flower of its birth
> So that it shone behind the dragon's wings?

The morning was fine and clear, with no rain and little mist to obscure the glory of the dawnflower Eiyai. Even Halai for all His passion knew that the Great Mother had many responsibilities besides Her lover's pleasure, and thus could not share His embrace every day.

Aleyara, though, could not avoid the attentions of males. True to Mirele's prediction, Yara's crests had filled out richly, seeming engorged even when they weren't. And this month they truly were engorged, proclaiming her fertility, so she could barely go anywhere without the young males puffing their bright necks, spreading their iridescent knee-length mantelets, and striving to outdisplay each other for her favor. Yara had made it clear that she wasn't ready for motherhood and would lie only with females until her fertile phase had passed; yet the boys still crowed and pranced for her nonetheless. She thanked Rulai that it only came six times a year.

So it surprised her when the males' amorous alalaes gave way to cries of wonder and thumb-claws pointed toward the rising sun Eídi. She joined the crowd that gathered to watch the approach of the mighty *ruyui*, its featherscales a gleaming gold rivaling the sun itself. Could it be Himoruyu the Dragon King on some divine errand?

But as the gleaming pterosaurian descended toward the village clearing, a Biauru became visible upon its shoulders. The golden-scaled rider was marked as male by his large, vivid red neckpouch and the intricate arabesques of red, orange, and green upon his long mantelets. The *ruyui* was also male, its teardrop head bearing two triangular crests whose scarlet hues increased the visual harmony between mount and rider.

By this point, the entire village recognized their visitor, and many called out the name he had earned: Byéliaruyu, the Dragon Minstrel. The Singer of the Skies was a legend; his travels took him across the world, spreading news and knowledge, trading songs for goods and skills, helping to bind the many communities of the rainforest together through the power of Meliala'ai, his dragon. Tamed ruyui were not rare, but they lacked the stamina and range of Meliala'ai's breed, whose allegiance was all but impossible to win.

As the mighty *ruyui* settled, grasping a thick branch firmly in his two taloned feet, the rider inflated his pouch and gave forth a mighty cry. For a moment the whole canopy seemed to fall silent, entranced by the beauty and power of his voice, confirming beyond all doubt that this was Byéliaruyu and no other.

Before the echoes faded, the matriarchs of Diurailya were bounding forward to greet their prestigious guest. They were shortly joined by Diurailya's chief minstrel, Ueribele Hiradai of Clan Lya, and her apprentice, Baralihu Narrayo Lya, a mahogany male of Aleyara's age. Narrayo threw an excited look at the gathered adolescents, who called to him in celebration. Narrayo's yellow neckpouch puffed with pride.

After the greetings had been exchanged, the Dragon Minstrel turned to the sky and sang thanks to Halai for supporting him through his journey, then crouched to the ground to thank Rulai for welcoming him back into her verdant arms. *The ritual has never sounded lovelier*, Yara thought.

With the prayers done, Byéliaruyu rose and addressed the assembled villagers. "My greetings to you all, new friends, and thanks for your bright welcome. I come from distant lands, have crossed the body of Rulai, to bring you news, exotic songs, and novel goods to trade."

"What trade do you bring?" asked the Rai matriarch. "And whence comes it?"

"From realms so far, they lie beyond the verdure of the Tree."

"Beyond Rulai?" cried young Narrayo. "What could lie beyond Her Who is all the world?"

Minstrel Hiradai patted his shoulder maternally. "He speaks of the *Nilyoro*, the Lifeless Ground."

"You mean... the land of Stone and Metal?" Narrayo lowered his head, his orange crests blushing. "I thought it just a fable."

"It's fabulous indeed, young bard," said Byéliaruyu, "and farther than the sky. But very real Nilyoro is — as tangible as this!" He gestured, and an object appeared between his clawed thumb and the middle finger it directly opposed. It was a disk three fingers wide, gleaming the color of Byéliaruyu's scales.

This was Aleyara's first glimpse of metal. Yet the Minstrel said this was no ordinary metal, but a rare and precious one named "gold," of which the medallion he passed to the villagers was just a sample. The people of the Nilyoro city whence it came had heard of the skill with which the Rulabiauru shaped the resinous blood of Rulai into so many different and beautiful forms and wished to combine that craft with their own goldsmith's arts. Byéliaruyu brought forth finely crafted lantern-frames of gold that he showed to Aleyara's mother. Meraliya asserted that it was strange stuff indeed but assured him she could learn to work with it in good time.

In return for Meraliya's service and the village's hospitality, the Dragon Minstrel promised to regale Diurailya that evening with tales of his distant travels. The villagers clamored for him not to wait, but he averred that his long journey had left him in need of food and rest. Meraliya invited him to take those things in her house as they discussed business. "And maybe you could repay me with a song or two," she cooed.

"I'll share my songs with all this evening meal, good resinsmith," smiled Byéliaruyu.

Meraliya moved close, stroking his dorsal crests at neck level. "Ahh, but couldn't you indulge me with a private serenade?"

The Minstrel's neckpouch puffed a bit, and a trilling chuckle emerged. "We shall see, my lady." Meraliya led him off, her hand sliding down his crests toward more sensual territory.

Aleyara turned at a barking laugh from her old rival Hanilitya Mirele, now an apprentice hunter-scout for Clan Diu. "Your mother's hunting for her next husband," Mirele mocked. "And she thinks she can snare the Dragon Minstrel himself from the sky!"

Yara glared at her orange-scaled clan-sister. "You should be glad if she succeeds, Mirele. If Byéliaruyu marries into Clan Diu, you might get *your* turn as his spouse in time."

"The Sky-Singer tamed and tethered to one village? You'd have as much luck training Motai to perform His tricks on cue."

"It's a brave one who mocks the Trickster." The new voice pleased Aleyara, for it was her childhood friend Daranui Tirenu of Clan Rai, a slender scarlet male with a bright green neckpouch and lavender crests. The comfort she felt in his presence always offset Mirele's abrasive nature.

"Are you prepared to face the tricks He plays on you?" Tirenu went on. "Or would you like me to pray to Himoruyu to hold Him back?"

"An apprentice nine months and you think you're a shaman," Mirele shot back. "I'll take my chances with Motai. I can take a puny dragonet any day, no matter how divine."

Before Tirenu could remind her of the Trickster's shapechanging skills, the gold medallion had made its way through the villagers' hands and finally reached their little group. "How strange," Aleyara gasped as she examined the unexpectedly heavy artifact. "To touch something that has never been alive."

She offered it to Tirenu, but he demurred. "I'm not sure I want to. It seems... unholy, somehow."

Aleyara was disappointed, barely noticing as Mirele snatched the metal from her hands. She had hoped her friend could share her excitement at experiencing something new and alien. It was a thrill she hadn't known since the day she'd gazed upon the Under.

Aleyara's hunger for the alien was richly sated that evening by the Dragon Minstrel's tales. He told the villagers of his journeys to the edge of the Tree, describing the peoples there and their exotic ways. Then he spoke of how the surface of the world sloped down, its foliage growing thin, until finally it gave way to the rocky ground of the Nilyoro, on which only smaller plants grew the way they grew atop Rulai.

Byéliaruyu told the Nilyobiauru's tales, passed down for generations, of how their forebears had settled the land. For ages the Biauru on the edges of Rulai had gazed out at the realms of stone, curious to see what wonders they held. But their forays always came to ruin, for the Nilyoro was populated by vast saurian beasts. Byéliaruyu sang of herbivores with bodies the size of clan-houses and necks longer than the body of Himitiye'ye the Serpent King. Then he chilled his listeners with descriptions of the predators who fed upon such awesome beasts: packs of fearsome ground-dragons the size of *ruyui*, whose keen sense of smell made it nigh-impossible for prey, once scented, to elude their deadly jaws for long. As he limned these savage hunters with his words, it became clear why the Biauru had avoided the stony lands for so long. How could they hope to survive amidst such giants?

But finally, the Minstrel sang, the people of the Tree learned how to craft the stone and metal they gathered in their forays, making potent new weapons that could take down a pack of ground-dragons or even their colossal prey. This, and the metal armor that shielded them from dragons' teeth, let them move out into the Nilyoro and make it their new home. Now, generations later, the Nilyoru lived in an uneasy truce with their unliving land and the behemoths who dwelt upon it.

With his tale done, Byéliaruyu invited questions from the children. Most asked about the saurians and the Nilyoru's battles with them. Some asked about the Nilyoru's religion, which perceived life as a contest between gods of good and evil. At one point, though, a child asked, "Does the Nilyoro have an Under?"

Aleyara looked up, startled by the thought. The rest broke out in laughter. "Foolish waif," Mirele muttered.

Byéliaruyu was more diplomatic. "Of course the Under gapes beneath Nilyoro, little one. In places there, the ground has cracks and holes, which they call caverns; they clearly are Eloro's maws, although the name is changed. They dump their bodies there to find their souls, just as we do."

"So," another child asked, "does the rock and metal rest upon the Branches, like the soil here?"

"Though strange to say, it seems to go beneath Rulai's green arms," the Minstrel answered. "Indeed, the Tree grows sparse, her legs appearing as mere treelets. But surely soon within the dark, the ground comes to an end, and gives way to the endless night of Lord Eloro's realm."

Aleyara pondered for a moment, then abruptly spoke, interrupting the next child's question. "How do they know?"

The others looked at her. "Know what, young Orihinu?" the Dragon Minstrel asked.

"That the ground ends within the forest. Have they seen the edge?"

"Oh, none would dare to delve so deep into the Under's cold. Or sure, if any fools have dared so far, they've not returned."

"So no one really knows what happens to the ground beneath the trees, do they?"

"We know it ends because it must, my curious dear lass. All know there's naught beneath Rulai but formless dark and death."

"Of course we all know this," an embarrassed Meraliye spoke up, taking her daughter's arm. "Now hush, Aleyara, and stop wasting Sky-Singer's time questioning what everyone knows."

Aleyara fell silent, satisfying her mother. But she didn't hear another word of Byéliaruyu's songs.

Yara slept fitfully and overlong, her rest troubled with dreams. She was disappointed when she emerged late from her house to see golden Meliala'ai receding into the distance and the villagers dispersing back to their daily lives. "Oh, Byéliaruyu is gone?" she moaned to her mother.

"For a while, my child. He's gone to share his news with the other villages hereabouts. But he'll be back within two moon-phases to pick up the goldwork I'm finishing for him." She chuckled. "What a word — goldwork."

"A shame," said Yara. "I think I had a vision in my dreams last night, and I wished to ask him about it."

"Well, surely a mother can do when no bard is to be found," Meraliya said, wrapping an arm and mantelet around her daughter's back. "What vision troubles you?"

"I'm not sure it troubles me — maybe it inspires me. At least it explains four years of wondering."

"Then please, share it with me!"

Yara turned to face her mother excitedly. "I dreamt the lifeless ground of Nilyoro did not end within the dark beneath the Tree. I envisioned it stretching on below us all, with the pillars of Rulai resting upon its back!"

Meraliya pulled back in shock. "What are you saying?!"

"Don't you see, Mother, it explains it all! If the Under is not the bottomless death we fear, but just another place where things live and grow, then all I saw back then makes sense! The living ghost, the birds deep down, the riddles are all answered!"

"You blaspheme!" Meraliya cried, pushing her away. "How can you say these things, you of all of us, who have looked upon the endless dark below!"

"But if it's so dark, how can we truly know it's endless?"

"Because it *is!*" Meraliya lowered her head in shame, her body trembling with rage. "I knew you were a dreamer, Orihinu Aleyara, but I'd hoped you weren't a fool as well. The greater fool am I for doubting it!" Without another word, she bounded away, deaf to her daughter's keens of pain and shock.

"But, Minstrel Hiradai, you must see the reason of it!" Aleyara exclaimed. "There's ground beneath the Tree to the south. There's ocean to the north. But that much water can't just rest atop the branches like the bathing-pool! Its weight would break the arms of Rulai and smash through, like any pool that grows too large! Only the solid ground could hold it! And if the ground is on both sides, then why not below as well?"

"Don't think to tell Rulai what She cannot hold," Hiradai warned. "None but Motai is fool enough to question the Goddess of us all. Motai and now you, I see.

"And what of Eloro's Roar?" the minstrel added. "If nothing's there save rock and soil, then who cries out in rage?"

"I heard the Roar up close that day, and I heard no rage within it. It was just a noise, like rain falling or a flock of birds taking flight. I don't know what it is, but I know what it isn't!"

"No. You *think* you know. The warped perceptions of a frightened child cannot outshout generations of song."

"But who wrote those songs? And how did they know what was true?"

"The songs tell us how to live, how to survive! If your soul is deaf to them, you may as well hurl yourself into the Under!"

"Fine," Aleyara cried, storming out. "You may just get your wish!"

Aleyara fidgeted as she waited outside the temple. Finally the door-curtain of wax-coated, flower-adorned leaves was pushed aside, and Tirenu emerged, his stance apologetic. "I'm sorry," the apprentice cleric told his friend. "The shamans refuse to hear you. Indeed, with the ideas you're spreading, they wish not even to hear your name."

Aleyara hissed in frustration. "Is all of Diurailya so deafened by old songs that they can hear nothing new?" she cried.

Tirenu moved closer, taking her hand. "You have to realize, Yara—these are strange and frightening things you're saying. They're in discord with everything we know."

"With everything we *think* we know," she countered. "We only know the songs say thus. I know what I've seen with my own eyes, heard with my own ears! I could sing to you a tale wherein a child named Aleyara fell into the Under four years past and died. But the song wouldn't erase the sight of me from your eyes, or the warmth of my hand from your touch!"

"But you could just as well invent a tale of seeing birds in the Under, and *elobyeru* who live and breathe!" Tirenu turned away and crouched upon a branch. Yara crouched alongside him as he spoke again, subdued. "Yara, you know I am your friend, and I admire your mind, your will, and your perceptions. But how can you ask us to hear the voice of one young Biauru more loudly than those of all our forebears?"

"You're right," Aleyara said. "One voice is not enough. That's why I need to go down into the Under and *prove* it has a bottom!"

Tirenu leapt to his feet, staring at her in shock. "*What?!* You can't mean that!"

"What other way is there?" Yara cried, leaping forward to clutch him by the shoulder. "If my voice won't convince them, I must bring proof. I'll lead a quest into the Under! We'll find the plants and animals that live there and bring them back! For surely different kinds of life have been found in every new place where Biauru have ventured, haven't they?"

"Uhm, yes, they have. But—"

"And we'll need a bard, of course, to chronicle the saga."

"Aleyara!" Tirenu cried. "All this talk of 'we'... are you asking me to come?"

"I couldn't do it without you, dear friend! There must be a cleric along. If we're going to find new life, we'll need an expert on the ways of living things. If we're venturing into danger, we'll need a healer." Yara tilted her head sardonically. "And if my certainty proves wrong, and the Under is but bottomless death after all... well, then we'll surely need a shaman."

"Aleyara, I can't!" Tirenu threw a nervous glance at the temple and moved closer to her. "If they knew I were even listening to you, I'd be in trouble. If I did what you ask, they'd never let me be a shaman."

Aleyara looked at him sadly, angrily, her dainty coral neckpouch trembling. "I really thought you were better than the rest of them, Tirenu. That your mind was open enough to hear new truths. That you wouldn't abandon me when I need your help, just so you can please the voices of tradition. Well, fine! I'll go alone if I must." She tried but failed to suppress a keen of sadness. "It seems I'll be alone here anyway." And she turned and hopped away.

"Aleyara! Wait!" came the cry moments later, drawing closer behind her. Tirenu caught up to her and held her by the arms. "If it... if you're so sure of what you believe, I can't dismiss it out of hand. I... I respect you too much for that. So...." He repressed a shudder of fear. "I'll go with you. You're right, you'll need me."

"Oh, Tirenu!" Yara threw her arms around him and nuzzled his head with hers. He nuzzled back, striving to keep his neckpouch from puffing up to full display.

Baralihu Narrayo whooped with laughter. "You want *me* to join you on this crazy quest of yours?" the apprentice minstrel cried. "Are you sure you haven't been fertile too long? All that blood engorging those lovely large crests can't leave much to spare for your brain."

"I'm nearly past my phase now, not that it's your concern," Aleyara told him curtly. "And my mind is clear in a way it hasn't been in four years."

"Well then, my mind must be addled for even listening to you. If you hadn't won Tirenu to your cause, I wouldn't even grant you that, beauty though you are."

"But Narrayo, I need a minstrel! My quest won't seem real if it isn't in a song. Without your help, they'll never believe me no matter what I find!"

"Your faith in me is flattering, my lady," the bard-to-be replied with a courtly flourish of his mantelets. "But I'm a singer and a lover, not an adventurer. Apprentice or no, I've sung enough tales of death to know I don't wish to be featured in one."

"You don't know there'll be death. If I'm right—"

"Ha! *If!* More deaths have come from *ifs* than arrowheads."

"Ahh," Aleyara purred, moving in close. "But if there were no *ifs*, would you have any songs to sing? An *if* is a risk, and risks can lead to glory and triumph. Think of it, Narrayo," she went on, stroking his headcrests. "If we come back from the Under alive, we'll be the first ever to do so. Our exploits will be sung down through the ages. And if you come with us... then *yours* will be the words they sing!"

Narrayo trembled in excitement, then whooped a raucous laugh. "You're a seducer, Aleyara, and you should've been a bard. You've played me like a lyre." He sighed. "I'll join you on your quest. It's mad—but madness oft is that with which the seers are blessed."

"You're a fool, Aleyara."

Yara hung her triangular tunic on the clothes-branch and waded into the village's bathing-pool. "I know, Mirele. I'm a fool for questioning tradition and going somewhere *everyone* knows is death, even though they've never been there like I have."

"No," Mirele shot back as she joined Yara in the communal bath. "You're a fool because, when you're planning a quest this dangerous, the *first* person you should recruit is a hunter-scout."

Yara gaped at her clan-sister. "Are you volunteering?"

"Well, you're stealing two of our most promising apprentices. Someone has to look out for them, even if you're expendable."

"Very droll, Mirele. With that attitude, I'll feel ever so safe with you watching my back." She splashed away in irritation.

"Hey, wait!" Mirele called, catching up to her. "Listen." She hesitated. "You... you never could resist a dare. It was my dare four years back that almost got you killed. Now that you're taking this even greater dare... well, I have to do what I can to keep you alive. And I know I can't talk you out of it, stubborn fool that you are. So that means I'd better come with you."

"Mirele, I... I don't know what to say."

"A pleasant change, believe me. Narrayo's told me of your winning way with words. Just...." She met Aleyara's gaze searchingly. "Just tell me that it's real. That you know what you speak of."

Yara answered plainly. "I know what I saw, and what I believe it means. The proof is in the quest itself. That's all I can tell you, Mirele."

"Oh, wonderful. Well, if nothing else, it's a bold way to die. I'd prefer nothing less, I suppose."

The secrecy of the expedition made it harder to equip themselves properly. Fortunately, Rulai was a generous mother, and the four young adults were able to make many of their own supplies from the flora and fauna of the greenwood. What they couldn't make, they contrived to borrow, in the flexible sense of the word.

But as soon as they were ready, the four youths gathered at the edge of Diurailya and called forth the villagers from their morning tasks. "We journey to the Under," Aleyara announced, "to prove that it does have a bottom after all. We will prove it is a place like any other, by bringing back samples of the life that dwells there."

The villagers were outraged. The foursome's parents all came forth and commanded them to remain. Aleyara made way for Narrayo to address them. "Your commands touch us, for they prove your love. But the time has come for you to face the fact, as all parents must, that we are babes no more. We are of age to make our own life choices; the peril of our choice does not change that. Take heart; we shall return. And should we not... well, in time, when you fall to Eloro's pull, you'll find us legends in the Under for the boldness of our quest."

Talayuni, the head shaman of Diurailya, hopped forward sternly. "It is true—we cannot stop you from choosing this mad course. But at least one choice is still in my hands. Tirenu," he intoned sadly, "if you join Aleyara in this blasphemy, then you reject your faith... and so the faith must reject you. If you do not stay with us, you will never be a shaman."

"What should it matter?" Tirenu countered. "If Aleyara's wrong, then I'll never return anyway."

"The choosing is what matters. If you reject the gods, then in death you will wander blindly through the Under, never knowing what is there, never reunited with your ancestors and loved ones. That is the path your friends have chosen. But it's not too late for you! Come back to us! Renounce Aleyara and her insanity! Eloro got His claws in her four years back, and now she is His toy, scheming to bring more souls into His grasp! She is cursed, and you must condemn her!"

"No!" Tirenu cried, the echoes bouncing across the canopy. "You're wrong about her," he went on more quietly. "I don't know if she's right... but I trust her enough to take the risk with her. She is special! She sees things you aren't willing to see! And if all you see in my friend is evil... then I cannot trust your sight. And I cannot follow your shaman's path. Forgive me, Talayuni."

"That is for Rulai to choose." Talayuni turned his back, dismissing Tirenu from his life. The clan matriarchs followed his lead, and the clans followed their matriarchs. Aleyara and her band had not yet left Diurailya, but now they were alone.

The other three looked to Aleyara, and she met their gaze firmly. "Truth doesn't come from numbers. Let's go prove them wrong."

Fortunately, there was now a closer access point than the Rift to the east. The year before, a region to the southwest had succumbed to parasites, the branches collapsing and forming a sinkhole into the Under. No one had yet used the site for burial of the dead (except themselves, Narrayo joked), but it had become a convenient place for garbage disposal.

"I can't hear Eloro's Roar through here," Tirenu said in puzzlement.

"No one can," Aleyara said. "So maybe it's not the howl of a god after all, but just some sound of nature. Odd that none have thought of that before, eh?"

She chose to descend more carefully than she had the first time. As they climbed down to the thick supporting limbs of the canopy, Aleyara, Tirenu, Narrayo and Mirele were tied together by a rope around their waists. This bound their lower mantelets, restricting their arm movements a bit, but it was an acceptable trade-off for safety. Hunter-scout Mirele took the lead, carrying one of their lanterns. The clouds were heavy this day, and it was dark even atop the canopy.

They followed the branchings of Rulai's limbs in reverse, knowing this would ultimately bring them to one of the vast columns that held up the world. "Tell me, Yara," Narrayo asked. "How far shall we travel before we decide there is no bottom and turn back? Or do you propose to make a life's career of climbing down the Tree?"

"We'll go as long as we can on the supplies we have and those we can find along the way."

"Just remember," Narrayo replied, "down is the easy part."

"Shush," Mirele hissed, and the party froze. "Watched, right and left," the scout whispered, using distance-language for its brevity.

Yara looked around, eyes straining to see what she'd been expecting to see. "Cloak light," she advised in farspeech. Mirele did so, and the party let their eyes adjust to the dim glow that remained from the enswathed lantern and the overcast sky.

Soon, Aleyara saw that her hopes were answered. "They're *elobyeru*," she whispered. "Watch them close, and see they are alive."

The Under-people seemed as curious about the Biauru as the reverse. Over a dozen watched from nearby limbs, keeping a cautious remove and tensed to flee at the snap of a twig. Aleyara met the eyes of one and was struck by the intelligence she saw.

"I hear their breath," Narrayo whispered. "And the rustle of their scales. You were right, Yara—they are alive!"

"So... what do we do now?" Tirenu asked at length.

"I'll go forward alone," Yara told him. "I'll call softly, see if they answer. Mirele, give me the lantern."

No answer came. "Yara!" Tirenu hissed. Aleyara looked and saw Mirele was gone. She'd slipped free of the rope and nestled the lantern in a crook between branches.

"Mirele, where are you?" Yara whispered sharply. She got no more response than she expected—until moments later, when a deafening battle cry pierced the darkness. The *elobyeru* froze, confused by the echoes, as Mirele fell from above and landed atop one of them. The others scattered, leaping from the branches and spreading their gliding membranes, as Mirele struggled with her quarry.

"Mirele!" Yara cried. "What are you doing?!" But the *elobyeru* had broken free and Mirele was starting after it.

"Don't worry!" she called back. "I got a rope around its waist; it can't spread its mantles!" Then she was gone, chasing it through the branches into the darkness.

"Don't hurt it!" called Aleyara. The only reply was a series of sharp, shrill yelps. "What is that?" Yara asked.

"The echoes tell her where the limbs are," Narrayo told her. "A trick for night-time hunting that I've heard about in songs."

Many eights of heartbeats passed before Mirele rejoined the party. Slung over her back was the *elobyeru*, bound hand and foot and trembling in terror. "Now we can look up close," the hunter-scout said, lowering her burden to the wide limb on which they stood.

Aleyara faced off angrily with her. "I did *not* say you could do this!"

"I didn't ask you to say!" Mirele shot back. "You forget I'm the eldest."

"And the rashest. You can't just attack every beast we find. What do you plan to do with this poor creature? Skin it and cook it for dinner?"

"It's alive, isn't it? You should thank me."

"Thank you for making our first act in the Under a predatory one? No, Mirele." She strode closer, staring down the taller Biauru muzzle to muzzle. "I'll thank you to remember that my vision drives this quest, and *my* voice!"

"Please, ladies," Tirenu urged. "The poor ghost is terrified enough without your shouting!"

Aleyara sobered. "He's right. We shouldn't add still further to his fear." With one last glare at Mirele, she knelt by the *elobyeru*, moving forward to untie it. Its terror increased and it began to struggle, so she fell back and simply studied it.

It was small, about three-fourths a Biauru's size. It was as huge-eyed as Yara remembered, and as colorless. "His mantles have no patterns, no scales," Tirenu observed.

"Ours had none until Eloro's Wager was lost," Narrayo reminded them. "Rulai endowed our shrunken mantelets with brilliant hues so we could look on them with joy instead of shame. The *elobyeru* can use their mantles still, so they have no need of colors."

"Maybe it's simpler than that," Aleyara mused. "They live in the dark, where colors can't be seen."

"They were supposed to be the dead," Tirenu breathed, and said no more.

Again Yara tried to approach the creature, but it was still too frightened. She sighed, pondering. "Friend," she told it softly in distance-language. "Friend."

"What are you doing?" Mirele asked.

"They live right under us; they must have heard farspeech all their lives."

"But they haven't seen what we've done while we spoke it."

"Ears and nares can tell as well as eyes." She continued speaking softly to the *elobyeru*. "Friend. No attack. We seek. No attack."

Maybe it was just the softness of her voice and manner, but finally the creature let her touch it and carefully undo the ropes. "You go," Yara told it. "Friend." She waved the party back. The *elobyeru* darted to the next branch, then watched them warily. "Let's move on," Yara said.

The living ghost's eyes remained upon them for a good way down.

The dactyls of the Tree grew vast as further down they climbed
Until Rulai's majestic lignous leg the heroes clutched.
So massive was this column that three eights and four Biauru,
Their arms stretched wide, could barely gird it 'round.

From here the climb was straight down to the foot, if foot there stood.
For safety's sake, the hunter-scout advised descent in pairs.
The leader and the healer and their lantern formed one chain;
From scout and bard did hang the other light....

As further they descended through the fabled realm of death,
The life in its diversity descended not one step.
Strange beasts and bugs of every kind did dwell within the Tree,
And many more familiar breeds besides.

The foursome proceeded down the massive bole with care, their thumb and toe-claws anchoring them firmly in the bark, with the finely textured scales at the tips of their digits providing extra traction. They stopped at many points to examine the insects, lizards, birds, and rodents they found living in burrows and fissures in the trunk, and those that flew past as well. Many of the insects had a surprising quality: they generated their own light. "Like the *nurruyui* who patrol the heavens," Narrayo laughed, "so the Under has its own bright planets."

"Quite small for dragons," Mirele countered.

"But truly children of a dark world," Aleyara beamed. "Let's catch some and keep them in one of the lanterns. Thus we'll hold some to take back home as proof, and benefit ourselves by saving firewax."

"There's no doubt now, Aleyara," said Narrayo as Mirele gathered the green-glowing insects, "that the Under is as rich with life as the Above. With each step I grow more certain of your rightness."

"It could still go down forever, for all we know," Mirele growled.

"You are a source of hope and joy to us all, fiery-scaled warrior."

"Oh, go jump into the Under," Mirele cursed, before realizing what she'd said. The others laughed heartily.

"Here, what's that below?" Tirenu cried, and the others looked down, Yara and Narrayo with excitement, Mirele warily.

"Let's draw nearer," Yara advised. They climbed down a few more body-lengths until the lanterns clearly showed the large fan shapes that grew out from the Tree bole. "It's not the ground," Aleyara sighed, not really surprised.

"But it might support our weight," Mirele said. "You all could use a rest."

To the climbers' relief, the fans were thick and sturdy enough to hold them and their supplies — although the two pairs stayed on separate ones nonetheless. There were dozens of fans wrapped all around the bole and extending who knew how far down. "Some sort of fungus," Tirenu judged after tasting a bit of the skin. "We can eat these, I'd say. If they continue, it could save us carrying so much food."

"But they might make the climb more awkward," Mirele added. "Our claws might rip through these. We'd have to find a new approach."

"May I suggest we find it in the morning?" Narrayo asked. "I don't know how far we are from nightfall, but we've surely done more than a full day's work."

The others acceded readily, making camp on the huge fungal shelves. Tirenu judged that they would burn easily, so cooking was out of the question; they limited their meal to plants, insects, and pieces of an adjacent fungal fan. Narrayo entertained them with songs and jokes until they decided to turn in.

Mirele advised using their dragonclaw pitons to secure their hammocks to the bole, rather than lying on the flat fungus and trusting that they wouldn't roll off. That left the question of how to share the two cocoons. "So which of you ladies will take my love tonight?" Narrayo asked, puffing his pouch seductively. "If you'd care to fight for the privilege, I'd deem it an honor."

Mirele grabbed his wrist and pulled him against her. "There'll be no contest. If Yara gets command, then I get the minstrel."

"Enjoy him with my blessing," Aleyara called as Mirele began to strip the willing male. Then she turned to meet Tirenu's gaze. "I have all the company I need this night."

"Aleyara!" Tirenu cried. "I... I would be honored."

"Is honor all you feel, my sweet?" Yara asked, stroking his lavender dorsal crests. They barely noticed the other two climbing noisily into their hammock.

"No," Tirenu sighed. "Delight as well." He shuddered as her caresses moved farther down his compact, masculine crests, her fingers darting below the low backline of his tunic. "And surprise, that you would choose me. I thought you only saw me as a friend."

"Once I did," Yara told him as she began to slide his tunic off. "But I admire you for your courage. You took a stand for me, Tirenu. You chose me even over your shaman's path." Now she had him nude and began to shed her own tunic. "Narrayo came for fame, and Mirele out of duty. But only you of all Diurailya could see with me that there might be more than dogma, that there was merit in searching for new truths. And I love you for that." She pressed her throat to his, coral against green, and fluttered her neckpouch, making him shudder. His own large pouch inflated, vibrating eagerly against her daintier one, and he let out a trilling cry of passion. He stroked the fine scales of her mantelets, their patterns less colorful than his yet equally intricate in their feminine way.

Aleyara gazed at him with a warm tilt to her head as she led him into the hammock. "Oh, Yara, my adored," Tirenu moaned. "I'm not worthy of this."

"You are worthier than any I've known," she assured him. Then her claws were against his crests, stroking their insides, sliding down the exquisitely sensitive dorsal membranes, clear down to where they met in a tapered, concave tail. Aleyara's claws scratched excruciating joy across its contours, and for the rest of the night Tirenu knew only ecstasy.

The next morning was still overcast, and Aleyara resigned herself to another day of climbing in darkness. Worse, there appeared to be a fog not far beneath them. "There won't be much to see beyond our arms' reach today. Let's hope this is a morning fog that clears before too long."

"Wait," Narrayo said as they gazed down from their fungal shelf. "Something's not right. Something with the sound."

Mirele's voice grew excited. "He's right. Fog dulls the echoes. This sends them back. Quick, a lantern!"

With the others holding her up, Mirele leaned out from the fungus and lowered the light as quickly as was safe. It neared the fog-bank, illuminating its lumpy grey surface. On reaching the surface, the lantern... stopped. The line grew slack and rested on the grey expanse.

The young Biauru stared at it for long moments, then stared at each other, eyes wide. Aleyara whooped in joy and began a hasty clamber down the fungal shelves. The others joined in her crowing and followed her down.

Then she was on the surface, fallen to her elbows and knees, feeling it, slapping her hands against it. The grey stuff seemed to be another sort of fungus, but underneath it was... "The ground! The bottom! This is *it!*" Aleyara shot upright and bounded clumsily yet eagerly across the strange surface, delighted to feel hard, level ground beneath her feet with each landing. Tirenu grabbed the pioneering lantern and hurried after her lest she become lost.

When the others caught up, she leapt one last time, clear over their heads, and pulled off three joyous flips before her feet touched the ground again. "I thought we'd climb for days before reaching it, even moon-phases!" she laughed.

Mirele stared. *"Moon-phases?!"*

"But here it was barely a dozen body-lengths below us all night long!"

"Amazing," Tirenu breathed. "It's really here... and so close below the Tree."

"How far do you think we climbed?" Narrayo asked.

"Nearly fifty-four body-lengths straight down the bole," said Mirele. "We're maybe seventy-two, seventy-six lengths below the surface."

"Where is the rock? The metal?" Tirenu asked.

"The stories of Nilyoro say they mostly lie below handspans or even body-lengths of soil," answered Narrayo, who apparently had been studying up on the distant realm.

"So how do we really know this is the same thing? It could be another layer of branches."

"Tirenu, have you ever known branches to make a surface as smooth as this?" Aleyara laughed. "Look at it! How flat it is, how uniform!"

"I can hardly stand," Narrayo complained. "There's nothing to clutch. And my claws get snared in fungus."

"Stay on your toes," Mirele advised, "with your claws held off the ground, like when you hop."

As the others practiced this art, Narrayo spoke a bit unsteadily. "So whither shall we set our course, noble and wise leader?"

"East," Yara decided. "I want to know what really makes Eloro's Roar."

"A worthy pursuit. But I pray what makes the roar is not as angry as it sounds."

The explorers made their way east slowly, for there was much to stop and look at along the way — starting with the ground cover. The fungus formed a cohesive mat; when Tirenu made a wide slit through it and pulled, it lifted easily off the ground. Aleyara made sure he took a sample, while Mirele examined the dirt beneath and its inhabitants. "Look," she cried at one point, snatching a writhing form into the air. "It's like a serpent but has no legs!"

"The bugs here aren't as tasty as in Rulai," Narrayo observed.

"The soil is less rich," Tirenu told him. "That would weaken the flavor."

Yara looked up at the dim, distant canopy. "I suppose the soil here, and its life, must depend on what falls from Rulai. With only the leavings to feed upon, no doubt the living things would be less robust."

They next turned their attention to the nearest of Rulai's pillars. Its base was almost a reflection of its capital, with large wooden buttresses sloping outward, helping to support the incomprehensible mass above. They spent some time digging away at the surrounding fungus and dirt, observing how the buttresses branched into the ground. "They're roots!" Aleyara realized. "Like the treelets above! Only so much huger."

"Not fully like them," Tirenu countered. "The treelets draw their nourishment from the body of our generous Mother. In turn, She thrives upon the life-force Her children provide her in death, completing the cycle. Down here the life-force is too sparse to nourish the body of Great Rulai."

"What if..." Aleyara began thoughtfully. "What if the pillars of the Tree begin as separate treelets? Then they grow to massive size, and their branches intermingle, growing tight and tangled, to form the canopy?"

"I... suppose it's possible," said Tirenu. "They could have been driven to it by competition from other treelets."

"But there are no other treelets here," Mirele put in.

"That's what spawns my thought. Perhaps the... the treelets of Rulai adapted, as all forms do, to win the contest by growing high and cutting off the light and rain, starving their competitors."

"Yes!" Yara cried. "And that could explain the *elobyeru*, couldn't it? Maybe both our races' forebears lived among the branches, and when they grew solidly together, some were trapped below! And in the dark they lost their colors and adapted to live in the vaults below Rulai instead of on Her surface." She looked to Tirenu curiously. "Does that sound true to your shaman's ears, my love?"

Tirenu resisted meeting her gaze. "I'm no shaman, Aleyara. Not anymore. All this new knowledge, my whole world remaking itself around me... anything could be true."

"Yes!" Aleyara hugged him. "Isn't it glorious?"

For lunch, Mirele captured several examples of an odd species that seemed to be one big muscular foot inside a spiraling conical shell. They proved surprisingly tasty; and after some work with his *hyeraloi*-horn knife, Narrayo was able to make their shells into serviceable wind instruments with low, plaintive voices. With Tirenu and Mirele accompanying on the shells, Narrayo treated the party to his preliminary, unfinished draft of "The Ballad of Aleyara's Descent." He and Yara got into some lively arguments over the content, particularly on the issue of factual reporting versus aesthetic embellishment.

In one respect, the amorous bard was eager for accuracy, plying Yara and Tirenu for the details of their previous night's lovemaking, which they laughingly provided. "Ahh, but to truly capture the experience," Narrayo purred to Yara, "I'd have to know your love firsthand. Will you have me, my song's beauteous hero, in the name of art?" He spread his mantelets and puffed his throat seductively.

"You're so obvious, Narrayo. That doesn't make my crests throb. Besides, Mirele's never liked to share."

"It's true," Narrayo sighed. "There's much negotiation ahead of us there." Mirele glared at him. "Well... certain things are expected of a male who sings for a living!"

Aleyara laughed. "No doubt why you became a bard! Obvious again, my friend."

"Ahh, but even were it not so, your splendorous violet scales would always make me crow."

"Well, if it's my scales you like," Yara said, "I'll let you have the next coat I shed." She stroked Tirenu's lavender crests. "I have the only lover I need right now."

"But he'll have to move on come the time for your second child. I pray you'll consider me for a sire then."

"I owe you the consideration, for all you've done for me. But whatever males may be my future husbands," she said, gazing at Tirenu, "my first one shall forever be my love."

A rain of sorts was falling from above. Halai must have been making love to Rulai once more, and some fraction of His seed trickled through the soil and branches of the canopy to drop upon the ground. It was a relief to the explorers to feel the familiar wetness upon their heads.

Another relief after the unTreely quiet of the Under was the growing volume of Eloro's Roar, now rivaling the everyday tumult of the canopy. It made Mirele even more alert for sounds of attack, and soon her vigil bore fruit. "We're being watched."

Aleyara turned to her. "From where?"

"Above. I was watching a flock of birds that made their own light. As they flew past one of Rulai's pillars, I saw pale forms clinging to its bark. I think they're *elobyeru*."

Yara beamed. "Wonderful!"

"How is it wonderful? They may be preparing an attack, in retribution for ours on them."

"*Yours*, Mirele. Remember that." That brought a glare from the sullen hunter. "No, I don't think they're hostile. They outnumbered us, but when met with danger, they fled. More likely they're curious. Maybe they even wish to be friends." She called up softly to the creatures, repeating "Friend!" in farspeech.

Mirele watched her askance. "Be as friendly as you like. I'll stay on my guard."

"You always do, Mirele."

"Really?" the taller female muttered. "Then what possessed me to come on this—*oof!*"

Suddenly Mirele fell backward, landing right on her sensitive tail. Aleyara winced in sympathy even as she wondered how the sure-toed hunter-scout could have stumbled. "Something tripped me! *Ow!*" Mirele cried.

Aleyara saw it—a large bump, nearly an arm span wide, rippled through the fungal mat. "Something must be crawling on the ground," Tirenu said, "under the fungus!"

"Not for long," hissed a livid-crested Mirele, gingerly rubbing her tail. "Whatever's there has damned itself for dinner!"

Mirele leapt upon the mound, but whatever creature moved below the mat slipped out easily from beneath her weight. The cloaked mass led Mirele on a merry chase, with the other three Biauru laughingly joining in the hunt. Mirele tried her bow, but the arrows' dragontooth points failed to penetrate the beast, merely becoming stuck in the mat.

"Let's steal its concealment and meet our foe!" Mirele howled. Drawing the carving knife from Narrayo's pack, the hunter cut a wide slice through the fungus and began ripping it away, soon creating a bare patch on the ground. The others managed to surround the lump and herd it toward the gap. Finally it emerged, a low-slung creature whose shieldlike shell was well-made for pushing around beneath the fungal mats. Mirele mounted it again, this time with no mycoidal carpet between them, and soon she managed to flip it on its back, revealing muscle-feet like those of the hornshells from lunch, rippling helplessly. Mirele took entirely too much pleasure in killing it, Aleyara felt. At least she remembered to sing a brief leave-taking prayer to Rulai first.

"I hope there isn't some other god I need to thank," Mirele said as she began to cut the meat out of the shell. "What god guides the spirits of things like this?"

"Eloro, perhaps?" Narrayo asked. "Any thoughts, Tirenu?"

Tirenu's pose was resigned. "I couldn't say. I—"

He broke off at a loud clamor from above. "The *elobyeru*," he called. "Something's agitated them!"

A large shape burst from behind a nearby buttress root and pounced upon Tirenu with a screeching roar. He fell, striving to keep its jaws from his neck.

Aleyara screamed his name, but then more creatures leapt from the shadows. Her keen eyes registered saurian quadrupeds with sinuous tails, long, flexible necks, and heads with forward-pointing eyes and needle-sharp teeth—like the *rutyu* that preyed on small birds and rodents in the canopy, but as large as *elobyeru*. Even as she registered this, one of the giant *rutyu* (*horutyu*?) pounced at her. She rolled with it, pushing the beast off with her feet. She leapt upright, but another creature was already lunging. She spun and kicked, gouging a deep furrow in its flank. The beast collapsed, a major muscle severed, and tried to limp away.

Her crests sensed the other *horutyu* lunging toward her back. She prepared herself for pain, but then she heard a *whish* and a *thunk*, and the *horutyu* fell dead alongside her, one of Mirele's arrows in its heart.

"Tirenu!" she remembered, turning to her lover's aid. The scarlet male still struggled beneath his attacker. He dug his thumb-claws into the *horutyu*'s neck, drawing blood. The injured saurian broke off its attack before Tirenu was forced to kill it, to his clear relief.

Narrayo, either the wisest or the luckiest of them, had leapt up to the fungal shelves surrounding the Rulai bole and was roaring with full pouch inflation at the *horutyu* who besieged him, trying to drive them off through sheer volume. One of the beasts managed to pull itself up onto the shelves, bringing its jaws within snapping distance of the minstrel; but another of Mirele's arrows pierced the roof of its maw, and it fell dead. Yara dove in slashing, and her claws left their mark on two more raptors.

The *horutyu* fell back but continued watching them, emitting throaty growls. "They just want the meat," Tirenu realized. "The crawler thing we killed. Let's move away and let them have it, and they should feel no need to fight us more."

Mirele hated to lose her culinary revenge, but she was warrior enough to know when to retreat. They bounded hastily away, and the pack did not follow.

"Interesting," Aleyara mused. "The *elobyeru* clamored just before the beasts attacked. Perhaps they meant to warn us, eh, Mirele?"

Mirele puffed her throat cynically. "You're a dreamer, Aleyara."

"That I am. And my dreams have spoken true so far."

As Eloro's Roar grew near, the darkness seemed to diminish. "Of course," Aleyara said. "We're nearing the Rift. More light is getting through from above."

Mirele peered forward. "I think I see a gap in the trunks ahead," she confirmed. "And... is that a gap in the ground as well?"

The others saw it too: a nearly straight line cutting across their field of view. "Come on," Yara cried, bounding ahead faster.

When she drew near enough to see it clearly, Aleyara's shock slowed her feet. She halted near the edge of a roaring chasm. Dozens of leaps across, the opposite side was a sheer wall of stone, more of the stuff than she'd ever imagined seeing in her life. It stretched to both sides, farther than her vision could reach even in the moderate light beneath the Rift. The huge anchoring roots of Rulai's pillars, both here and on the other side, grew outward from the edges of the gorge, beyond the layers of dirt and fungus, and bent sharply down to hug the stony walls. Dug deep into the stone were numerous vertical fissures, making the chasm wall seem like a crosswise strip of bark enlarged a thousandfold. Water trickled steadily down those furrows, as though they had been carved as its conduits.

As Aleyara and her friends peered down, they saw the destination of that water. The bottom of the gorge, dozens of body-lengths down, was filled with the stuff, and it flowed with raucous haste to the north. "So this is the voice of Eloro's rage!" Narrayo cried. "A river! But running not through a channel in Rulai, like those we know of, but through the stone instead!"

"But Rulai rests upon the stone," Aleyara countered over the roar. "And rivers are found where Her body dips far down, as far as this. Maybe those rivers run in the ground as well, and the canopy descends to meet them!"

"So why does this look so different?" Mirele countered.

"It's just a thought," said Aleyara.

"At this point, wise lady, I question nothing you envision," Narrayo told her with a gesture of homage.

"So now you know what makes the Roar," Mirele said. "What do we do now? I tell you this heartbeat, I'm not trying to cross *that*."

Yara pondered. "Let's head north, following the flow. After all, if the water rushes so madly to get there, its spirit must have some fine cause for going."

As they went, they had to climb and leap over the many thick roots that grew out from the trunks and snaked beyond the rim. After so much flatness, it was a relief to travel almost normally again.

"This proves for sure," Tirenu said as he gazed down at the river, "that this ground is not just a crust with bottomless Eloro beneath it. The stone is even thicker than the canopy!"

"But then what do stone and metal rest upon?" Narrayo asked. "And what pulls down on us, if not Eloro's covetous clutch?"

"Perhaps the answers lie down there," Aleyara suggested. "We thought this ground was deep, but that river's deeper still. Maybe there are yet more levels to be found."

"Remember, Aleyara," Mirele warned, "the farther down we go, the harder the climb back up! I thought we'd come to prove the Under was *not* bottomless!"

Soon they made a new discovery, one whose surprise came in its familiarity. "They're bones," Mirele said as she knelt to examine them. "Biauru bones!"

"Are you sure?" Aleyara asked. "They're so decayed and broken."

"She's right," Tirenu confirmed somberly. "I know these shapes from the shamans' scrolls. These are undoubtedly the bones of our own kind."

"The Rift," Narrayo whispered, looking above. "Where the dead are sent down to be reunited with their spirits."

"This must be... where they land," Yara continued, feeling weak.

"Many must fall into the river," Mirele supposed. Even she was subdued at the sight. "But the Rift is wide. I reckon most of the bodies land on the cliffs." She looked up, blinking in the rain. "These must be from Autyurei Village. I'd heard they'd had a deadly fever recently. These bones must be recent, else they'd be more eaten."

"Eaten?" Tirenu cried. He leaned weakly against the Rulai root beside him. "Oh, Mother Rulai, sustain me," he sobbed.

Aleyara hopped to his side, caressing his arm. "What troubles you, dear love?"

He met Aleyara's eyes, his gaze unsteady. "Aleyara... I've been trying not to think on what all this means. I've tried to treat it simply as a puzzle, a study of nature."

He whirled, gesturing angrily at the bones. "But this... this shows our fate upon our deaths. No reunion of body and soul, no eternity. Our corpses just fall and shatter on the ground and get devoured by scavengers!

"Where is Eloro's Realm?" he shouted. "Where are the souls of our forebears?" He looked up, his head darting frantically around. "Our Mother is just treelets. The Death Lord is just a river, His realm just dirt and stone. Our ghosts are just animals, pale travesties of ourselves!

"Where are the gods, Aleyara? Do they even exist? Do our souls exist?" He leapt over to the scattered bones and picked up a decaying skull. "Or is this our only fate? An ignominious plummet, tossed out like the trash? A destiny as fetid fare for burrowers and bugs?"

"Tirenu, I don't understand," Aleyara told him. "I thought you shared my urge to find new truths."

"I never wanted to find *this!* To find that all I've believed was but a fancy-song like those we use to tease our children!"

"You don't know that!" Aleyara said more sharply. "All we see here is that things are different than we thought. We haven't disproved the divine or stripped the meaning from life."

She took the skull from his hand. "This skull that once walled a proud Biauru head is rotting away, that's true. But that means it's becoming soil and will cradle and nourish new life. Its essence will help sustain this mighty trunk that rises above us. This trunk is a part of Rulai our Mother Tree, who sustains us. And so it forms a cycle: She feeds us, and we feed Her. It's no different from what we see above.

"What this means, Tirenu, is that the spirit of the Goddess and the spirit of the Biauru are one. That the spirit of all life is one. Does that mean we have no souls? Or does it just mean that our souls' path is different than we thought?"

Tirenu was silent for a long moment. "I don't know," he finally said, slumping by the Rulai root. "Your words sound fine, but this quest has shown that words are not enough to know the truth. The words of all our ancestors sung in chorus can still sing false. So how can I know what's real?"

Aleyara sat beside him, pondering. "Maybe nothing is real until you've witnessed it yourself. Maybe the truth is something you must discover piece by piece."

"But then what is left to believe in?"

Yara contemplated that for a time, then wrapped her arm around him. "I believe in you." He met her gaze, and she tilted her head warmly. "If we can believe in ourselves, and in the ones we love, then maybe the rest will follow."

Tirenu sighed softly and returned her embrace. She pressed her throat against his—but they were distracted by Mirele's cry. *"Yara, jump!"*

They looked up to see a massive serpent head descending. Yara leapt aside, pulling Tirenu with her, barely avoiding the clash of its jaws. She rolled to get a look at their attacker. It was the very root they'd been leaning on, she realized—or rather, a huge serpent whose scales mimicked the bark of a root. Its head must have been hanging over the cliff edge, lying in wait for prey to settle against it.

As they ran, the serpent pursued them, its body tearing free of the fungal mat grown over it. *It must not usually have to chase after its meals,* Yara thought. She hoped its skill at the chase was thus limited.

Mirele shot arrows at the beast, but few penetrated its bark-like hide. One shot hit a vulnerable spot, and it reared back. Mirele crowed in triumph—but the root-serpent had merely reared back to strike, which it did with awesome speed. Mirele scrambled back, but fell over a Biauru ribcage, perhaps a grisly presage of her own fate. The monster's jaws clamped about her leg, and she screamed.

The root-serpent pulled, but Mirele dug her claws into the ground, and Narrayo gripped her arms with all his strength. Mirele cried as if her leg would be torn off any moment—as indeed it surely would.

But then shrieks came from above, and loud thumps began around them. Something hit the serpent's head, then another something. It roared and released Mirele's leg, and Narrayo pulled her close.

Above them, to Aleyara's astonishment, the *elobyeru* glided, leaping from the vaulting limbs of the Rift to hurl broken branches upon the serpent. Their aim was keen, and their projectiles fell from such a height as to hit with great force. It wasn't enough to stun the beast, but surely enough to enrage it. The serpent lunged after them, its whole body tearing free of the fungus.

By now some of the *elobyeru* had glided to the ground. Some were scaling the Rulai boles with all their speed, but others scampered across the fungal mat, trying to outpace the serpent. Aleyara picked up Mirele's bow and resumed shooting at the beast; Tirenu gathered some of the ghosts' projectiles and hurled them himself.

As the serpent's tail went by her, Mirele leapt upon it, heedless of Narrayo's cries, and dug her claws into its hide. Yara and Tirenu ran alongside, bombarding its head. One *elobyeru* stumbled and squealed as the serpent reared up to strike. But Aleyara made one mighty leap, spinning in midair, and landed between them, firing one last arrow right into the creature's mouth just as Mirele had done with the *horutyu* before.

The serpent convulsed, roaring. Mirele crowed, "You've killed it!" But in its death-throes, its tail lashed out beyond the cliff, taking the hunter-scout with it.

"Hang on, Mirele!" Narrayo cried, reaching for her desperately as the tail began sliding more rapidly over the edge. Aleyara and Tirenu leapt upon the beast, trying to hold it back, and the minstrel got a grip on his lover's wrist. But the serpent convulsed one last time, sending its dying body and the four Biauru over the edge.

"Leap clear, grab the roots!" Yara cried, acting on her own words. She pushed off toward the nearest root, spreading her mantelets to slow her fall. She caught the root, and her claws dug deep furrows as she braked herself. She looked down to see that the others had followed her lead... but Mirele clung near the bottom of a root and Narrayo hung from her good leg, with only sheer stone within his reach.

"I can't hold on long!" Mirele cried. Yara and Tirenu began climbing down toward them. But Mirele was weakened by her wounds, and just before Tirenu reached her, her grip gave way. She and Narrayo plunged into the turbulent waters below.

Without hesitation, Aleyara leapt after them. "Yara!" Tirenu cried, then sighed and followed her down, praying the fall was survivable.

There were moments of wet, roiling darkness; then Yara's head breached the surface, and she sucked delicious air. She felt a hand upon her and recognized Tirenu's scarlet scales with joy. Then Narrayo and Mirele pulled them up onto a floating branch they'd managed to find, and the party was together once more.

Aleyara heard distant cries above and searched for their source. The *elobyeru* scampered along the cliff edge, calling out to the Biauru.

The cries had no consonants that she could make out... but their vowels and their cadence matched the farspeech word for "friend."

The sheer stone cliffs to either side, like great rectangular teeth poised to crush them, ensured they'd not be leaving the river soon. Luckily there was enough driftwood in the current for them to capture and lash together into a crude floating platform.

Sadly, many of their supplies and samples had been left up on the cliff. At least Tirenu still had his healer's supplies, which he used to mend Mirele's leg as best he could. "Will I hop again?" she asked, afraid of the answer.

"I think you will, but I don't know how well. It depends upon the care and rest you get over the days ahead."

"Worry not, hunter," Aleyara told her, a comforting hand upon her shoulder. "You will bound fast and far before long. You're too stubborn to accept any less."

Mirele placed her hand wordlessly upon Yara's. Finally she spoke. "I suppose I owe you an apology. About the *elobyeru*."

"It's them you owe the apology."

"Yes," Mirele sighed. "And my life." She met Aleyara's gaze. "There are wonders here beyond any in the songs. And your vision brought us to them. I'm glad I chose to follow it."

"We'd not be here to see these visions if not for you."

"Not me alone. That shot that felled the serpent was superb."

"I only mimicked you, Mirele. So again you saved us all." Mirele lowered her head abashedly. Then she pulled Aleyara into an embrace of astonishing tenderness.

By now, darkness was rapidly falling, and one lantern had been lost. Fortunately they retained the one that housed the glowing insects. By its cool green light, Aleyara made her way across the raft to where Tirenu crouched in thought. She wrapped a mantelet around him and fluttered her throat against his headcrests. "How are you, love?" she asked.

"Unworthy of your love," came his soft answer.

"Never!"

"Yes!" The tilt of his head was ashamed as he faced her. "You said you loved me for my courage, my openness to new things. For being the one who truly believed in your vision. But I never did, not until we came here."

"But you made the choice to come, against all the pressures of community and faith."

"But not because my mind was open." He looked away. "I only came because... I wanted to impress you. To please you. To be near you. I let you think I shared your vision, but all I wanted was to share your body and your love. So if you love me for my insight, then your love is based on a lie."

Yara pulled him closer. "No, Tirenu," she said after a pause. "To defy tradition, to speak out against the chorus and choose this path... that took courage, no matter what drove the choice." She turned his head to face her. "And if you loved me enough to follow me even into the realm of death... then I must love you all the more."

He shuddered and threw himself into her arms. "Ohh, Aleyara!" he cried, pressing his throat against hers. They stayed that way well past the fall of total blackness.

Paradoxically, sunrise was beautiful in the Under. The radiance of Eídi burst through holes in the Rift, piercing through the early-morning fog to create sharp-edged shafts of gold descending from the heavens.

It was the only source of pleasure the Under gave the party for some time. The river remained rough, the cliffs remained high, and food was scarce. The denizens of the canopy had little skill in fishing. They made do with what insects they could extract from the branches of their crude raft.

Yara spent much time examining the jagged cliffs, for there was little else to see. With the water ever spilling through the deep, vertical furrows, she wondered if the water itself could have carved away the stone. Could soft water affect solid stone so deeply? Though after her fall into the river, Yara mused, she would never call water "soft" again.

After another day of travel, the cliffs finally began to fall away, and the canopy above their heads grew closer and more sparse. Finally it reached a point where the limbs of Rulai grew right into the water, perhaps filling the role of roots to help sustain the vast compound organism that had once been Aleyara's entire world. "This is why the Biauru never saw the ground, even around the rivers," Tirenu said. "The canopy grows out well beyond the edges, hiding the ground."

Those branches began to impede their raft's travel; but better still, they enabled the party to leave the raft altogether. Here the canopy was thin compared to what they'd passed through before. Soon the four explorers stood atop Rulai once more, basking in the brilliance of the sun and the beauty of the vivid blue sky. "I feared never to know the light again," Narrayo crowed, spreading his arms to the sky. "O Great Eídi, fruit of the Dawnflower, rain your luminous nectar down upon me! My eyes have never known a taste so glorious!"

He turned to the others. "This moment must be celebrated, my friends. In honor of the sun who warms us, and in honor of our valiant leader," he said, bowing to Aleyara, "I improvise these verses of our ballad:

"When Motai in his mischief snatched the sun's flame with his tail,
Rulai said, 'Let it burn,' so Trickster dropped it in his pain.
Tihi'inaru found it, and with wisdom tamed its rage
And brought the boon of fire to all his kind.

"So daring Aleyara snatches secrets from the gods;
So brave Mirele bears the pain that such a theft does bring.
So Yara plumbs the darkness, and with wisdom sees its light
And brings the Under's truth to all her kind."

Aleyara's crests blushed, but she and the others crowed in appreciation at the end.

"But this raises one great question," Mirele interjected. "I've no idea how far we've traveled. How will we get home to bring these truths?"

Aleyara looked to the northwest, where their river met a larger one, and where a movement caught her eye. "The answer may be before us," she told the others. "Come!"

They were slowed by the need to carry Mirele, but soon they were close enough to make out a flock of wild *ruyui* with brightly colored featherscales. "They could be our ride back home," Aleyara proposed.

"*They* could?" Mirele asked skeptically. "True, they're not of Meliala'ai's breed, but they're still wild. Riding-drakes are bred for allegiance. With these, we'll have to earn their trust. And that's no easy thing."

"Tirenu knows how, with his shaman's arts. Don't you, love?" Aleyara asked.

Tirenu hesitated. "I know the principles, yes. There's Tihi'inaru's Song, with which he tamed the *ruyui*. And the rituals Aeli'inaru used to appease Himoruyu Dragon-King to give his leave to ride them." He sighed in dismay. "But what good can they do? The myths spoke false, we know that now. How can I win the *ruyui* over with a lie?"

Narrayo stepped forward. "There are many truths to be found in a song, good shaman. Even a song of make-believe can hold meanings that affect our real lives."

Aleyara took his hand. "What we've found doesn't destroy everything we've known before. It just forces us to look at it differently. There's much in the ancient songs that works. Songs of planting, of harvesting. Songs of what's safe to eat and what kills. Songs that tell what herbs can save a life or ease the pain of the dying. Maybe the reasons behind these songs aren't what we thought... but they still work.

"Don't the shamans' songs speak of the cycles of life? Don't they tell that all living things must grow and change, and must be able to adapt to the changes of the other life around them to survive, just as a singer must follow the changing chords of a song to remain in harmony?"

"Yes," Tirenu said, "they do."

"Then surely changing our beliefs does not destroy them. Instead, it helps them to adapt, to endure, even to thrive. And what is good within them will live on."

She fluttered her throat briefly against Tirenu's. "Sing Tihi'inaru's songs, my love. Make Aeli'inaru's rituals. Maybe they don't work by appeasing the gods; maybe they simply please the *ruyui*. But they work. You can make them work... if you believe in yourself, as I believe in you."

"As we all believe in you," Narrayo added, taking his hand.

Mirele took his other hand and tilted her head warmly. "All of us."

Tirenu's throat fluttered with emotion. "All of us," he finally trilled. With a deep breath, he took a hop toward the *ruyui*.

If there was one thing any Biauru could appreciate, it was a dramatic entrance.

When Aleyara and her comrades descended into Diurailya Village atop four iridescent *ruyui*, it created a stir even greater than that caused by the return of the Dragon Minstrel the day before. Far from the cold farewell they had been given, the revenant youths were met with crows of joy and tight embraces from their families and friends. Mainly it was just relief at seeing their loved ones returned to them... as Aleyara now understood that their harsh farewell had sprung from fear at the prospect of their loss. There had been moments on the journey when Yara had feared never seeing her kin again, and so she understood and forgave what the villagers had done.

But when they began to tell of their adventures, the ears and arms of the villagers began to shy away once more. Still fearful of blasphemies, they refused at first to hear the ballad that Narrayo had refined during the long flight home. But Byéliaruyu interceded, saying he would gladly hear the tale. And if the Dragon Minstrel wished to hear another bard perform, then the villagers could hardly refuse.

When Narrayo sang "The Ballad of Aleyara's Descent" that evening, the villagers marveled at the sound. His experiences had deepened the roguish bard, giving him an understanding he'd never had before of adventure, of beauty, of pain, of fear, of love; and these fresh insights filled his voice, giving weight and substance to the words. The villagers trembled at the terror of their first descent; laughed at their whole night spent not knowing they were just above the ground; puffed their throats at the detailed erotic passages (which made Mirele's crests blush, for they flattered her deeply); thrilled at their battles with vicious predators; sighed as lovers reaffirmed their love; and cheered at the heroes' triumphant flight back home. At the end, Byéliaruyu led the villagers in a rousing cheer for the returned champions, and Aleyara's spirit soared with joy.

But soon it came back down to Rulai. "It was a fine tale," Minstrel Hiradai said to Narrayo, clapping her student proudly on the shoulder. "You have truly surpassed your teacher, my apprentice. A wilder work of fantasy I've never heard — and told with such deep feeling! Your imagination will doubtless take you far."

"Imagination?" Aleyara cried. "This was a true tale!"

"Every word," Narrayo affirmed. "For Yara would allow no embellishments — even those that would have helped the song." They exchanged an affectionate glare.

Hiradai shook her head. "Oh, Narrayo. This is how you meet my praise... by clinging to her lies."

"If you call her a liar," Mirele hissed, "you blight the honor of all of us! Do you challenge my claws, old one?"

"Perhaps it is too harsh to call them lies," interjected the Lya matriarch, coming up alongside her clan-sister Hiradai. "'Delusions' would be a better word."

Tirenu shoved into the group and held up some of the few things they'd brought back from the Under, including a hornshell and the glowbug lantern. "Are these delusions that you see in my hands? If we are mad, then surely all of you who see these are mad with us."

"And how do you explain our journey?" Aleyara added, taking in all the gathered villagers with her voice. "We climbed into the Under through a hole southwest of here. Then half a moonphase later we return from the north on *ruyui*'s backs! How can you explain this if not by our tale?"

"That is not difficult to see," said the shaman Talayuni. "The visions you beheld in the Under overwhelmed your minds, filling them with delusions. Merciful Rulai took pity on your youth and madness, and convinced Himoruyu to send His dragons to spirit you away from Eloro's clutches. A pity She could not clear your minds as well."

"Our minds are the only clear ones here!" Yara cried. "You're all a bunch of rigid fools!"

But none would hear her. The gathering broke up, and the villagers returned to their homes, muttering sadly. Soon Aleyara and her three companions sat alone upon the branchy ground. "All we did, and it counts for nothing," Aleyara mourned.

"Not for nothing." The four youths looked up in surprise at the voice of golden Byéliaruyu, who stood behind them. "I must tell you, young Narrayo, I have rarely been so moved by a tale."

"But you think it just a fiction," Narrayo shot back.

"No. A true song has a harmony that no deceit can equal. I heard that ring of truth within your ballad. Surely more than in the villagers' denials."

Aleyara rose to her feet, gazing in wonder at the gleaming bard. "Then you believe us? You accept the truth of what the Under really is?"

Byéliaruyu was slow to answer. "A traveler finds many truths, not all of which agree. I've heard such tales from bards who've flown from lands I've never seen. An Under filled with life, with stone beneath…" He puffed his throat uncertainly, leaving the line unfinished.

"Then… we are not the first? Why didn't you say?"

"Our people have our own songs, harmonious with the lives we lead, the values we strive for. The songs from other lands have their own harmonies and rhythms, melodious to the native-born, yet discordant to our ears. We minstrels rely on the appreciation of our audience, so we hone our songs to suit our listeners' tastes."

Tirenu's nostrils flared. "Then you knew the truth all along, and sang lies to buy our food and favors?"

The golden bard met his eyes calmly. "I know only that I have heard different truths from different lands. It was not my place to say which one was truth for all." He turned to Aleyara. "But while you may not have been the first to venture into the Under, I think you have brought back something truly new, far beyond shells and glowbugs."

"We showed all that we brought back," Mirele said, confused.

"You showed me more than things, brave guardian. You showed a new path to truth. A path, not through ancient lore and faith, but through your own efforts, your own senses. Instead of telling the Under what it should be, you *asked* it what it was and heeded its answers. Maybe that is the way to find which truth is true for all. Perhaps, if enough people learn to ask instead of telling, they may climb down their varied branches and find they all emerge from the same trunk. That way of asking, more than the solid ground and fierce *horutyu*, may be the greatest truth I heard within your song."

"But is it a truth you'll sing to others?" Tirenu challenged. "Or do you fear to offend their ears?"

Byéliaruyu cocked his head. "I'll gladly sing Narrayo's tale across Rulai's green face. You saw how well it was received, even without belief."

Narrayo did not look flattered. "But without belief, what is the point? Your gift for fiction is legend. The people are too frightened to hear what goes against their beliefs, even when spoken in so noble a voice as yours."

"Indeed," the Minstrel told them, "the bulk of Biauru will hear no more than fiction. But perhaps some young ones, less set in their thinking, will be inspired to ask, to seek, to test and amend their guesses as you did in the Under. Perhaps they will go to see the Under for themselves and bring back more of its life. Perhaps they will raise their children to question and test and amend as well. And slowly, as the generations pass, more will think as you do.

"And one day, all the world will know the Under has a floor. And people will look back on those who lived today and say, 'What fools they were to think the Under bottomless! Except for Aleyara and her friends, who were the wisest of them all! How simple a truth they found when others failed — that knowing comes after finding out, not before.'"

The Minstrel took her hands and met her shining eyes. "And your name, brave Aleyara, will be sung down through the ages, when those of all the cynics are forgotten."

But these four heroes, deepened by the wonders they had known,
Could never bear returning to Diurailya's shallow life.
"So join me in my flight," the Dragon Minstrel bade the four.
"A broad and lovely world awaits your eyes."

So with the dawn's next flowering, five dragons bright and brave
Strained stalwart wings to lift their heavy burden to the skies.
But this great weight would raise the souls of all Biauru high;
For truth herself was lifted on their wings.

Afterword

Aleyara's Descent and Other Stories differs in a couple of ways from my previous collection, *Among the Wild Cybers: Tales Beyond the Superhuman*. While all but one of the stories in that collection took place in what I now call the Arachne-Troubleshooter Universe (the shared continuity of *Only Superhuman*, its related Troubleshooter stories, and the *Arachne* novels), this volume features a more eclectic mix of realities: four stories in the ATU, two in a continuity I call "Braneworlds," and five standalones. Also, only four of the eleven have been published in magazines, three in *Analog* and one online in *Amazing Stories*. "Early Warning Systems" makes its debut here, and the remainder were published on my Patreon page at https://www.patreon.com/christopherlbennett, which has so few subscribers that those stories will be brand new to most of this volume's buyers.

Nonetheless, I've revised most of the stories for this volume to offer a little something new. Mostly it's just a few minor textual edits, but I did a substantial polish on "The Moving Finger Writes" and refined some rough phrasings in "What Slender Threads." In "Conventional Powers" and "The Monsters We Make," I restored some material I'd deleted for space, about 300 words' worth for the former and a paragraph for the latter. In "Growth Industry," I added a few jokes I didn't think of until after the story's Patreon publication.

"Aleyara's Descent" is my thirteenth story to appear in *Analog Science Fiction and Fact* over the course of 25 years (and my longest to date), but I actually wrote it only a few months after my 1998 *Analog* debut story, "Aggravated Vehicular Genocide" (collected in *Among the Wild Cybers* and expanded and revised into the first half of *Arachne's*

Crime). I didn't believe at the time that "Aleyara" was appropriate for *Analog*, for although it's a hard-SF story, the Biauru's rich mythology and Bronze Age setting gave it the feel of a high-fantasy quest. But only a couple of other magazines at the time would take a story of its length, and I was advised in its first rejection letter that the standards for such a long story were unusually high. Thus, I decided to set it aside and try to sell some shorter Biauru stories first to lay groundwork for it. When that didn't pan out, I decided instead to incorporate it into a novel. But my original novel career didn't take off as I'd hoped either, so I lost track of the story for a long time. I finally dusted it off in 2022, since I'd run out of other short fiction to put on the market and decided I had nothing to lose. I didn't actually expect *Analog* to buy it, so I was delighted when they did, for it's one of my favorite things I've ever written. I wonder now what might have happened if I hadn't talked myself out of submitting it to *Analog* in 1998.

Writing this story took a lot out of me. The Biauru are a grand, Shakespearean people, so I had to raise my use of language to its most refined level. I strove to be as poetic as I could by focusing on the rhythm of my words and refining the flow of images and ideas. My goal was to produce the kind of story that's best enjoyed when read aloud.

One of the hardest parts was describing the characters' emotional displays, since Biauru don't have human facial expressions, using mainly tone of voice and body language, especially head positioning and the inflation of the neckpouch. Avoiding human references also deprived me of a lot of metaphors. On the other hand, I regretted it when I had to step a bit out of the Biauru's perspective and explain things they'd find obvious, such as their anatomical features.

Since "Descent" is set in the Biauru's past (and ours, about 1100 Earth years ago), there's no explicit connection to the rest of the Arachne-Troubleshooter Universe, beyond the mention of Madeleine Kamakau, a character featured in "Twilight's Captives," "Comfort Zones," and *Arachne's Legacy*, as the translator of the titular ballad. But I created the Biauru for that universe and hope someday to depict their future interaction with humans and other species. For now, I'm working on plans to continue my exploration of the Biauru's history.

Thanks to Xuân Stanek, my best friend from college, for inspiring elements including the Biauru's farspeech, the dragonet deity Motai, and Mirele's name.

To give some context, a Biauru "body-length" represents their average height of 2.1 meters, so the Rulai canopy is about 150-160 meters above the ground, a Rulai trunk about 20 meters wide (c. 60 m in circumference). The tallest reliably reported tree in Earth history was 126 m. Their planet's year is 1.464 Earth years, making Aleyara 11-12 Earth years in the opening scenes and 17 in the bulk of the story. The Biauru's rate of maturation is evidently fairly close to humans'.

"Conventional Powers" was inspired by my trips to New York Comic-Con in its first several years. I remember mentioning it to fellow authors or editors at one NYCC—possibly even the 2012 one where *Only Superhuman* debuted, or the earlier one where I first pitched the novel to its editor Greg Cox. Somewhere along the line, I got to wondering what a superhero/sci-fi convention would be like in the Troubleshooter milieu where superheroes actually exist as a profession, and where superhero fiction has been embraced as a sort of foundational mythology by the transhuman Strider culture. I figured it would be a hybrid of a sci-fi convention and an industry trade show where professionals got together to compare techniques and offer new technologies to potential investors. Merging the two types of convention was too fun an idea to pass up.

I tried to cover a lot of aspects of the convention experience, including a satire of some of the controversies in the fan community over the preceding years, particularly the "Sad Puppy" and "Rabid Puppy" movements that tried to stack the voting of the Hugo Awards in favor of material that fit their political ideology. At the same time, I took the opportunity to explore the larger community of transhuman "mods" and superpowered crimefighters beyond the Troubleshooters, and to delve more into the behind-the-scenes workings and support staff of the Troubleshooter Corps itself. I'm pleased by how much worldbuilding texture this story adds to the Troubleshooter setting.

"Legacy Hero" is an attempt to diversify the Troubleshooter series beyond Emerald Blair, though I included Emry to ease the transition. I wanted to set up Ekundayo DeMarais as a potential lead in her own right, maybe one who could headline more intellectual and mystery-driven stories than the Green Blaze's action-packed adventures.

When trying to choose Kunda's Troubleshooter name, I noted her similarity in powers and methods to Lydia Muchangi/Lodestar, who became the Corps's director at the end of *Only Superhuman*. I realized I had an opportunity to explore a new superhero dynamic, the legacy hero. I decided to combine that with another story concept contrasting progressive and authoritarian approaches to superheroics. It evolved into a commentary on police brutality and authoritarianism in the United States. In order to make it into a mystery, I came up with a contrasting take on the idea of a shared superhero identity, giving the story a nice thematic resonance.

The final Arachne-Troubleshooter Universe tale in this collection, "Nilly's Choice," was written for my Patreon as a character study of R'nilinnath, the young Chirrn apprentice mediator introduced in the second half of *Arachne's Crime*. She was one of my favorite characters to write in that novel and *Arachne's Exile*, and I realized I'd never established her background and the motivations for her career choice. This tale also let me flesh out more details about the Chirrn, and several of its ideas found their way into the upcoming third novel, *Arachne's Legacy*.

I was initially hesitant to include "Nilly's Choice" herein, concerned that it was too much an extension of the *Arachne* novels. Upon rereading it, however, I felt it could stand reasonably well on its own. It makes an interesting companion piece to "Aleyara's Descent," as Nilly is about 19 Earth years old in most of it, so both are coming-of-age stories about adolescent nonhumans on the verge of adulthood.

The only other stories in this volume that share a continuity are "What Slender Threads" and "Though Worlds Divide Us," belonging to a multiverse I call "Braneworlds." This was my first stab at the multiverse concept featured in my audiobook-exclusive superhero trilogy *Tangent Knights*. When GraphicAudio invited me to pitch a trilogy proposal, I was already planning to outline a novel trilogy around one of my old superhero-comics concepts from college. The problem was that I'd already written "What Slender Threads," a prologue story focusing on the trilogy's supporting characters before they met its protagonist. The open-call anthology I wrote it for didn't take it, but I was shopping it to magazines when GraphicAudio's offer came. If the story had sold, I wouldn't have been able to use that universe for an original, GA-exclusive production.

The solution, fittingly, was to split the concept into two separate realities. I excised the characters and concepts featured in "Threads" from the trilogy premise, leaving just the main character's arc as the spine of the narrative, and cannibalizing more of my unused comics ideas to replace the supporting cast and worldbuilding. As it happened, I'd already reworked the physics of the premise sometime in the early 2000s, replacing its quantum-based "phase worlds" with parallel brane universes based in string theory. Thus, I could divorce the audio trilogy from the short story simply by going back to quantum theory as the foundation for its parallel worlds. I made other changes to differentiate *Tangent Knights* from "Threads," like making inter-world contact public knowledge from the start.

As it happens, "What Slender Threads" didn't sell after all, ending up on my Patreon. Yet when the current incarnation of the long-running *Amazing Stories* Magazine put out a call for flash fiction about colonizing the Solar System, I recalled wondering how instantaneous travel to habitable parallel Earths would impact space colonization, and the idea for "Though Worlds Divide Us" arose readily from that. It's an oblique way to approach the theme, but it worked well enough to get purchased for the online edition of the magazine.

"Though Worlds Divide Us" is my only professionally published work of flash fiction to date (only 1500 words long, though the revised version herein is slightly longer). It was published online just a couple of weeks before "Aleyara's Descent" hit the shelves in *Analog*, which means my shortest and longest short-fiction sales both came out in the same month. Not only that, but "Aleyara" had the longest interval from writing to publication for any of my non-Patreon fiction (26 years), while "Worlds" surely had the shortest (a little over 3 months).

The only other story herein that's been previously published outside my Patreon is "Abductive Reasoning," appearing in *Analog* in 2017. This was my previous record-setter for the longest interval to publication. I wrote the first version some twenty years earlier for a story contest, under the title "An Update from the Flying Hubcap Front." It was little more than a self-indulgent polemic trashing UFO beliefs, so when I revisited it, I recognized the need to give the main character more motivation and investment in the core debate. I ended up rewriting it from top to bottom, injecting a number of new scientific concepts I'd picked up in recent years, such as Cornell University's research into microchip "Sprite" satellites and the late Jordin Kare's proposal of interstellar microsail probes (both of which I learned about from Paul Gilster's *Centauri Dreams* blog). I added more emotional and philosophical depth and completely changed the climax and resolution. It's essentially a whole new story, and I was pleasantly surprised to sell it on my first try.

I intended the title "Abductive Reasoning" as a pun on alien abduction and deductive reasoning, only learning after publication that there actually is such a thing in logic as abductive reasoning, in which you "take away" (abduce) a best-guess conclusion from an observation, drawing an inference that may or may not be correct but seems likely given your understanding. It's actually one of the most common forms of reasoning, the way we determine the likely cause of an observed result. It's how detectives determine who to charge with a crime, how doctors arrive at diagnoses, and how scientists form hypotheses.

However, abductive reasoning is only as good as the assumptions you make, so it doesn't guarantee a correct result—which is why hypotheses and diagnoses need to be tested and criminal charges need to be proven in court. Two people observing the same situation with completely different worldviews will probably abduce completely incompatible inferences. In that sense, I suppose, the title actually has more relevance than I'd intended.

When I wrote *Arachne's Legacy*, I reused several key concepts from "Abductive Reasoning" in a modified way. Thus, when I revised the short story for this collection, I briefly tried rewriting it to take place in the Arachne-Troubleshooter Universe, since I would've liked to have more than four ATU stories in the book. I belatedly realized it wouldn't work, because the premise of "Abductive" requires a universe without faster-than-light travel, so that crewed starships of the sort that UFO lore claims to be visiting Earth could not exist. Thus, like "No Dominion" in my previous collection, it ends up as a near-miss, a story that's conceptually quite close to the ATU but doesn't fit the continuity. (In principle, there's no reason "Abductive" couldn't take place in the same universe as "No Dominion," but there's no particular reason to think it does.)

"The Moving Finger Writes" is another very old story. It began as my second attempt to write a story under the title "The Cat Who Chased Her Tail Through Time," the name of the first story I ever tried to sell — a self-indulgent hard-SF/fantasy hybrid starring my family's new kittens as cosmically powered beings. I published that story on my Patreon as a nostalgic exercise, almost exactly as I wrote it back in 1991. While searching my files for that story, I accidentally opened this one, which I'd virtually forgotten about. Originally written in late 1996, it was a merger and expansion of two 1991 vignettes inspired by a June 1989 *Discover* Magazine article about Kip Thorne and Mike Morris's theoretical model for a time-travel wormhole. I was pleasantly surprised by how well the story held up, so I decided to publish it on Patreon as a companion piece to "Chased Her Tail," since it also paid homage to my beloved cats, this time as felinoid aliens. I revised this one extensively, incorporating some more current ideas about time travel and its ramifications, and renaming it to avoid confusion with the previous story (a pity, since I really like the "Chased Her Tail" title).

I'd also forgotten that this story featured the first version of the character that would eventually evolve into Tsshar Murieff in my Hub series in *Analog*, based on my beloved cat Natasha. The original story named her and Miar's species Marwadji, after my family's "wadgie" nickname for our cats, but I changed it to Marrhwai to make it a bit more distinct from the Hub's Mrwadj species.

In retrospect, I feel this story in its current form is one of my best, and I wish I'd tried marketing its rewritten version to magazines rather than publishing it on my Patreon first. I'm quite proud of it and glad that more readers will now have the chance to experience it.

My editor wanted at least one brand-new story in this collection, so I kept "Early Warning Systems" off my Patreon. I originally wrote it in 2017, but I wasn't satisfied with it yet, and I was concerned that its subject matter involving auto accidents might be inappropriate in light of then-recent news about terrorists deliberately hitting pedestrians with their cars. When I revisited it after a few years, I found ways to make it more personal and character-driven; the intervening COVID pandemic let me add some heft as well. (Foreman's anecdote about her "solution" to trisecting an angle is a true story from my own adolescence. It was one of the nicest things my sister ever did for me, so I wanted to commemorate it.)

I based both "Moving Finger" and this story (as well as *Tangent Knights: Gemini Ascendant*) on the same scientifically grounded model of temporal physics, more realistic than the usual "changing history" cliché for the reasons discussed in both stories. I suppose there's no specific reason why the two stories couldn't be part of the same reality, although I wrote "Early Warning Systems" assuming a less cumbersome method of time travel than timeholes. The stories also differ slightly on the feasibility of creating parallel timelines, but then, Pandit is arguing from conjecture while Miar has far more advanced knowledge.

Indeed, strictly speaking, there's no proof in "Early Warning Systems" that any time travel has actually occurred, only a strong implication. I enjoyed writing the sort of ambiguous story you might have seen on an old anthology show like *The Twilight Zone*, a two-hander driven by a conceptual and philosophical debate between two people in a room, with no special effects needed.

One thing I like to do in my fiction, as seen with *Only Superhuman* and *Tangent Knights*, is to take a fanciful genre like superheroes and explore how it might work in a plausible hard-SF context. "The Monsters We Make" is my attempt to do the same with the giant monster genre. I remember having the idea on a subway during a convention trip or family visit, which must have been before 2013, because I recall feeling that I'd been beaten to the punch when *Pacific Rim* came out in that year.

Maybe that's why I didn't pursue the idea in earnest until 2017. I chose to make the story an allegory for the growing cultural and political conflicts in the United States, in the way that the best Japanese kaiju movies are often allegories for nuclear war, environmental destruction, or political and social issues.

Telling a kaiju story in a relatively hard-SF way meant acknowledging how utterly devastating their existence would be to civilization, unlike in most of the movies where the world tends to carry on pretty much unaltered despite the periodic monster-induced cataclysms (although the *Monarch: Legacy of Monsters* TV series has featured some interesting explorations of the long-term social and physical impact of a kaiju attack). Thus, "The Monsters We Make" came out as my most dystopian story ever, with only a few slim rays of hope. Still, I did have some fun developing the science behind the kaiju, as well as coming up with punny names for the various species. (I had a harder time with the title, though. Rejected titles include "The Maintenance of Monsters," "The Monsters You Know," "The Kaiju in the Room," and "Flies to Wanton Gods.")

My friend and fellow novelist Dayton Ward, a veteran of the U.S. Marine Corps, advised me on the story's depiction of military procedures and tactics. Any errors that remain are my own fault, not Dayton's.

"Growth Industry" is a very different riff on the kaiju and *tokusatsu* genres, an affectionate spoof of the long-running *Super Sentai* superhero franchise from Toei Company, Ltd. and its American adaptation, *Power Rangers* (originally from Saban Entertainment, then Disney, then Saban again, and now Hasbro). The specific inspiration came from *Denji Sentai Megaranger*, the basis for the sixth American season, *Power Rangers in Space*. Every season of both franchises has its own mechanism that the villains use to grow their monsters to giant size, and in *Megaranger*, it was a small comic-relief monster who would bite defeated monsters to infect them with a growth virus. It crystallized my problem with the other Sentai/Ranger villains I'd seen who had to physically approach the monsters in order to make them giant: namely, why didn't the Rangers just shoot them *before* they got there, saving themselves the trouble of having to deal with giant monsters ever again? This story was my chance to express that perennial annoyance, and to comment on other silly conventions of the long-running international franchise (for which I nonetheless have considerable affection, particularly toward the original Japanese version).

For further discussion and annotations, visit my website at christopherlbennett.wordpress.com.

Chronology

Bibliography

"Abductive Reasoning" in *Analog Science Fiction and Fact*, Vol. CXXXVII Nos. 9 & 10 (September/October 2017), pp. 138-145.

"Conventional Powers" in *Analog Science Fiction and Fact*, Vol. CXXXIX Nos. 9 & 10 (September/October 2019), pp. 118-131.

"The Moving Finger Writes" on Patreon (www.patreon.com/christopherlbennett) at https://www.patreon.com/posts/fiction-moving-35679628, posted April 5, 2020.

"Growth Industry" on Patreon at https://www.patreon.com/posts/fiction-growth-38016786, posted July 10, 2020.

"The Monsters We Make" on Patreon at https://www.patreon.com/posts/52689808, posted June 20, 2021.

"What Slender Threads" on Patreon at https://www.patreon.com/posts/fiction-what-56732165, posted September 29, 2021.

"Nilly's Choice" on Patreon at https://www.patreon.com/posts/fiction-nillys-57994899, posted October 29, 2021.

"Legacy Hero" on Patreon at https://www.patreon.com/posts/76873089, posted January 6, 2023.

"Though Worlds Divide Us" in *Amazing Stories* Patreon, https://www.patreon.com/posts/though-worlds-us-80497954, posted April 3, 2023. Reprinted in *Amazing Stories* online magazine, https://amazingstories.com/2023/04/though-worlds-divide-us-by-christopher-l-bennett-free-story/, posted April 10, 2023.

"Aleyara's Descent" in *Analog Science Fiction and Fact*, Vol. XCIII No. 5 & 6 (May/June 2023), pp. 8-29.

About the Author

Christopher L. Bennett is a lifelong resident of Cincinnati, Ohio, with a B.S. in Physics and a B.A. in History from the University of Cincinnati. A fan of science and science fiction since age five, he has been a semi-regular contributor to *Analog Science Fiction and Fact* (home of his "Hub" series of comedy adventures) since 1998 and has also been published in *Galaxy's Edge, Amazing Stories*, and others. Since 2003, he has been one of Pocket and Gallery Books' most prolific and popular authors of *Star Trek* tie-in fiction, including the epic *Next Generation* prequel *The Buried Age*, the *Enterprise — Rise of the Federation* series, and the Original Series prequel *The Captain's Oath*. He has written two Marvel Comics novels, *X-Men: Watchers on the Walls* and *Spider-Man: Drowned in Thunder*, as well as creating two original series combining superheroes and hard science fiction: the Troubleshooter series, including the novel *Only Superhuman* from Tor Books (*Library Journal's* SF/Fantasy Debut of the Month for October 2012) and assorted short stories, and the full-cast audio novel series *Tangent Knights* from GraphicAudio. His original science fiction also includes the *Arachne* trilogy and the collection *Among the Wild Cybers* from eSpec Books. Christopher's Patreon page at https://www.patreon.com/christopherlbennett features original short fiction, behind-the-scenes notes, and classic TV reviews. More behind-the-scenes material and the author's blog can be found at https://christopherlbennett.wordpress.com/.

Among the Wild Cybers

Being a hero never falls out of style!

When the line between life and technology blurs, humanity must adjust its understanding of the universe. From bestselling author Christopher L. Bennett comes *Among the Wild Cybers*, eight tales portraying a future of challenge and conflict, but also of hope born from the courage and idealism of those heroes willing to stand up for what is right.

• An intrepid naturalist risks her future to save a new form of life that few consider worth saving.
• An apprentice superhero must stand alone against an insane superintelligence to earn her name.
• A cybernetic slave fights to save her kind from a liberation not of their choosing.
• A seasoned diplomat and mother must out-negotiate fearsome alien traders to save a colony's children.
• A homicide detective serves in a world where curing death has only made murder more baffling.

These and other heroes strive to make their corners of the universe better—no matter how much the odds are stacked against them.

The Arachne
Omnibus

Setting off to explore new worlds, only to encounter old problems!

What a Tangled Web…

The crew of the interstellar colony vessel *Arachne* is roused from artificial hibernation to face a horrific reality, as an alien boarding party takes them into custody to answer for the deaths of tens of thousands of sentient beings.

Her crew commit themselves to a lifetime of penance to repay their debt, but not everyone agrees. As tensions rise and opposing factions come into play, a brutal act of vengeance forces them into exile in a distant part of the galaxy.

Drawn into a cosmic conspiracy spanning millennia, the colonists learn that the Chirrn's ancient choices have exacted a terrible toll on human history. Now, their only way to win true freedom may be to carry out a perilous theft aboard an extraordinary megastructure orbiting a neutron star.

Will Arachne and her crew pull off the heist of the millennium? Or are they being manipulated into committing a far more awful crime... one for which all humanity could pay the price?

https://especbooks.square.site

www.ingramcontent.com/pod-product-compliance
Lightning Source LLC
Chambersburg PA
CBHW060717190726

48289CB00002B/723